ADVANCE PRAISE FOR

RETRIBUTION

"*Retribution*, Wendy Whitman's worthy successor to her exceptional debut novel, *Premonition*, is a tautly-constructed, page-turning thriller. Driven by a fascinating and frightening villain, the intrigue and suspense are unrelenting. Buckle up—you're in for a breathtaking ride!"

—**Jack Ford**, Emmy and Peabody Award–Winning Journalist and Bestselling Author of *Chariot on the Mountain*

"*Retribution*, the sequel to Wendy Whitman's powerful debut crime thriller *Premonition*, takes the reader on a demonic journey filled with smartly written plot twists. Whitman's true crime background shines through each and every page as she takes us into the mind of a demented serial killer. Clearly Whitman has penned another unique and unforgettable thriller, masterfully written and one that will leave you at the edge of your seat."

—**Rita Cosby**, Renowned Emmy-Winning TV Host and Bestselling Author

"Wendy Whitman does it again! Her first book, *Premonition*, was a fast and furious page-turner. This sequel, *Retribution*, is every bit as real and frightening. Wendy's background in the world of true crime gives her a solid foundation to build a tale of suspense that keeps us all riveted. She deeply sees into the minds of her characters on the right and wrong sides of the law. Her serial killer is utterly diabolical and the cops who are out to get him are dogged and determined. This is a terrific thriller—at each and every moment!"

—**Rikki Klieman**, CBS News Legal Analyst

"There is nothing better than another novel that enhances the excitement created by author Wendy Whitman in this sequel to her debut crime thriller *Premonition*. *Retribution* carries the day as a powerful continuation of the characters of the previous book, filled with new intrigue and adventures of crime and mystery. Once again Whitman has drawn the reader into another riveting adventure."

—**Gerald P. Boyle**, Jeffrey Dahmer's Attorney

"Wendy Whitman's newest novel, *Retribution*, part two in what I hope is a long series, is a fast-paced cat and mouse game between a cop and a serial killer, who may have more in common than is first evident. Making excellent use of her years of experience as a producer for Court TV, where she covered the highest profile criminal cases in the nation, Ms. Whitman deftly teases out fact by tantalizing fact in the breadcrumb trail she leads the protagonist—and the reader—to follow. You don't need to have read her clever debut, *Premonition*, which introduced rival main characters, the 'Deer Killer' and Detective Hank Nowak, to fully enjoy *Retribution*. But I guarantee you will want to! So sit back and enjoy the ride as *Retribution* cleverly takes you right up to the brink where you can't wait until Ms. Whitman delivers her next scintillating thriller."

—**Deborah Goodrich Royce**, Award–Winning Author of *Reef Road*, *Ruby Falls*, and *Finding Mrs. Ford*

"*Retribution* is a serial killer thriller extraordinaire, a pulse-pounding exercise in suburban terror. Court TV alum Wendy Whitman brings her vast experience to bear in a seminal tale that takes us to the depths of human depravity and despair, as well as the heights of compassion and heroism. A neo-noir of the highest level, *Retribution* echoes of Thomas Harris at his best, stretching a tapestry stitched in blood across a riveting, suspense-riddled landscape."

—**Jon Land**, *USA Today* and *New York Times* Bestselling Author

"*Retribution* is a brilliant, thrill-a-minute roller coaster ride through the mind of a serial killer as Det. Hank Nowak, private investigator Vito Loggia, and Sgt. Joseph O'Malley race against the clock to stop him from murdering again. A stellar, immersive follow-up to Wendy Whitman's outstanding debut novel, *Premonition*. Well done!"

—**Brian Cuban**, Author of *The Ambulance Chaser*

Retribution is a top-shelf serial killer chiller with a twist I did not see coming. If you've ever wondered what it's like to be in the mind of a psychopath, this is the crime novel for you."

—**Tessa Wegert**, Author of *The Kind To Kill*

ALSO BY WENDY WHITMAN

Premonition

RETRIBUTION

RETRIBUTION

WENDY WHITMAN

Post Hill
PRESS

A POST HILL PRESS BOOK

Retribution
© 2023 by Wendy Whitman
All Rights Reserved

ISBN: 978-1-63758-944-1
ISBN (eBook): 978-1-63758-945-8

Cover design by Conroy Accord
Interior design and composition: Greg Johnson, Textbook Perfect

Post Hill Press
New York • Nashville
posthillpress.com

Published in the United States of America
1 2 3 4 5 6 7 8 9 10

ONE

Now that Cary Mackin was gone, he would have to water the plants for the foreseeable future and take in his own mail until he found a new tenant—a small price to pay for all the entertainment she had provided him over the past several months. He had been all stirred up that night, so what better way to release a little energy than to rid the world of a couple of useless deer? What a surprise when following the *unexpected* witness home landed him back at his own place. He hadn't recognized Cary's car in the dark, nor her face, for that matter. He just saw it was a woman. *Talk about a small world.*

He had never planned on harming Cary. But sometimes, life took unanticipated twists and turns, and you just had to go with it; spontaneous plans were always the best. Antoinette "Toni" Moretti was the number one real estate agent in Fairview County, and she had managed to keep a steady stream of tenants coming and going from his guesthouse over the years. Not that he needed the money. The young women simply provided him with fodder for his imagination. And he had even let them live—well, except for that *needy, aspiring model nutjob* who fell in love with him. And Cary, of course. If only she had kept her nose out of everything. But Cary just couldn't leave well enough alone. The foursome had gotten too close, and his options had dwindled. He had no choice; he had to look out for himself.

The other murders, well, they were on him. He loved the synchronicity, the perfect balance of it all. The deer, the girls; a puppy, then a baby; and then everything all at once: a family and their dog. He couldn't help but wonder if all his hard work had been appreciated. If the police, Eve, and all the others realized how much thought he had put into his crimes. He was an actor, after all. Theatrics came naturally to him. He had big shoes to fill: William Holden, John Huston, and Matthew Broderick all turned automobiles into deadly weapons, intentionally or not. Yes, big shoes indeed.

Brandon wondered how much time it would take before Cary was officially declared a missing person. With a detective as a girlfriend, he guessed it wouldn't be very long. There was nothing on the news yet, but it was still early. He decided a lot could change by the end of the day. There was no way to know how quickly Cary's cohorts would start putting it all together. No worries. No one was going to find her any time soon—her *body*, that is. Brandon had made sure of that. What an exhausting night it had been. A quick shower and a much-needed nap would fix everything. Then maybe he'd swing by the diner and have an order of pancakes in Cary's honor—a small enough gesture but a thoughtful one. She deserved at least that. He had always been good at the details.

As Brandon made his way through the winding streets of Wooster on his way to breakfast, he couldn't help thinking about a few notorious killers who had inspired him. Dennis Rader, a.k.a. "BTK," was one, and the two men who massacred the Clutter family of Holcomb, Kansas, back in the '50s were another. Rader murdered Shirley Vian on March 17, 1977, but not before giving her a glass of water to comfort her after she got nervous and threw up. Likewise, Perry Smith and Richard Hickock, the ex-cons who nearly wiped out the Clutter family, put a pillow under fifteen-year-old Kenyon Clutter's head before they shot him to death in the basement. These were compassionate people. And although some killers tricked their victims into a false sense of security, Brandon believed everybody had a soft side. He would have to up his game, but pancakes were a good start.

* * *

It was 6:00 a.m., and Hank woke up knowing she had a challenging, full day ahead of her. The room was still dark at this hour. Hank didn't want to wake Cary, so she preemptively turned off the alarm set for 6:15 a.m. She wondered where her other alarm clock was—that is, Barry. Hank found her loyal dog's morning antics far more reliable than her iPhone, as several power outages over the years would have caused her to be late for work if not for Barry's wet nose. But this morning, he was nowhere to be found. Hank figured he must've gotten a jump on the day and was probably already at his favorite window attempting to spot a squirrel, UPS truck, or school bus, unaware of the early hour.

Hank snuck out of bed and headed for the bathroom. She'd let Cary sleep in until she left for work and would take care of Barry once she was showered and dressed. The steaming hot water felt good on her upper back and shoulders. Last night had been particularly erotic. Hank feared thoughts of another sensuous evening with Cary would distract her from her duties today. After drying off, Hank grabbed her hair dryer and clothes and made her way to the powder room off the kitchen to finish getting ready.

Tiptoeing toward the refrigerator, Hank grabbed a yogurt and went to look for Barry so she could take him out to do his business. Calling to him in a whisper elicited no response, so Hank headed to the large wall-to-ceiling window in the den. But Barry was not at his usual post this morning. Uncertain of what to do next, Hank decided to wake Cary up with a kiss. As she bent down near Cary's side of the bed, Hank reached for her, barely making out the blanket in the dimly lit room. It only took a moment for Hank to realize no one was there as the kiss landed on Cary's pillow.

As Hank opened the blinds, she saw nothing but an empty bed in front of her. Hank's first thought was that Cary must have woken up early and taken Barry for a walk. Hank knew Cary had trouble sleeping these days. So Hank decided she would fix Cary a quick breakfast before she took off for police headquarters. Getting impatient, Hank decided to go outside and see if she could find them. She couldn't be late this morning. O'Malley had called a special meeting on the "Deer Killer" case, and among others, Vito would be there.

It was now almost 7:15 a.m., and Hank knew that if she didn't leave soon, she would likely miss at least the beginning of the meeting, factoring in traffic. Frustration setting in, Hank called out to her lover and best friend but got no response from either. And then Hank noticed her car was nowhere in sight. Could Cary have taken Barry for a ride so early in the morning? Unlikely was the only answer that made sense. *What the hell?* Hank asked herself. The detective in her knew what the next logical step was: to call Cary's cell phone. So Hank went back into the house to get her own phone and placed the call. Almost immediately, she heard a ringtone coming from the bedroom. Hank entered the room only to find Cary's phone on the floor next to the bed, flashing an incoming call signal. Although she decided there was no reason for Cary to take her phone with her just to walk Barry, the additional absence of Hank's car was troubling. And so *now* Hank was worried.

Panic setting in, Hank's next call was to Vito. After one ring, he picked up.

"Hank?" Vito began. "I'm on my way to the station. What's up?"

"I...uh...nothing...it's just Cary and I spent the night...at my place..." Hank started to explain, but Vito cut her off.

"Yeah, we know. Cary left us a note. Glad you guys are back together...worked it out. What's going on? The meeting starts in less than an hour, and the traffic into the city is a bitch as always," Vito continued.

"I don't know. It may be nothing.... It's just...my car is gone. And there's no sign of Cary...no sign of my dog.... I'm starting to get worried. Something's not right," Hank added, sounding atypically alarmed. "Where's that guy who's been guarding her?" Hank asked. "What's his name? Cliff?"

"He showed up at the cottage right on time this morning, so I told him to wait there...that Cary was in good hands and would probably be back home in a bit," Vito explained. "He'll stay there till she shows up."

"Okay, good.... But, Vito, on top of everything else, I'm stranded. I need to be at that meeting—especially now. I hate to ask you, but... think you could..." Hank continued, rambling on.

"I'll call O'Malley...tell him something unexpected came up...that your car's missing, and we might be a little late. I'll be there as soon as I can," Vito assured her.

"Thanks, Vito. I don't know what to make of all this," Hank declared.

"We'll figure it out. There's gotta be a simple explanation. I'm sure they'll turn up soon," Vito responded. And then Hank had a thought.

"Vito, what if she took him to the dog park...Barry, I mean...think Cliff could..." Hank continued.

"Good thinking, Hank. I'll give Cliff a call and tell him to check it out. Sit tight. On my way."

* * *

Pancakes were the only way to start the day. He needed to indulge more often. Xanthe had been especially attentive this morning. *She must think I'm on my way to stardom*, Brandon contemplated. In reality, despite his good looks, Brandon had decided that being a character actor suited him best. If he picked his roles carefully, he would be unrecognizable on-screen and, therefore, off-screen, and that's how he liked it. Brandon didn't give a rat's ass about being famous and having annoying people approach him on the street. Indeed, traditional fame would have infringed on his true passion: *murder*.

How ironic that *Barry* came out just a couple of years ago. But far from being a copycat killer, Brandon had actually committed his first murder before the series ever aired. It was naturally his favorite show, and in a delusional way, he credited himself for inspiring it even though he knew better. So far, his acting had been limited to an off-Broadway play or two, some community theater, and a couple of online advertisements, the kind that everyone sits through for the first few seconds only to hit the Skip Ad button as soon as it appears.

The Hulu series Brandon had told Cary about would have been his first big break, even though he had a relatively small part. And no one would have recognized him in it as he was to play the role of a disfigured victim of a suspicious fire: *heartbreaking*. It got pushed back, however, which ended up working in Brandon's favor. But Cary didn't need to know that. She thought he was away on location while, all that time, he was stalking her. Therefore, over the past several months, it had been easy to fool Cary into thinking he was away filming the show—the perfect cover.

As Brandon doused his pancakes with maple syrup, his mind drifted to more important matters, such as whether he was a psychopath or a sociopath. He had never been sure of the difference. And then he did a little research. Apparently, psychopaths make up a mere 1 percent of the population, while sociopaths make up 4 percent. While both fall under the heading of antisocial personality disorder, psychopaths tend to be more manipulative, charming, and able to live a generally "normal" life. Sociopaths, on the other hand, exhibit erratic, rage-prone behavior. Psychopaths tend to minimize the risk of getting caught, while sociopaths seem to be a little more careless. According to experts, psychopaths have no conscience, and sociopaths are capable of limited empathy. So where did that leave him? *Clearly*, Brandon concluded, *I am a proud, card-carrying psycho*: manipulative—*check*, charming—*check*, *good at not getting caught*—*check*. And, most importantly, he loved being in the top 1 percent. *Never tell a psychopath they're a psychopath*. But Brandon didn't mind. He had diagnosed himself.

As Brandon went to the cash register to pay, he felt satisfied. Hard work was always rewarded. He returned to the booth to leave a more-than-generous tip for Xanthe. Brandon was on a post-kill high and wanted to spread the joy around. As he got into his Tesla to return home and regroup for the day, another thought crossed his mind. If he did his calculations right, so far, he had killed seven females, two deer, and three dogs—if you didn't count his youthful indiscretions. *Not bad*, Brandon told himself, but not great either. However, he figured that made him a serial killer. The thought raised his spirits. He had a competitive nature, but he had a long way to go if he planned on breaking any records.

❋ ❋ ❋

Vito took the turn into Hank's driveway too fast and almost spun out, honking his horn in the process. A frazzled-looking Hank came out of the house with the most worried expression Vito had ever seen on her face. The first word Hank uttered as she got into the car was an expletive.

"Shit...fuck...shit...fuck. I can't find my phone, Vito. Goddamn it," Hank declared in an uncharacteristically shaky voice.

"Must be in the house, Hank. Calm down...calm down...one step at a time," Vito continued, trying to help.

"Just give me a sec. I'll be right back," Hank said as she ran into the house.

Vito looked at his watch. It was already 7:30 a.m., and the meeting was supposed to start in half an hour. He needed to make another call to O'Malley as they would be even later than he had anticipated.

"Hey, Vito. What now?" O'Malley asked matter-of-factly.

"Just got to Hank's. We should be there by 8:15 if the traffic isn't too bad. Hope that doesn't mess up your day," Vito replied.

"Just get here as soon as you can," O'Malley answered. "Not a problem."

Vito suspected O'Malley had a soft spot for Hank. He even wondered if anything had ever gone on between them but wouldn't think of asking. As Vito looked up from his phone, he saw Hank locking the side kitchen door and running toward him.

"Got it," Hank declared. "Let's get out of here."

* * *

As Brandon pulled into his driveway, he recounted the past twenty-four hours in his head. Everything had gone pretty much according to plan, but he hadn't expected Cary to have a dog with her and was now second-guessing his decision to leave the frantic canine in the car—*alive*. Now that he thought about it, the smarter move might have been to eliminate all loose ends. *Well, too late now*, Brandon told himself. He wouldn't dare go back to the scene in broad daylight. For all he knew, the police might have already rescued the poor animal.

Brandon loved his new *discreet* smart car: the latest addition to his fleet of automobiles. It made stalking people all the easier. When Hank surprised him by picking Cary up last night, he was practically in the bushes, so they didn't have an inkling of what was to come. Caution always paid off. The only major disappointment of the evening had been the closed bedroom blinds that denied Brandon his guilty pleasure: *voyeurism*. Cary's return trip to Hank's house had almost derailed Brandon's plans for the night. But it turned out to be just another futile attempt on Cary's part to protect herself—gun versus car, no contest there. Cary's death was quick, but he had made sure to give her just enough time to absorb what was happening. No one should go to their demise confused and clueless.

* * *

Vito and Hank pulled into the station a little after 8:20 a.m. and headed straight to O'Malley's office. Vito wondered where everyone else was, but as soon as they saw the sergeant's face, they got a bad feeling.

"Sorry we're late," Hank said, but O'Malley cut her off.

"Think you guys better have a seat," he began.

As Hank and Vito sat down, O'Malley dropped a bombshell on them. "They found your car, Hank," was all he said. Hank's face went white. As Vito put his arms around her, Hank braced herself for O'Malley's next words.

"We got a call about ten minutes ago from the Sullivans, the couple who own that little farmers market off of King's Road in Wooster. They found your dog, too." O'Malley rambled on. "Inside," he added.

"I don't understand," Hank began. "Is Barry okay? Oh my God," she said in a shaky voice.

Vito had never seen Hank like this. He decided it was time to intervene. But before he got as much as a word out, O'Malley and Hank said in unison, "Let's go."

TWO

Vito and Hank drove in silence, following O'Malley in his vehicle. The ride was interminable. Normally, it took about half an hour to forty minutes to get from Stamford to Wooster, but the traffic on I-95 heading out of the city was a bit heavier than usual this morning. It would likely take them at least that long to get to the Sullivans' place, which only intensified Hank's anxiety.

"Everything will be okay," Vito began, breaking the tension.

"You don't know that, Vito," Hank answered. "None of this makes any sense."

And then, Hank added, "Vito, I'm scared."

Those words broke Vito's heart, so he grabbed Hank's hand and held it tightly.

"Me, too," was all he said in response.

When they arrived at the farmers market, Hank and Vito pulled in behind O'Malley, by the side of the road. The general store was a small, quaint, New England-looking building with a parking lot out front that held less than a dozen vehicles. At the moment, the only car in it was Hank's. As they got out of Vito's car, O'Malley approached them.

"Crime scene is on its way. Don't touch anything, not yet. Not sure what we're dealing with here. Let's go find the Sullivans. Maybe they can help," O'Malley declared.

But before either of them could answer, Hank noticed the elderly couple coming from the rear of the store, Barry in tow. When he spotted Hank, Barry's tail wagged ferociously, and he began to tug on the leash. As the couple struggled to control him, Barry broke away and ran straight into Hank's arms. She was overcome with emotion.

"Hey, good boy...my sweet boy.... Oh my God. Vito, what's going on?" Hank asked.

Vito simply shook his head, a worried look on his face.

Then the couple approached.

"Edgar Sullivan here," the man said, putting out his hand. "This is my wife, Doris. We own the place. Found your car here early this morning...um, then saw the dog...in the front seat...wasn't locked," he continued, trying to find the right words. "Our house is just down the road. We got a late start today...usually get here in the middle of the night you know what with the baking and all."

Hank was already losing patience with Edgar, well-meaning though he was. O'Malley noticed.

"We have a few questions if you don't mind, Mr. Sullivan," O'Malley said.

Then, introducing himself, he added, "I'm Sergeant Joseph O'Malley. Nice to meet you."

"Call me Edgar. Please," the man responded.

"Sure, *Edgar*, did you see anyone last night...I mean, early this morning when you got here. Touch anything?" O'Malley asked.

"Can't say that we did. I mean we didn't see anyone. But sorry, guess I must've touched the door handle of the car when we went to get the dog out of it. The car wasn't locked," Edgar repeated.

"Well, whatever went on here last night, odds are whoever's involved didn't go near the car...maybe...we'll know more when the techs get here," O'Malley said.

"Sorry, didn't mean to cause any problems," Edgar said meekly.

"You have a very sweet dog," Doris interjected, speaking for the first time. "He was shaking when we went to get him out...get him out of the car. Didn't have a leash on so we got one of our own...used to have a dog. Afraid he's been cowering ever since...until you got here," she added.

Hank was starting to get light-headed. She turned toward O'Malley.

"Joe," Hank began, "can we..."

"Edgar, Doris, can you give us a minute?" O'Malley asked them.

"Of course," the couple replied simultaneously.

Vito, Hank, and O'Malley walked toward the road, Barry at Hank's side.

"What the hell is going on, Joe? Vito?" Hank implored.

"I don't know," O'Malley answered.

"Me neither," Vito chimed in.

And then it dawned on Vito. He wondered if O'Malley even knew that Hank and Cary were involved and that Cary was the one who was driving Hank's car. He and Hank had some explaining to do.

"Hank, can I have a word alone?" Vito asked her, glancing at O'Malley.

"Um, sure," Hank responded, not sure what Vito was up to.

O'Malley appeared to be suspicious but nodded as if to say, "Go ahead, do what you have to do." He gave them some privacy and headed back to his car to grab a cigarette. Once they were alone, Vito took the opportunity to say what was on his mind.

"Hank, don't mean to get into your personal business, but does O'Malley know about you and Cary?" Vito blurted out.

Hank seemed taken aback by the question, but Vito could see she understood why he had brought it up.

"I, uh," Hank began. "It's complicated. No, I guess I never told him. I mean, it's really none of his business," Hank continued.

"But we have to tell him now," Vito added. "I mean, O'Malley has to be told who was driving the car, at least."

"Yes...yes...I know...guess I wasn't thinking. Vito, can we just say it was Cary and not get into it right now?" Hank asked.

Vito suspected there was more to the story, but all he said was, "Just for the time being. You know, Hank, he's gonna have to hear the whole—" Vito went on, but Hank cut him off.

"Fuck it. Let's tell him now. Tell him everything," Hank declared. "We don't even know where in God's name she is."

As Hank uttered those words, two patrol cars pulled up. O'Malley greeted them.

The officers, one of whom appeared to be a crime scene technician, began to process the scene. While they were doing so, O'Malley began walking toward Vito and Hank, assuming he had given them enough time to discuss whatever it was they needed to.

"So, we all good?" O'Malley asked as he approached them.

"Yeah," Vito answered, looking at Hank.

"Joe, we know who was driving the car...who was with Barry..." Hank began. "It was Cary."

"Cary? Cary Mackin?" O'Malley asked.

"Yeah," Hank answered.

"I don't understand," O'Malley continued. "Why the hell would Cary have your car...be driving your car in the middle of the night... with your dog no less?" O'Malley asked.

"Joe...Vito, do you mind?" Hank asked.

"No, just tell me," O'Malley said pointedly.

"Cary spent the night...at my place, I mean. She didn't have her car..." Hank rambled on, trying to avoid getting to the point.

Vito sensed he was in the middle of an awkward conversation he wanted no part of, but before he could figure out the best way to proceed, Hank understood what needed to be done.

"Joe, it doesn't matter. All that matters is we need to find her...find her now," Hank said in a desperate tone.

If Joseph O'Malley was good at poker, you wouldn't know it from the expression he had on his face. It was a combination of jealousy, betrayal, and a tinge of anger.

"We'll put out an APB stat," he responded curtly. "We just need a picture of her if you have one," O'Malley said. The response was clearly a dig at Hank, but she didn't seem to notice.

"No problem," Hank replied.

And then Hank collapsed into Vito's arms before crouching on the ground to give Barry a much-needed hug. It was going to be a very long day.

* * *

As Brandon got into bed for his second nap of the day, he admired his newly acquired gun courtesy of Cary's paranoia. After dragging her into his car, the back seat of which was covered with plastic, Brandon went to take a piss by the side of the road. That's when he noticed a shiny object on the ground. Like most killers, he enjoyed collecting a souvenir from each of his kills whenever possible. Returning to the scene afterward was such a pain. Fortunately for Brandon, nobody was around when Cary met her fate. So he was able to grab the weapon and place it under the front passenger seat in secret.

Brandon checked the area before he drove away from the scene, as he was always careful not to leave any incriminating evidence behind. It amused him that a killer as prolific as Danny Rolling forgot his wallet at one of his victim's apartments and had to go back to retrieve it. *Dumb fuck.* Christa Hoyt was the third student Rolling murdered in Gainesville, Florida, back in 1990. Although Brandon lost a bit of respect for Rolling for being so careless, he had to admire how Rolling turned the near debacle into a victory of sorts. Upon returning to Hoyt's residence, Rolling took the opportunity to decapitate and disembowel her, placing Hoyt's head in a manner that would freak out the police when they eventually were called to the apartment by Hoyt's landlord. Rolling turned lemons into lemonade. Brandon had to give him credit for that.

When Brandon woke up, he checked the time: late morning. He had slept longer than expected. He decided it was time to turn on the television and see if there had been any developments regarding Cary's disappearance. After flipping through the channels, Brandon settled on News 12, the local Connecticut station. As he watched the screen, the words at the bottom of it caught his eye. The crawl read: "Missing woman last seen in Fairview, last known location King's Road in Wooster.... About five foot five inches tall, with reddish-brown hair.... Anyone with information should call the hotline: 203.555.4444." *Looks like the cops broke their twenty-four-hour missing persons rule*, Brandon told himself. *But local news, I mean, please. What a comedown from the national spotlight of Eve's show*, he bemoaned. It didn't appear they were releasing Cary's identity just yet, however. And with no body, Brandon wondered what he could do to blow the case up—without getting caught, of course. He had done enough for one day. Tomorrow, Brandon would sort it all out. There was a fine line between being notorious and ending up in a jail cell.

THREE

Anna woke up to six missed calls on her iPhone, all from Vito. She had turned the ringer off before she went to bed and, consequently, overslept. Vito had managed to slip out of the guesthouse without waking her on his way to meet up with Hank and O'Malley. The lack of progress regarding the "Deer Killer" case was starting to frustrate all of them.

Anna made herself a strong cup of coffee and then sat down to play the messages.

"Anna, call me."

"Anna, pick up."

"Anna, I'm here with Hank..."

"Anna, I need to talk to you NOW. Please call me."

"Cary's missing. Call me."

The last message got Anna's attention. She put her mug down on the kitchen counter, nearly spilling her coffee in the process, and returned the call.

"Anna, thank God. Hank and I are on our way. Stay put," Vito said abruptly.

"What the hell is going on?" Anna asked.

"Just hang on. We'll be there in fifteen, twenty minutes, tops," Vito replied.

"Vito..." Anna began, but the call ended.

What the fuck? Anna asked herself. Her heart started to race as she headed to the bathroom to get washed up and dressed before Vito and Hank arrived. As Anna finished putting on her clothes, she heard Vito's car pull up and come to an abrupt halt in front of the cottage. Anna ran outside to greet them. As Vito and Hank got out of the car, Barry made a hasty departure as well, running straight toward Anna.

"Anna, let's go inside," Vito said with a worried look on his face.

"Vito," Anna began, "what's going on?"

As the three of them made their way into the guesthouse, the tension in the air was unbearable.

"Anna, is there a bowl I can use? Barry's thirsty," Hank said, breaking the silence.

"Sure," Anna replied, grabbing a plastic container from one of the kitchen cabinets. "We used this one for Obi," Anna said ominously.

"Why don't we all sit down?" Vito suggested.

As Anna, Hank, and Vito made their way to the sitting area off the kitchen, Barry followed suit, curling up at Hank's feet for a much-needed nap.

"Anna, we don't know where Cary is. She's gone," Vito began to explain.

"I don't understand," Anna replied.

"Hank," Vito said. "Think you can bring Anna up to speed?"

"Sure. I got up this morning, you know, to get ready for the meeting. I couldn't find Cary or Barry.... Then my car was gone. Cary's phone was still in the bedroom. I called Vito, and he picked me up. But when we got to O'Malley's office, he told us that my car had been found at this farmers market. Vito and I followed O'Malley to Wooster. This couple had Barry, and my car was in the parking lot. But we don't know where Cary is..." Hank concluded, breaking down.

"Oh my God," Anna answered, holding her head in her hands. "Vito, what are we going to do?"

"Crime scene is processing the area right now. It's too soon to file an official missing-persons report, but we got O'Malley to put the word out to the local stations. Let's see what we can find out," Vito said. "Let's not go jumping to any conclusions just yet."

Then Anna had a thought. "What about Gayle? Cary's mother? Have they been notified?"

"God, no, we weren't thinking. Vito?" Hank asked, turning to him.

Vito nodded and picked up his phone to place the call to Gayle. When she answered, he simply said, "Gayle, we're all at the cottage. Think you could get over here...now?"

Sensing the urgency, Gayle replied, "On my way," as she hung up her phone.

* * *

Brandon wasn't sure how to kill the rest of the day. He could visit Cary, but it was too soon. Brandon had decided not to move her again for a while. He liked having his victims close by. After all, they had an unbreakable bond. He could decide on a final resting place later.

Brandon was hungry. Killing always got his adrenaline going and hence his appetite. He used to joke to himself that it was amazing most serial killers didn't have a weight problem. So Brandon went to the kitchen to fix himself a sandwich and then made his way to the den to relax. He put on his favorite music, poured himself a drink, and sprawled out on the couch. There was a chill in the air, so putting his glass down carefully on the coffee table, Brandon went outside to grab some wood to build a fire. As he stoked the flames, he was reminded of the first time he met Cary.

If memory served Brandon right, Moretti had brought Cary to see his guesthouse on a crisp, late fall afternoon. Brandon already knew what she looked like as it had become standard operating procedure for the real estate agent to provide him with a picture of any potential tenants before he met them. Brandon had already signed off on Cary as a possibility, so the meeting was mainly for her to assess the living quarters. Of course, Brandon had the right to turn the applicant down should she not make the cut in person.

Brandon's first impression of Cary had turned out to be pretty accurate. In spite of her relatively good looks, he hadn't sensed any chemistry between them when Moretti initially made the introduction. But Brandon liked a challenge, and he enjoyed finding common ground with his prey, so when Cary's face lit up at the sight of the fire, it stirred something in him.

"What a lovely fireplace," Cary said. "So cozy."

"Why, thank you," Brandon replied. "Makes you want to have a stiff drink and grab a good book."

"Sorry, I don't drink...I mean, usually," Cary responded.

Then Brandon noticed a ring Cary was wearing on her middle finger on her left hand. Bronze in color with a unique yet understated opal in the middle, it was striking. But before Brandon could compliment the piece, Cary seemed to pick up on his interest in it.

"It's from my great-grandmother. The ring," Cary said awkwardly as she began to fidget with it.

Brandon said nothing in response, only nodding to Moretti that Cary had passed the test. And yet, Brandon lost interest in Cary shortly after she moved in. There was something about her he failed to connect with. The other women were different. He loved messing with them. But not Cary. And yet, she was one of the few who ended up dead. Oh, the irony. For now, he had decided to leave the ring on Cary's finger. It would eventually, however, make for a perfect keepsake.

* * *

It only took Gayle about twenty minutes to get to the guesthouse from her office. Barging in, she saw Vito, Anna, and Hank pacing around the kitchen with worried looks on their faces. When he heard the front door open, Vito turned around and looked straight into Gayle's eyes.

"Vito, what's going on? Where's Cary? Why isn't she here?" Gayle asked.

"Let's all have a seat," Vito answered, uncertain of where to begin.

As Vito made eye contact with Anna and Hank, he got the feeling they were all thinking the same thing: had Gayle seen anything about Cary on the news? But the missing woman's identity hadn't been released yet, just a brief description, and as Gayle had been at work, Vito figured she likely hadn't watched any television this morning.

"We don't know where Cary is," Anna said bluntly. "She's missing."

"I don't understand," Gayle responded. "What the hell is going on?"

It fell to Hank to explain.

"Cary stayed at my place last night," she began. "Um...when I woke up, she...uh...she wasn't there. Neither was Barry. I called Vito, and when we got to the station, O'Malley told us they found my car at this farmers market in Wooster. But when we got there, Cary wasn't there, only Barry," Hank continued. "We don't know where she is. What happened."

"Oh, God," Gayle said. "My mother...who else knows about this?"

"The police...there's no official missing-persons case yet...have to wait twenty-four hours, but they put out a bulletin on News 12 with a description, last known location, that sort of thing, but nothing about it being Cary," Vito explained.

"We've gotta tell my mother before she sees anything," Gayle said with an anxious expression on her face.

"Sorry, afraid we got our wires crossed on this...weren't thinking..." Vito continued. "Wanna call her?"

But as Gayle reached for her phone, it rang. Stuart, the reliable paramedic who always responded to her mother's emergencies, was on the other end.

"Gayle," he began, "I don't mean to worry you, but think you could get over here right away? Your mother's having an episode."

"On my way," Gayle answered. Then, turning to Vito, she added, "I think she knows."

FOUR

As Gayle pulled up to her mother's condo, she had a pit in her stomach. Felicia had a sixth sense and was as sharp as a tack for her age. If she had seen anything on television, she could have easily put it all together. But Gayle hoped she was wrong. When Gayle opened the door, she spotted her mother lying on the living room couch with a blood pressure cuff on her arm and Stuart by her side. As Gayle touched him on the shoulder, he nodded to her to step outside, and another paramedic took over.

"Gayle," Stuart began. "Your mother thinks..."

"I know," Gayle answered. "...that something happened to Cary."

"Yeah," Stuart responded, confused. "How did you know that's what I was going to say?"

"It's complicated," Gayle began. "How is she?"

"Okay, I guess. We gave her a sedative, some water. She's resting comfortably now," Stuart explained.

"Is it all right if I go talk to her?" Gayle asked.

"Guess so, but try not to upset her...I mean, any more than she already is," Stuart said.

"I'll do my best, but she needs to know," Gayle answered.

The two of them made their way back inside the condo and bent down next to Felicia. Taking her mother's hand, it was Gayle who spoke first.

"Mom, how are you feeling?" Gayle asked in a concerned tone.

"Cary?" Felicia began, clutching Gayle's hand.

"Mom, it's me: Gayle," she responded.

Felicia was pretty out of it, but as she turned to Gayle and fully opened her eyes she recognized her daughter.

"Where's Cary?" she asked. "The news...I saw something on the news...a missing woman. Is it Cary?"

Felicia's sixth sense had clearly kicked in. Mothers always know. Gayle figured it must have been the description and general location that caught her mother's eye.

"We don't know anything yet," Gayle said. "Not sure where she is, but you need to stay calm. I'm sure everything's going to be all right. I have to go back home. Vito, Anna, they're waiting for me, but let me see if Marcy can come over and stay with you, okay?"

"Oh, Gayle...what are we going to do?" her mother asked. "I can't even begin..."

"Just try to get some sleep. I'm gonna call Marcy now," Gayle responded. "I'll check on you later."

"Promise?" Felicia asked.

"Promise," Gayle reassured her.

Gayle waited until Marcy got to her mother's condo before leaving and brought her up to speed on what was happening. As they had discussed over the phone, Marcy might need to spend the night so she brought an overnight bag with her. Gayle wasn't sure she'd be staying at her mother's tonight, depending on what the rest of the day and evening would bring. Felicia loved Marcy. She was her go-to aide and seemed to bring her great comfort no matter the circumstance. And then, just as Gayle was about to depart, her phone rang. It was Vito.

"Gayle," he began, "we need you back here stat."

* * *

Brandon wasn't sure if it was too soon to commit another murder. While there was an upside to overloading the police with an additional case to solve, he wanted them to focus on Cary. *What to do?* he asked himself. As afternoon approached, Brandon was getting bored and a bit stir-crazy. He therefore decided to risk it all and do a drive-by of Gayle's house to see what was going on. Living on the edge kept your adrenaline pumping. So Brandon got in his smart car and headed toward Gayle's.

When he arrived, Brandon decided it would be best to leave his car a couple of blocks away and make his way on foot to the guesthouse. After all, this was his movie. He had written the script, and they were just unwitting, improvisational actors in it. Watching the now three-some try to solve Cary's disappearance would undoubtedly provide Brandon with endless entertainment. Vito, Anna, and Detective Hank would be going in circles like mice on a wheel, clueless as to what he had planned for them. He would always be one step ahead.

Just as Brandon was about to take cover in his favorite bush, he heard the sound of a car driving a bit too fast down the narrow path that connected the main house to the cottage. He had come to know the place well. As Brandon peeked through the brush, he saw Gayle get out of her car and make her way to the front door. One quick knock, and Vito was at the entrance to let her in. Then they both disappeared from view. For a second, Brandon considered calling Cary's cell phone, but something stopped him. Maybe it was knowing that it was just a cheap trick already used by Joseph DeAngelo, the "Golden State Killer," and many others to call your victims posthumously. Brandon knew he was better than that. He would need to be more careful and watch every move he made, every step he took, and every word that came out of his mouth for the foreseeable future or risk getting caught. Unlike killers like Dennis Rader, who Brandon felt were responsible for their own demise, Brandon cherished his freedom, and he had several roles left to play.

As Brandon waited patiently outside, wondering what his next move should be, he couldn't help thinking about the woman who was murdered by her gardener decades ago in a Pennsylvania suburb. The man got caught because the victim had the presence of mind to write his name with her own blood. *How sloppy can you get*, Brandon asked himself, *leaving a woman alive at the scene, not even bothering to check if she was dead or not? Absolute amateur hour.*

Meanwhile, inside the guesthouse, Vito, Anna, Hank, and now Gayle were pacing around, deep in thought. It was Hank who spoke first.

"Guess I better get that photo of Cary to Joe," Hank began. "Gayle, you wouldn't happen to have one on you, would you?"

"I can run to the house…" she began to answer, but Vito stepped in. "Just tell me where it is, and I'll go grab it," he said.

Gayle hadn't been in her own home since Obi was killed, and Vito didn't think it was such a great idea under the current circumstances. Gayle acquiesced and told Vito to take whichever one he thought best from the wall unit in the den.

As Brandon watched ever closely, he spotted Vito heading out the front door and kept his eyes on him as he made his way up the hill to the main house. Brandon then followed Vito circumspectly. Vito entered the house through the side door, the same entrance Brandon had used when he went looking for Obi. After a few minutes, Vito emerged from Gayle's holding something in his hands. Brandon, always prepared for the unexpected, took out a small pair of binoculars and zeroed in on Vito's hands. He could just make out that it was a photo, seemingly of Cary. Brandon decided things were moving along.

When Vito got back to the cottage, out of respect for Gayle, he showed the photo he had chosen to her to get her approval.

"This one okay?" Vito asked discreetly. "If you'd rather…" he continued, but Gayle interrupted him.

"Oh my God. That's Cary's favorite picture," Gayle responded, beginning to shake. "Her and Obelus…Obi." And then she broke down.

"It's okay, Gayle. Really. We don't have a clue what we're dealing with yet," Vito said as he put his arms around her. "Let's try to stay positive."

Then Vito handed the photo to Hank.

"I'll get this to O'Malley stat," Hank said. "They won't release Cary's identity yet, but they need to have this."

As Hank was about to leave, there was a knock on the door. It was Cliff. Vito and Hank had almost forgotten they sent him to the dog park to search for Cary. It appeared he came up empty-handed.

"Sorry...guess I should have called, but I figured I'd swing by and see if I could catch you or see if Cary was here," Cliff started to explain. "No sign of her at the park."

"Thanks, Cliff," Hank said with a concerned look on her face. "I'm Hank, Detective Nowak. Been working the 'Deer Killer' case. Don't think we really expected to find her there."

It fell to Vito to continue the introductions. "Cliff, this is Gayle, Cary's sister. We're all pretty worried, I'm afraid. Not sure what's going on."

"If there's anything I can do, just let me know," Cliff offered.

Then Hank had an idea.

"We need to get this photo of Cary to police headquarters right away. If you'd be..." Hank continued, but Cliff stopped her.

"Be happy to. Who should I leave it with?" he asked.

"Sergeant Joseph O'Malley in Stamford," Vito answered. "Really appreciate it. Have our hands full at the moment," Vito declared.

"On my way," Cliff answered. "Will check in later."

And with that, he was off.

"What are we supposed to do now?" Gayle asked, frustration setting in.

"O'Malley will let us know if they find anything at the crime scene...I mean, the place where they found my car," Hank began. "Once twenty-four hours have passed...I mean, we hope that doesn't happen...but Cary will officially be declared missing. But we can start checking her phone...credit cards...things like that...Vito?"

"Yeah, the police are doing everything they can right now. We just have to wait. But I have an idea. Gayle, do you have the keys to Cary's place? I know she hasn't been staying there much lately, but it couldn't hurt to check it out, see if we find anything," Vito added.

"Cary gave me an extra set a while ago," Gayle replied. "It's actually on my key chain if you can believe it."

Vito, Hank, Gayle, and Anna exchanged looks and nodded in agreement that that was the next step.

"Let's take my car," Vito suggested. And so, they exited the guesthouse, Barry right by Hank's side.

As the posse of four got into Vito's car, Brandon raced toward his own so he could follow them. *God knows where they're headed*, he pondered. *Likely on a wild goose chase*. It didn't take long, however, until Brandon got his answer: Vito pulled up to none other than Brandon's own home. *I should have seen that one coming*, Brandon contemplated, as he made his way down an alternate path so they wouldn't see him.

As Brandon took cover, he watched from afar as Vito punched in the code that opened the exterior gate to the estate. *Guess Cary shared that little bit of information with her sister*, Brandon told himself. He reluctantly decided that it made sense for them to go through Cary's things while they were waiting to see if she turned up on her own. *But that certainly wasn't going to happen*, Brandon told himself. Not in this lifetime.

Cary's death, albeit at Brandon's hands, was just another reminder of how fragile life is. Where you decided to live could make all the difference. If Cary had just gotten an apartment somewhere else, she'd probably still be alive. But you can only fight fate so much. Years ago, Brandon heard about a young woman who lived in a building where a murder took place. She decided to move as a result. Relocating turned out to be a fatal decision, as the girl was slain herself in her new home. Sometimes it's better to leave well enough alone.

The gate opened, and Vito drove through the entranceway until he reached Cary's quarters. It was about a five-minute drive from the main house. The property was well maintained and looked particularly inviting this time of year. The fall colors were apparent everywhere you looked. As they stepped out of the car, there was a feeling of apprehension shared by all.

"Well, let's get to it," Vito said as he unlocked the door. "Might be best if just Hank and I go in for now...gotta be careful not to compromise anything...don't know what we're gonna find. Anna, why don't you stay out here with Gayle and Barry," he suggested.

"Sure. That okay with you, Gayle?" Anna inquired.

"I guess, but I can't just stand around doing nothing while Cary is God knows where," Gayle responded.

"Just give us a minute," Vito replied.

And so, Vito and Hank made their way inside Cary's makeshift home of sorts, leaving Anna to distract Gayle, unaware that Brandon was watching their every move. Brandon had cameras installed in the carriage house well before he ever began renting it out. The decision had served him well, and from the looks of it, so far Batman and Robin seemed clueless. *Cops are stupid*, Brandon told himself. It wasn't even a fair fight.

"Anything jump out at you?" Hank asked Vito as they began to look around.

"Nothing yet," Vito responded, pulling up the shades so that they could get a better look.

Cary's OCD was clearly on display in her little home. Everything was in its place. The bed was made and decorated with colorful throw pillows. The bathroom was immaculately clean, and the sink and refrigerator in the kitchen looked almost like they had never been used. Except for an expired container of milk and some cheese and eggs, the fridge was empty, as Cary had basically stopped staying there while the "Deer Killer" was still on the loose.

As Brandon observed from his study, he wasn't worried. He opened a desk drawer and admired Cary's gun and wallet, which he had taken from the scene. He was saving the spot next to them for the ring he had spotted on Cary's finger the first time he met her. Vito and Hank weren't going to find anything that mattered, even if they searched Cary's room for eternity. He had gotten there first. While they were gushing over what an organized home Cary kept, Brandon would have loved to point out that he was the one who made the bed. No good deed goes unpunished, and it often goes uncredited as well.

Brandon watched the monitor until the frustrated duo turned off the lights and exited the guesthouse, empty-handed. A few minutes later, he heard a knock on his front door. Brandon checked another screen only to find the foursome and a traumatized English sheepdog on his porch, waiting for someone to answer. As he sat patiently, hoping they would leave, Brandon's prayers were answered. Vito, Hank, Anna, and Gayle exchanged looks and headed back to their car, a rather large canine in tow.

Once Brandon was certain they had departed, he made his way to the main entrance of the home. As he opened the door, a card fell to the ground. On the front, it read "Detective Harriet 'Hank' Nowak" and had her official work contact information. She had taken the time to write her personal cell number on the back. Brandon told himself not to stress over the impromptu visit. But if they became a chronic nuisance, he would have to take matters into his own hands. It might just be time to give them something else to worry about besides him.

FIVE

As Vito and the others headed back to Gayle's place, they realized none of them had eaten since breakfast. It had been a long, stressful day that would likely end in the wee hours of the morning with Cary being officially declared a missing person. Vito and Hank's search of Cary's home had failed to produce anything remarkable. The coming days would likely test their fortitude.

"Why don't we swing by the diner and pick up an early dinner?" Vito proposed.

"That sounds like a great idea, Vito," Anna responded. "I'll call it in if everyone tells me what they want."

When they arrived at the diner, Vito and Hank volunteered to go inside and pick up their order. Then they all went straight to the guesthouse. Anna and Gayle distributed each item to its rightful owner, and with the exception of Gayle, they began to eat.

"I just can't...not yet..." Gayle said preemptively, knowing Vito was about to push her to have a bite.

"You need to keep your strength up," Vito began. "This could go on...I mean...for a while," he added, regretfully.

"Later...maybe in a bit..." Gayle replied. Then, changing the subject, she added, "So what are we supposed to do now? How do we know if Cary's all right or not or where the hell she even is?"

"Once or um...should say if we hit the twenty-four-hour mark, they'll declare Cary a missing person. Then things will change," Vito answered. "Right now, there's not a lot we can do, unfortunately."

"Hey, I'm gonna take Barry out," Hank said, interrupting Vito. Then, turning to Gayle she said, "Wanna come with me?"

"Um, sure. Give me a second. Let me just grab my jacket," Gayle answered hesitantly.

The two of them made their way outdoors, Barry at Hank's side. When they had gotten a short distance up the dirt path that led to the main house, Hank revealed her agenda.

"Gayle, I don't know how much Cary's told you about us...that we're back together...or how much you even knew about what went on between your sister and me, but I need you to know something," Hank continued in a rambling manner.

"What is it?" Gayle asked gently.

"Your sister...Cary...she...she's the one. I can't explain it.... I don't see how..." Hank said in a shaky voice as she tried to get the words out.

Gayle understood what Hank was trying to say, and so, she took Hank's hand and simply said, "We'll find her. It'll be all right. I promise."

And with those words, they exchanged worried looks before going back inside.

The first thing Vito said to them as they entered the cottage was, "O'Malley just called. Nothin' to report...still running tests from the scene...he'll keep us posted."

And then, as Gayle was about to get something to eat, there was a knock on the door.

Vito stood up, walked to the entryway, and opened it, only to find a small envelope lying on top of the mat. Vito picked it up and raced outside to see if he could spot anyone running away, but there was no one in sight. So he went back inside, clutching the delivery in his hands.

"What the hell?" said Hank, as they gathered around him.

Vito opened the packet as carefully as he could with his thick fingers, careful not to disturb it any more than he had to. Inside were a dozen pieces of plastic, all the same shape and size. Vito placed the fragments on the kitchen counter and began to put each in its proper place as if he were working on a jigsaw puzzle. When he was finished, a haunting image stared back at them: Cary's driver's license.

"Oh my God," shrieked Gayle, as she stood there in shock.

Then Hank looked directly into Vito's eyes and said abruptly, "Get O'Malley here now."

* * *

As Brandon made his way through the brush back to his smart car, he wished he could have seen their reaction. *Game on*, he thought to himself. Brandon wondered what Vito and Hank's next move would be. After all, they were the professionals. Cary's sister and best friend were just useless window dressing. Brandon had been careful not to leave any fingerprints on Cary's ID, so he was relatively certain that there would be no way for the duo to figure out who destroyed the driver's license and delivered it in pieces. They were nowhere close to putting it all together.

Brandon felt he deserved a reward for making the first move. So he went down to the wine cellar and selected the most expensive bottle of Malbec he owned, the one he had been saving for a special occasion. Then he could figure out the best time to commit his next murder. Before Cary's would-be rescuers knew it, they would find themselves overloaded, with clues and crimes coming at them from all directions.

Brandon ate his dinner by the fireplace in his favorite room— the den. He decided to catch another episode of *Mindhunter*, then head to bed for a good night's rest. He knew that he would wake up in the morning to the news that Cary Mackin was missing and that her devoted friends, family, and lover were nevertheless optimistic that she was still alive. The purpose of the first clue—the dismembered driver's license—was to plant the idea that Cary may have been kidnapped. Clue two would provide Vito, Hank, and company with more false hope.

* * *

A frazzled Joseph O'Malley arrived within thirty minutes of Vito's call, donning sweatpants, a tee shirt, and a light jacket. Upon hearing the news about Cary's license, he abandoned the baseball field where he was coaching a game for underserved youth and headed straight for Gayle's. When O'Malley arrived, four clearly on-edge people greeted him.

"Vito, let me see it—now," O'Malley said.

"It's on the counter right over here," Vito replied.

Sgt. Joseph O'Malley made his way to the kitchen area and stared down at Cary's reassembled license. Hank thought she knew what he was thinking.

"She's alive," Hank began. "That's what it's gotta mean, right?" Hank asked, turning to O'Malley.

"I don't know," O'Malley started. "It could mean anything. But yeah...guess someone might have her," he concluded.

"*Someone might have her*," Hank responded. "What the fuck, Joe? We all know who's responsible for this," she added in an agitated tone.

"Slow down, Hank," Vito interrupted. "Afraid we don't know anything...not just yet."

"Listen," O'Malley said. "Let's keep this under wraps for the time being. If she...if Cary doesn't show up by the morning, we'll put out an APB and turn the case over to Missing Persons. I'll take her driver's license with me for now...have a tech run some tests on it...fingerprints...all that. Then we'll see where we are."

"It's him. It's the 'Deer Killer.' Let's just stop pretending we don't know what the fuck is going on here," Hank blurted out in a panicky voice.

"Oh, God," said Anna and Gayle simultaneously. "Oh my God."

"Look, I'm gonna run back to the station...see if they found anything on your car, Hank," O'Malley replied. "Anything that might give us something to work with. I'll keep you all posted."

"I'll see you out," Vito said, turning to the sergeant.

The two stepped outside, and Vito thanked O'Malley for coming over on such short notice, then left him with the following words.

"Joe, you know she's right," Vito began. "It's gotta be him."

As O'Malley went to get in his car, he simply nodded in agreement, a troubled look on his face.

SIX

The first thing Brandon did when he woke up was turn on the television in his bedroom. Within minutes, the morning anchor on News 12 Connecticut was announcing that local resident Carole "Cary" Mackin had vanished. Brandon needed to do something to ignite national interest in the story. He would figure it out. A press conference was scheduled for 10:00 a.m., where Sgt. Joseph O'Malley and a representative from the district attorney's office would provide further details. That would give Brandon just enough time for a quick jog, a shower, and breakfast. The presser would no doubt be appointment viewing at its best.

As Brandon completed his morning routine, news of Cary's disappearance was spreading throughout the community. While Vito and Anna were being informed directly by O'Malley, across town, a different scene was unfolding. Gayle and her mother sat in disbelief as the man on television announced that Cary was nowhere to be found. Meanwhile, Hank and O'Malley were glued to the television in his office, monitoring the media's take on the situation.

"We'd better call Gayle," Vito said to Anna.

"Yeah, they must be worried sick. Her and her mother," Anna agreed.

Vito picked up his phone to place the call. Gayle picked up immediately.

"Hello. Vito?" she asked.

"Yeah, Gayle...Anna and I...we were thinking you should come over here. We'll all watch the press conference together."

"My mother...I can't leave her..." Gayle responded.

"That's okay. Bring her along," Vito said, as if that settled the matter.

"Are you sure...never mind, Vito. That's a great idea. She shouldn't be alone right now, and I'd rather watch with you guys," Gayle declared.

"Great. It's at 10:00 a.m. We'll be expecting you," Vito replied, then ended the call.

* * *

Brandon finished his eggs, toast, and protein shake before heading to his study to catch the press conference. At the same time, Gayle and Felicia were arriving at the guesthouse to join Vito and Anna, while O'Malley was reviewing his notes before going on camera. Everyone was in their place.

When Gayle knocked on the door, Felicia beside her, Anna answered almost immediately. Their nerves were raw, but Anna graciously let them inside.

"So nice to see you, Felicia," Anna started. "Wish it was under better circumstances. Here, let me help you."

"I don't need any help. I just need my daughter," Felicia responded in her usual ornery manner.

"Oh my God. Enough! Anna's just trying to help," Gayle replied, scolding her mother.

"It's okay, Gayle, really," Anna responded. "I get it."

Felicia brushed by Anna as soon as she spotted Vito in the kitchen area.

"Give me a hug," she said to him, taking off her coat.

"Felicia, so good to see you," Vito said, glancing at Anna. "Why don't we pull up a couple of chairs and we can all watch? We have a couple of minutes before it's supposed to start."

* * *

"Brooke, make sure we're rolling. We all set?" Gene asked, as O'Malley's press conference was about to begin.

"Yeah, we're good," Brooke responded. "They never start on time anyway," she added.

"Can't afford to miss any of it, that's all," Gene declared.

LNN had put the "Deer Killer" case on hold for the time being, but Cary's disappearance was a whole other matter. There was no way Eve and Gene weren't going to give the story wall-to-wall coverage. It was too soon to suggest on air that there was a connection between the two cases, but it was hard to think otherwise.

At the moment, only a small group of microphones from various television stations surrounded an empty podium. Before long, however, Sgt. Joseph O'Malley would be standing in front of it. Eve's staff stared at the frame sync, genuinely worried about where this story would lead. Cary was family after all, albeit intermittent.

As O'Malley took the stage, front and center, Brandon, Vito, Anna, Gayle, Felicia, and Eve's producers and operations techs watched the proceedings from three different locations. Wooster Mayor Ned Callahan took it upon himself to introduce the sergeant. *Never let a good crisis go to waste,* Brandon thought to himself. *Politicians have no shame.*

As O'Malley thanked the mayor and adjusted his microphone, Hank came into view behind him. Vito wasn't sure if she had been planning to be at the presser, but now, he had his answer.

"I'd like to thank everyone for being here this morning," O'Malley began. "I'll bring you all up to speed on the case, and then we'll take a few questions."

But before O'Malley was able to say another word, several members of the press started interrogating him.

"Like I said we'll take some questions after we're finished—if you guys can wait that long," O'Malley shot back at them. "And if you behave yourselves, Detective Nowak will be happy to provide you with some answers as well. As you all know she's been working the 'Deer Killer' case."

O'Malley's last comment, which he immediately regretted making, triggered one young reporter, who, unable to control himself, yelled out, "Are you saying the cases are related?"

"I'm saying no such thing," O'Malley responded. "Please, can I continue?" he asked, fearing he was losing control of the crowd. "Thank you. Appreciate it. Now, as you all have probably heard by now, a young woman, Carole Mackin, has been missing for the past twenty-four-plus hours. She goes by Cary. We have a team looking into her disappearance and will update everyone as soon as there's anything to report. At this time, we're going on the assumption that she is still alive. And now, we'll take a few questions."

But before O'Malley could call on anyone, a reporter blurted out, "Todd Zeff here. Who was the last person to see Cary alive?"

Gene MacMaster, the executive producer of Eve Arora's LNN show *Crime Watch*, had sent Zeff to see what, if anything, he could get out of them. Zeff did his job well, unintentionally rattling the sergeant and detective with the inquiry. As far as Hank knew no one on the show, with the possible exception of Eve, was aware of her relationship with Cary. So the question really threw her.

The last thing O'Malley wanted to do was kick off the investigation with a lie, so, thinking on his feet, he opted to do damage control by dodging the question.

"Sorry, Todd, but we're not giving out those details at the moment," O'Malley began. "Don't want to jeopardize the case. All I can say is we believe the last known location of Ms. Mackin was at a market in Wooster...probably around two o'clock in the morning."

The response threw the media into a feeding frenzy, wondering why the sergeant had skirted Zeff's question. It appeared they weren't buying the default 'don't want to jeopardize the case' explanation, chronically overused by law enforcement. O'Malley, appearing increasingly uncomfortable, glanced at Hank and then shut it all down.

"We're done here for the time being. We'll make sure to let you know as soon as there are any new developments. That's all folks," he said abruptly, and then exited the podium.

As it was, Hank had been struggling to keep it together during the press conference, as she was worried sick about Cary. O'Malley and Hank had decided not to bring up the driver's license, and now, by avoiding Zeff's question, she felt they were on their way to hiding important facts from the public. Hank couldn't process what the reaction would have been if she had responded to Zeff's query. *Um, I was the last person to see Cary. She was in bed with me.*

Distracted by her thoughts, Hank was startled by a tap on her shoulder. O'Malley stood behind her, a "we better talk now" expression on his face.

"Over here," he said, moving toward a side door used for deliveries at the station.

"Joe," Hank began, "I didn't mean for..." but he stopped her.

"Look, Hank," O'Malley responded. "This is turning into a mess, and it's only been twenty-four hours. It's all gonna come out. We're not gonna be able to hide any of this. When people find out about you and um...well, I'm not sure we'll be able to keep you on the case. It's probably not such a great idea anyway...under the circumstances, I mean." Hank knew O'Malley was right. God only knew how everyone would react when they found out that the missing woman and lead detective on the "Deer Killer" case were involved, especially the media and the higher-ups on the force. *What have I gotten myself into?* Hank asked herself rhetorically. And then it hit her. I'm doing the same thing Cary did: failing to disclose critical information. But right now, all Hank could think about was getting Cary back alive. The fallout in terms of her career could wait.

* * *

Hey Todd, Brandon said to the television. *I was the last person to see Cary alive.* But Brandon thought Hank should have stepped up and told the truth. The fact that neither she nor O'Malley had the guts to answer the reporter's all-important question was a clear sign that Brandon was winning. On the other side of town, Vito and Anna were trying to process what they had just witnessed. The exchange wasn't lost on Gayle either, but fortunately, for now, Felicia was still in the dark. Vito, Anna, and Gayle were all thinking the same thing: Cary's relationship with Hank was going to come out, get sensationalized by the media, and overshadow the investigation.

With that thought in mind, Vito picked up his phone to call Hank. The call went to voicemail. Vito was about to hang up, then decided to leave the following message.

"Hank, call me," Vito began. "You gotta get ahead of this thing, or it's gonna blow up in your face."

* * *

Brandon decided it was time to visit Cary, get the ring, and maybe go to a movie. He needed to relax before he made his next move. It was intermission. Brandon always enjoyed his walks to the cabin at the edge of the property. That's where he kept his souvenirs of sorts. As Brandon opened the door, he failed to detect the foul smell he expected would greet him. He guessed his decision to keep the windows cracked had paid off. Bending down over Cary, he carefully removed his favorite ring and placed it in his pocket. For the foreseeable future, Brandon would keep it in the drawer in his study, next to Cary's gun and wallet. Then, eventually, he would move all three keepsakes to their final resting place.

As Brandon was about to leave, he had an idea. Just for his own amusement, he decided to mimic a trick he had seen in an old black-and-white film. He went over to a shelf where he kept odds and ends and picked up a small mirror. Then he placed it under Cary's nose. The glass fogged up immediately. Brandon jumped up and started pacing around the room. That was not what he was expecting. It was just supposed to be a macabre joke, but Cary was still alive, if only barely. Unbeknownst to Brandon, just hours earlier, Cary had briefly regained consciousness, waking up with the mother of all headaches. Her state of awareness was short-lived, however, as she drifted in and out of cognizance.

What threw Brandon most, however, was his carelessness, not the fact that Cary had miraculously survived the attack. *How could I have been so sloppy and arrogant?* he asked himself. Had he really sunk to the level of that guy in California who cut off the arms of the girl he supposedly murdered, only to find out that she survived the brutal assault, walking for miles until she found help. Then there was the woman in South Africa, left for dead by her would-be killers, who dragged herself to the nearest hospital, clutching her intestines. And, of course, there was HG, the woman who survived the Carr brothers massacre, even though she was shot in the head and run over with a truck. Those murders were supposed to be slam-dunks. Cockiness landed one in a prison cell. Never underestimate the power of adrenaline.

Rattled from the discovery, Brandon locked the door to the cabin and made his way hastily back to the main house. He headed straight for the den and poured himself a double scotch. He needed to think. As Brandon saw it, he had the following options. He could leave Cary to die and continue with his fake kidnapping plot; he could proactively finish her off; or he could acknowledge that she won this round and dump her at an emergency room. Of course, a fourth possibility presented itself as well. Brandon could let Cary live and keep her, which would amount to an actual kidnapping. But in Cary's current state, that would require medical attention. A well-trained veterinarian would surely suffice. Oh, the irony. What to do?

Brandon was certain that Cary wouldn't be able to identify the person who did this to her—that is him—as his headlights had blinded her. There was simply no way she could have gotten a good look at him or the car. And now that she was safely tucked away in Brandon's estate, plainly out of it, he was in control.

Brandon needed to clear his head. What he decided to do with Cary would be one of the most important decisions of his life. So he made himself another drink, stoked the fire, and turned on his favorite playlist, which included songs such as "Anchor" by Novo Amor and Moby's "In This World." Brandon dozed off to the melodies, only to wake up twenty minutes later. He had made up his mind.

SEVEN

It was nearly dinnertime, and Vito and Anna decided to order takeout Chinese and turn on Eve's show. Tonight, they would be prepared for anything. As they began to eat, they heard Eve's voice in the background.

"Breaking tonight," she began. "*Crime Watch* producer Cary Mackin is missing, and we will have all the latest on the case that has rocked the tristate area. Who saw Cary Mackin last? Where is Cary Mackin now? And is Cary Mackin even still alive?" Eve asked, teasing the audience. But although Eve was putting on a brave front, doing her job, she was worried sick about Cary, just like everyone else.

"Oh God, Vito," Anna said. "I can't eat any of this. What's going to happen to Cary? Where the fuck is she?"

"I don't know...we don't know...something will turn up. They're still running tests on the license...Hank's car...it'll break...something will change everything," Vito answered, a bit incoherently.

The next words out of Eve's mouth took them by surprise.

"Hold on," Eve began. "Breaking right now, we take you live to a press conference friends and family of the 'Deer Killer' victims are holding. Todd Zeff, what can you tell us?"

"Hello, Eve," Zeff said. "Yes, family and friends of the 'Deer Killer' victims are demanding justice...."

As Zeff rambled on, Vito and Anna looked up at the television. Huddled around several microphones were Kim Hunter, Siobhan Browne, Rebecca and James Caldwell, Tom Cooper, and Richard Riordan. Tim Shaw was nowhere in sight.

Vito decided to place another call to Hank. This time, she picked up immediately.

"Hey, Vito," Hank answered. "It's been a long day."

"Yeah, how you holding up?" Vito asked her.

"I'm okay. Well, not really. What is it, Vito? Trying to get some rest," Hank responded.

"Nothing...just, did you get my message? Are you watching the presser right now? Eve's covering it," Vito added.

"What presser?" Hank answered.

"Turn on Eve's show," Vito said. "Better yet, can you get over here now?" Vito asked. "There's something I wanna talk to you about anyway. Left you a message," Vito repeated.

"Sure...okay. I'll be there in fifteen," Hank said, and the call went dead.

* * *

Hank didn't realize how exhausted she was until she went to get out of her car. *I'm not gonna make it*, she told herself. When she knocked on the door, Vito let her inside.

"Come here," Vito said, putting his arms around her. "It's gonna be all right...it will...everything will..."

And then Hank broke down.

"Here, let me get your jacket. Why don't you have a seat? Anna, would you get Hank some water, please?" Vito asked.

"I'm fine, Vito, really. You guys don't have to worry about me," Hank declared.

"That's not how I'm seeing it," Vito responded.

Hank looked up at the television screen and saw Kim Hunter speaking. Then the camera pulled out to reveal the rest of the players.

"What's this all about?" Hank asked Vito and Anna.

"The 'Deer Killer' families...friends...guess they feel the case has been put on the back burner. Trying to keep it alive, I figure," Vito added.

"We're still working it," Hank began. "I'm personally overseeing..."

"Yeah, I know," Vito responded. "That sort of brings me to what I wanted to talk to you about, Hank. You didn't answer the question. Who was the last person to see Cary alive," Vito said. "You gotta come clean...control the story, or God knows the press will eat you alive once they find out—and they will."

But before Hank could respond, Vito's phone began to vibrate. When he picked it up, O'Malley was on the other end. He dropped a bombshell on Vito, not unlike the ones Eve was known for on her show. When Vito was done listening, his face went pale, and he got off the phone with a simple, "On my way."

"On my way where?" Anna asked him nervously.

"That was O'Malley," Vito started. "A woman was dropped off... abandoned...dumped at the emergency room in Stamford. They think it might be Cary."

"Let's get the fuck out of here," Hank said as she grabbed her jacket.

* * *

Brandon drove away slowly, not wanting to attract attention. He had checked to see if anyone was around before removing Cary from his car and leaving her by the curb. Any minute now Cary's cohorts would likely be notified that a woman matching her description had been found at the ER. What a mistake it had been for Brandon to mix scotch with some Oxy the night he attempted to eliminate Cary. The way he figured it, it almost made sense for him to drive drunk as he had planned on having an accident of sorts anyway. But the Oxy messed Brandon up, and consequently, he failed to take notice that Cary, while severely injured, was still alive. The current predicament

Brandon found himself in could have been prevented had he been sober. Lesson learned.

Brandon knew the smart thing for him to do was to go home and, in the privacy of his study, monitor the news for any word on Cary. But he liked a challenge and couldn't resist the urge to hang around the hospital in hopes that Cary's loyal entourage would show up. Brandon found a parking spot between two streetlights and pulled over to wait. Before long, a car pulled up to the emergency entrance, and Vito, Hank, and Anna got out.

The trio rushed through the sliding door and went straight to the information desk. A young woman in purple scrubs appeared to be in charge.

"Can I help you?" she asked, taking note of their anxious expressions.

"I'm Detective Nowak, Carlee," Hank said, flashing her badge as she noticed the girl's name tag. "We're here to see the woman who was just admitted...left on the street, apparently."

"She's in critical condition, unconscious at the moment, but let me page the doctor who's on tonight," she said.

A woman in her late forties with a stethoscope dangling from her neck approached them.

"Dr. Denizer," she said, introducing herself. "How can I help you?" Hank held up her badge again, but this time, it was Vito who spoke.

"We're here about the woman who was just dropped off," Vito began.

"Yes, I'm afraid no one can see her yet.... She hasn't been identified.... She's in the ICU.... Police are on their way," Dr. Denizer answered. "May I ask why you're here?" she asked, pointedly.

"I'm Detective Nowak...Hank...we think she may be the missing woman we've been looking for: Cary Mackin," she explained.

But before Hank could say any more, O'Malley, followed by four uniformed police officers, came through the door. He immediately spotted Vito, Anna, and Hank and came right over.

"Glad you're all here," O'Malley said. "Sorry couldn't get here sooner."

"Joe, this is Dr. Denizer. The woman's in bad shape. They're not letting anyone in at the moment," Hank declared.

"When can we see her?" O'Malley asked, turning to the doctor. "We have to find out who she is."

"She's critical, but we've stabilized her for now...may have to do surgery...but if one of you wants to see if she's your missing woman, come with me," Dr. Denizer answered.

The four of them looked at each other and knew who it had to be. Hank looked into the doctor's eyes and said, "Let's go."

Although Hank was only going to look through the room's glass wall, she still had to enter the ICU, so Dr. Denizer handed her a gown and cap to put on before they went inside. Hank didn't think she had ever been this tense in her entire life. As they approached the room, she steeled herself for what was to come. Making her way to the window, Hank peered through the glass only to see her beloved Cary, barely recognizable with all the tubes and bandages.

Dr. Denizer knew immediately from Hank's expression that this was the woman they were looking for. She took Hank's hand and said, "Come on, let's get back to the others and tell them. I'll give you all an update on what we expect to happen medically."

When Hank and the doctor returned to the waiting room, they went directly over to the group. From the look on Hank's face, O'Malley, Vito, and Anna knew at once that the woman was Cary. Vito gave Hank yet another one of his bear hugs, and she collapsed in his arms. Dr. Denizer took it from there.

"I have to be honest with you," the doctor began. "She's in very bad shape. But we'll do everything we can. We're going to need to know who her next of kin are," she added, sympathetically.

"Her sister, Gayle Mackin...she's a doctor—well, a dermatologist— and her mother Felicia," Vito answered. "Didn't wanna get their hopes up until we knew anything. I'll call them now."

Vito couldn't help but wonder who had dropped Cary off at the emergency room. He nodded to O'Malley, and the sergeant walked toward him. Hank noticed and joined them.

"What are you guys talking about?" she asked.

"Um...well...how the hell did Cary get to the hospital? I mean someone had to take her here," Vito began.

"We all know who it is," Hank began. "The 'Deer Killer' is behind this."

"But why would he bring her here?" O'Malley asked, confused.

"Who knows? This guy's crazy," Vito answered. "If it's him."

* * *

Gayle arrived at the hospital, charging through the emergency room door, clad only in her pajamas. It was nearly one o'clock in the morning, and Vito's call had woken her out of a deep sleep courtesy of Ambien. Gayle spotted Vito and the others in a corner, pacing around in front of a vending machine. She ran over to them in a panic.

"What's going on?" Gayle asked, looking directly at Vito. "Where's Cary? Can I see her? Oh my God..."

"Gayle, why don't we go sit down?" Vito said. Then, looking around, he asked, "Is your mother with you?"

"No, just tell me. Is she going to be all right?" Gayle asked.

"I saw her," Hank interjected. "I saw her," she repeated, flatly.

Vito thought Hank was going into shock. He and Anna would have to stay strong and get them through this nightmare.

"I'm gonna get Dr. Denizer," Vito said. "Just give me a minute. She'll explain everything...where we are medically. Cary may need surgery..." Vito added. "She's unconscious...not with it," Vito continued, rambling on.

Responding to Vito's request, the girl in the purple scrubs paged Dr. Denizer. It only took the doctor a moment to respond. She made her way over to Cary's little group of friends and family to give them the big picture. False hope was not her thing.

"Dr. Mackin?" she asked, turning to Gayle. "You're her sister, I assume? Cary's sister? Please, call me Naz," Dr. Denizer added.

Vito thought telling Gayle to call her by her first name was Dr. Denizer's way of extending some kind of professional courtesy. It was a nice gesture.

"I'm the ER doctor," Dr. Denizer explained. "Cary's being evaluated by a neurosurgeon right now: Dr. Han. We should know more soon. But she's not responding at the moment...has internal injuries... broken ribs...lot going on. We'll let you know if she's going to need surgery as soon as we find out more."

"Vito...Hank...she can't just lie around defenseless while God knows who is out there hoping she's going to die," Gayle said.

O'Malley stepped in to ease her concerns.

"It's all taken care of," O'Malley began. "A uniformed cop will be standing guard around the clock. No one's gonna be able to get near her," he added.

Then, grabbing Dr. Denizer's arm, Gayle asked bluntly, "Is she going to make it?"

"There's always hope," Dr. Denizer responded, but the look on her face said otherwise.

* * *

It was now morning, and news that Cary was alive and in the hospital spread quickly. Eve and Gene planned on leading with the story tonight, and Brandon, of course, already knew. He wanted to do something dramatic while Cary was unconscious and fighting for her life, but what? Then Brandon got an idea. *Less is more*, he told himself. Why not start small, then throw so much shit at them that they won't know if they're coming or going?

O'Malley was able to get a couple of hours of sleep before heading to the station. Vito, Anna, Hank, and Gayle stayed at the hospital until the wee hours of the morning, and then went their separate ways. Vito and Anna headed back to Gayle's guesthouse, while Gayle returned to her mother's condo, where she was still staying, to update Felicia on Cary's reappearance and medical condition. That left Hank, who went home to regroup, check on Barry, and make herself some breakfast and a strong cup of coffee.

Cary's reappearance spared Hank the necessity of publicly announcing their involvement, at least for the time being. But in addition to worrying about and checking up on Cary, Hank knew the shit would hit the fan today. She would likely split her time between the hospital, press conferences at the station, and possibly Eve's show. Pressure was mounting regarding the "Deer Killer" investigation as the families were running out of patience. And Hank was certain that O'Malley and Vito knew her instincts were right, that he was the one who went after Cary and likely left her at the hospital. Hank didn't see much sleep in her future.

* * *

It was a little after 8:00 a.m. when Hank's phone began to vibrate. Vito was on the other end.

"Hey, Vito," Hank answered.

"It's Cary," he said. "Gayle just called. They're taking her into surgery."

"On my way," Hank uttered simply in response.

* * *

When Hank arrived at the hospital, Vito, Anna, and Gayle were already there, deep in conversation with Dr. Denizer.

"Hey, what's going on?" Hank asked the group.

"Cary's getting prepped for surgery," Dr. Denizer said. "Dr. Han will be here in a minute to explain the procedure," she added.

Dr. Charles "Chuck" Han appeared, wearing standard surgical garb, ready to operate. He made his way over to the group.

"Dr. Han," he said, putting out his hand to greet them. "I'll be performing the procedure on Ms. Mackin this morning. Afraid she may have a brain bleed and internal injuries that Dr. Denizer will be assisting with," he clarified.

"When will she be out of surgery?" Vito asked.

"Can't say at this point...depends on what we find when we go in... no need to wait around. We could go well into the afternoon," Dr. Han responded.

"I'll stay," Gayle said. "You guys help find this guy," she continued, addressing Vito and Hank.

"Vito, can I talk to you for a minute?" Hank asked.

Hank and Vito stepped away from the others to get some privacy. When they were safely out of earshot, Hank spoke.

"Vito, how can we leave Gayle here by herself while Cary is barely clinging to life?" she submitted.

"Anna will stay," Vito volunteered.

"Thanks, Vito," Hank responded, relieved.

"Good thinking. Gayle's not wrong," Vito said. "We need to catch this guy. Nothin' we can do here, and God knows how long Cary will be in surgery. Let's catch up with O'Malley and see where things are. We can check back with Gayle and Anna later." And then Vito added, "This guy's dangerous, Hank. We gotta get him."

"This guy," Hank said to Vito. "You mean I was right...you mean..."

"Yeah, it's the 'Deer Killer,' Hank...gotta be," Vito concluded, an apprehensive look in his eyes.

* * *

It was now early afternoon, and Cary was still in the operating room under the care of Drs. Denizer and Han. Vito and Hank had spent most of the day with O'Malley, attending yet another press conference to update the public and media on Cary's whereabouts and condition. They had checked in with Gayle and Anna several times, but there was nothing new to report. When Vito and Hank got back to the hospital, they found Gayle sitting on a chair near the vending machine, drinking coffee. She looked exhausted and emotionally drained.

"Hey, Gayle," Hank said, taking her hand. "How are you doing?"

"I don't know. They're not saying anything yet. Oh God, what are we going to do if she..." Gayle continued.

"Don't think like that," Vito interjected. "Cary needs us to stay positive...can't give up hope. Right, Anna?"

Then, just as Vito was giving his pep talk of sorts, an elderly man ran into the emergency room, screaming incoherently. He made his way to the information desk. As Vito, Hank, Anna, and Gayle looked in the direction of the sliding doors, they saw a young woman being wheeled in on a stretcher. All they could make out were the purple scrubs.

EIGHT

Brandon had put a great deal of thought into his next move. *Why not make it convenient for everybody?* he had asked himself. Brandon therefore decided that the hospital could provide him with a wide array of potential victims. How unfortunate for Carlee that her shift ended as Brandon was stalking the entryway. Cary needed a roommate, someone who would understand, and so, Brandon's plan was to merely graze the young woman, not outright kill her. But as he got out of his car to check on her, Carlee seemed unresponsive. Brandon, always looking for a keepsake, spotted her name tag and removed it, sliding it into his rear pocket. *If you throw enough shit at the wall...* Brandon joked to himself. *Let's see how the cops react to this one.*

* * *

Vito, Anna, Hank, and Gayle froze as the gurney rushed by them and through the doors of the ICU. Hank went into detective mode, her eyes trained on the unfortunate woman. It took Hank a moment to recognize Carlee, as her face was severely bruised. Hank's instincts told her this was no accident.

"Hank," Vito said. "Isn't that..."

"It's the woman from the information desk...Carlee..." Hank answered, interrupting Vito.

"What the hell is going on?" Gayle added, confused.

"Don't know," Vito replied. "Hank, better get O'Malley on the phone—*now*."

As Hank was about to place the call, Drs. Han and Denizer emerged from the OR. The look in their eyes didn't portend good news. Dr. Han spoke first.

"Um, why don't we all go over here?" the doctor said, as he guided them toward a more private corner of the room. "That's better," he declared.

"Where's my sister?" Gayle asked in a distressed tone.

"She...uh...we've done everything we can," Dr. Denizer replied.

We've done everything we can were the last words any of them wanted to hear.

"I don't understand," Gayle said, ignoring the explanation. "How is she?"

"Cary's sustained very serious head trauma...internal injuries... afraid she's unresponsive at the moment.... We don't necessarily expect her to..." Dr. Han concluded.

"Oh my God," Gayle said. "I wanna see her now."

"What Dr. Han is trying to say," Dr. Denizer began, "is that we don't expect her to make it through the night."

Vito, Hank, Anna, and Gayle exchanged looks. They couldn't process what they had just been told.

"This can't be happening," Gayle said in an anxiety-ridden voice. "There must be something you can do...anything.... I can't lose my sister, I can't," she implored them.

Vito stepped in to try and diffuse the situation.

"We need to see her. Can that be arranged? Can we go in now... before it's too late?" he added, whispering to the doctors.

Dr. Denizer and Dr. Han looked at each other and nodded. Vito, Anna, Hank, and Gayle followed them into what should have been the recovery room but would more likely be the last place Cary spent on earth.

"We'll give you some time with her," Dr. Denizer said compassionately. "Just let us know when you're finished."

The foursome surrounded Cary's bed. She almost looked ghostlike. Gayle pulled up a chair, took Cary's hand, and broke down.

"Please don't die, Cary. Please...please," Gayle said, as tears streamed down her face.

Hank made her way to the other side of the bed and sat down on top of the covers. She touched Cary's head, brushing her hair aside. Then Hank kissed Cary's forehead as her eyes welled up with tears. Anna looked away. The expression on Vito's face belied his tough exterior. He walked over to the window, stared vacantly, bent over ever so slightly, and began to shake. Then he heard Gayle shriek.

"Her eyes, Hank. Did you see her eyes?" Gayle asked, hysterically.

Hank touched Cary's face, and before she knew it, Cary was looking right at her.

Vito, Anna, Hank, and Gayle surrounded Cary as she struggled to speak. Cary reached for Hank, but all she had time to utter was, "Get him." And with those final words, Cary said goodbye to the four most important people in her life, while she moved one step closer to eternity with Obelus.

Hank and Gayle stayed by Cary's side, frozen and in shock. Only Vito had the presence of mind to call for the doctors. When Dr. Han and Dr. Denizer entered, they rushed over to Cary, took her pulse, and pulled the sheet over her head.

"She's gone," Dr. Han said.

"I'm so sorry," Dr. Denizer added. "I'm so very sorry."

* * *

O'Malley's phone rang as he was driving back to the station. After the latest press conference, he had gone for a run to de-stress, then decided to swing by his apartment for a quick shower and change of clothes. As O'Malley glanced at his phone, he saw it was Vito calling.

"What's up?" O'Malley asked, matter-of-factly.

"Afraid I have some bad news," Vito started to explain. "Uh...it's Cary.... She didn't make it," he said, his voice cracking with emotion.

"Shit, Vito. I don't know what to say.... I know how close you guys were."

Then, taking in the full import of the news, he added, "How's Hank?"

"Not good. We're all in a bit of shock. But, Joe, there's something else," Vito said.

"A woman was brought into the emergency room while Cary was still in surgery. Carlee...don't know her last name. She actually works there...at the hospital.... We think she was hit by a car."

"Stay put, Vito. On my way," O'Malley responded. "Tell Hank I'll be there in twenty."

* * *

O'Malley arrived at the hospital to find Vito, Hank, Anna, and Gayle huddled together in the waiting room, attempting to console each other. But it was an exercise in futility.

The sergeant walked straight over to them to express his condolences.

"I'm at a loss," he began. "We'll get him...we will...you have my word."

Hank looked up at O'Malley with desperation in her eyes. She stood up, walked over to him, and said, "Then we all agree. It's the 'Deer Killer.' He did this to Cary, and he's probably responsible for what happened to that girl...Carlee...who was just brought in. We better talk to the old man who found her. Where is he anyway?" Hank asked no one in particular, trying to stay focused.

"I'll find him," O'Malley said. "Unis are cordoning off the scene right now. You and Gayle stay here. Vito and I will have a look around. There's one other thing," O'Malley said. "We're gonna need to hold another press conference about Cary. Update everyone. We need to take control of the story," he added.

O'Malley's words snapped Gayle out of a fog. *My mother*, she said to herself.

Then, turning toward the sergeant, she explained, "I have to tell my mother. Can someone..."

"We'll have her picked up, bring her here. Anna, think you can..." Vito stated.

"Yeah, sure, of course," Anna replied, knowing Vito wanted her to escort Felicia back to the hospital.

"Then we'll explain what happened," Vito continued. "That Cary... well, didn't make it. You won't have to do it alone. Joe, think you can hold off on that announcement until we get her here?" Vito asked, knowing the answer.

"Yeah, sure, of course," he answered. "No problem."

* * *

It seemed like an eternity before Felicia Mackin made her grand entrance in the emergency room, Anna trailing behind. Cary's mother appeared to be on the verge of hysteria as she made her way toward the sole remaining daughter she was on speaking terms with. Felicia didn't know yet that Cary had died, so Gayle gave her a break regarding her self-centered theatrics. Vito, sensing Gayle wasn't up to delivering the news, intervened, introducing Cary's mother to the doctors, who would convey the awful truth.

"Felicia," he began. "This is Dr. Denizer and Dr. Han. They've been taking care of Cary."

"Where's my daughter?" Felicia asked, as she tried to process the morose expression on Gayle's face. "Where is she?" Felicia repeated, dramatically.

"Ma," Gayle began. "Oh, God...I can't even..." she continued, disjointedly.

"Mrs. Mackin," Dr. Denizer said, addressing Felicia. "We did everything we could."

But before either of Cary's doctors could say anything more, Felicia understood what had happened, collapsing on the floor in front of them.

"Oh my God...her blood pressure," Gayle said, turning toward the doctors.

Hank and O'Malley rushed over from the corner of the waiting room they had positioned themselves in so that Cary's family could have some privacy.

"Get a stretcher," Dr. Denizer yelled out to an intern who was passing by.

Felicia was whisked out of view, as the doctor told Cary's entourage that she would keep them posted.

As Vito, Anna, Hank, O'Malley, and Gayle were trying to absorb what had just happened, a uniformed police officer approached them.

"Sergeant O'Malley," he began. "We located the old man who found the girl: Carlee. He's been sitting right over there, the guy in the green jacket."

"Thanks, Brian," O'Malley responded. Then, turning to Vito, he added, "Let's see what he knows."

Vito and the sergeant approached the elderly man, who appeared shaken and confused as he sat bent over with his head in his hands. O'Malley spoke first.

"I'm Sergeant Joseph O'Malley," he said, as the man looked up. "We'd like to ask you a couple of questions about the young girl you found."

"Mickey...Mickey Shanahan," the man answered, staring blankly at his two inquisitors.

"We'd just like to know if you saw anything or anyone that might help us figure out what happened. Take your time," Vito added, sensing the man's reluctance to speak.

"I, uh, I, uh was walking my dog. Guy almost hit us...the girl was leaving the hospital. He was kinda following her...then he hit her. Got the feeling he did it on purpose," Shanahan stated uneasily.

Vito and O'Malley exchanged glances. They both knew what the other was thinking.

"Did you get a look at the car...plate?" Vito asked.

"Can't say that I did," Shanahan answered. "My dog...he broke away...I chased after him...grabbed the leash...made sure he was okay...pulled him onto the sidewalk. Happened so fast," he explained. "Looked up...she was lying in the middle of the road, so I ran inside to get her help," he said, defending himself.

"Where's your dog?" O'Malley asked him, a bit suspiciously.

"Tied him up outside," the man answered. "Can someone go bring him to me? Name's Ben."

"Yeah, of course," O'Malley answered, backing off his accusatory tone. "Brian, I need you to do something for me," O'Malley called out to his subordinate.

Within minutes, the officer returned to the waiting room, being dragged by a rather large golden brown Leonberger who ran straight into his owner's arms. O'Malley and Vito decided they had gotten as much information out of Mickey Shanahan as they were going to for the time being. So the sergeant handed his card to the old man, with the proviso that he should get in touch if he remembered anything more. It was time to check on Felicia and Carlee. O'Malley and Hank would have a lot of explaining to do at their next press conference.

NINE

When Brandon got home, the first thing he did was pour himself a scotch and turn on the television. As he changed channels, a breaking news alert appeared on the crawl at the bottom of the screen. It read: *Missing Woman Press Conference LIVE at 5 p.m. ET*. Cary, of course, was no longer missing, but the media was notorious for sticking with whatever moniker it thought would rate the best. For the time being, that meant Cary would be referred to as such.

Brandon decided the best way to kill time before the presser was scheduled to begin would be to make himself a snack and listen to some music. He sat in anticipation, wondering how his latest victims were doing. The handsome sergeant and Detective Hank would surely provide him with the answer. Meanwhile, back at the hospital, Felicia was recovering from her spell—to the relief of Gayle and company—as Carlee was fighting for her life.

* * *

It was now approaching 5 p.m., and O'Malley and Hank were about to step in front of the podium to update the public on recent events. As the sergeant walked toward the microphone, his phone began to vibrate. O'Malley signaled to Hank, and they both stepped away. Dr. Naz Denizer was on the other end.

"What's up?" O'Malley asked the doctor. "We're about to go on."

"I just...it's about Carlee...we lost her. I'm afraid she didn't make it," Dr. Denizer responded, dejectedly.

"Glad you caught us before we tripped ourselves up," O'Malley began. "We'll be heading back your way as soon as we're done here."

Hank didn't know what O'Malley had just been told and by whom, but she knew it wasn't good. Before she could ask him, he turned to her and said, "Carlee...the young woman at the hospital...she um...she didn't pull through...afraid she's gone."

"Oh my God," Hank said. "What should we do, Joe?"

"Let's sit on it for now," O'Malley answered. "Until we know what we're dealing with. Make this quick...stick to Cary. You good with that?"

"Sure, Joe," Hank replied. "Think you can handle the brunt of this? I'm not up to..." she explained.

"Yeah, of course," O'Malley responded. "I get it. I mean I *got* it."

O'Malley was still processing the fact that Hank and Cary had been involved romantically. He was struggling with the news and fighting several emotions, including jealousy, but he knew Hank was hurting, and he cared enough about her to get her through this nightmare.

And so, O'Malley took his place at the podium, with Hank beside him and Mayor Ned Callahan in front, never one to miss the opportunity to interject himself into anything he thought might help his career. There was no love lost between O'Malley and the mayor, but you'd never know it from their demeanor. Callahan graciously introduced the sergeant to the crowd, then stepped aside.

"Thank you, Mayor Callahan," O'Malley began. "We're here to bring you all up to date on what's been going on, to give you the latest information on the Cary Mackin case. Ms. Mackin passed away... succumbed to her injuries this afternoon. We are doing everything we can to find the person responsible. As soon as there are any more developments, we'll let you all know."

A hush came over the audience, but as O'Malley and Hank abruptly walked away from the microphones, a familiar voice rang out.

"Sergeant O'Malley, can you tell us what happened to the woman who works at the hospital, Carlee Delgado?" Todd Zeff asked, knowing the answer.

Zeff had managed to rattle the sergeant and Hank just as they were making their escape. Apparently, an intern from Eve's show had been staked out at the hospital and relayed the news to Zeff right before the presser began. Taken aback, O'Malley glanced at Hank, made his way back to the podium and answered with a simple, "No comment."

The unexpected question and evasive answer sent the press into a frenzy as O'Malley and Hank made their way through the crowd and back to the sergeant's car. As they drove to the hospital, O'Malley broke the awkward silence.

"Fuck," he said, an exasperated look on his face. "Damn, I really fucked that up."

"It's okay, Joe," Hank responded. "He really threw us. We'll have another chance to explain...to explain everything."

* * *

Brandon sat quietly, processing the news of Cary's death. While he had given her a second chance, her time was clearly up. It was like when a bug suddenly appeared in your home and your conscience got the best of you and you managed to capture it and put it outside, only to discover that it had no life left in it. Yes, that's what Cary's death was like—an insect given a final feeble opportunity to live. How sad.

Brandon put down his drink as O'Malley and Hank made their getaway, wondering about the fate of Carlee. The sergeant had dodged the question and appeared to have been blindsided by Zeff's inquiry. That boded well for Brandon. Although he had intended to injure, not kill, the young woman, after the near debacle with Cary, Brandon wasn't sure if Carlee was actually dead when he left her. But if she had died at the scene, or was on her way to her demise, Brandon could live with that. He would find out the truth soon enough.

* * *

In the meantime, on the Upper West Side of New York City, all hell was breaking loose on the eighth floor of WorldWideCommunications headquarters. The staff of *Crime Watch* was in shock. They gathered in the conference room, where a call with Eve was about to begin. The "Deer Killer" case had all but stalled out, so Eve had returned to LA along with Annie Cline, the head of booking. With the news of Cary's death, however, that was certain to change.

Gene and Brooke, his second-in-command, took their seats at the head of the table. When the phone rang, Clyde, Eve's assistant, was on the other end.

"Hey, everyone," Clyde said in a quiet tone. "I don't know what to say."

"It's okay," Gene responded. "We're all in a bit of shock. How's Eve doing?"

"I'm right here," Eve answered, her voice cracking with emotion.

"Eve, I'm so sorry. What do you...I mean, how..." Gene began, but Eve interrupted him.

"We're all coming to New York on the red-eye after the show tonight—Clyde, Annie, and me," Eve declared.

"How do you want to handle things?" Brooke asked Eve, leaning into the speaker.

"I think Eve's gonna wanna do some kind of a timeline on the case," Gene interjected, missing the mark.

"No, nothing about the case," Eve said, definitively. "Tonight is all about Cary. Ellyn, Lee, put something together for the staff; Brooke, handle graphics, photos, all that. Clyde's going to put a script—a tribute—together for me. And Gene, get the funeral info from Todd. We're all going," Eve concluded.

* * *

When Hank and O'Malley got to the hospital, only Vito remained there waiting for them. Gayle and her mother, along with Anna, were on their way to Felicia's condo. Then the plan was for Anna to meet Vito back at the guesthouse.

"Let me go grab Dr. Denizer," Vito began. "She can fill you guys in on Carlee."

While Hank and O'Malley were anticipating the doctor's arrival, a young woman approached them.

"Sergeant O'Malley, Detective Nowak, I'm Caity Murphy. You may not remember me. I work for *Crime Watch*," she said, introducing herself.

They both understood at once that Caity was the person who tipped off Zeff about Carlee. But they weren't sure if she knew yet that the girl had died. The next words out of Caity's mouth confirmed their suspicions.

"I'm so sorry about Cary...and the woman from the hospital," Caity said, sympathetically. "Wondering if I can get a statement from either of you."

"Look," O'Malley began. "We're about to be briefed on Carlee Delgado by her doctor. We'd appreciate it if you wouldn't—" he continued, as Caity interrupted him.

"No worries," Caity answered. Then, turning to Hank, she added, "Eve would love to have you on the show tonight. It's going to be a tribute to Cary."

As Hank stood there, unsure of her answer, Dr. Naz Denizer approached them, exhausted and drained.

"Caity, do you mind...think you could give us some privacy?" Dr. Denizer asked the aspiring journalist.

Apparently, in just a few hours, Caity had become a fixture in the emergency room.

"That's okay," O'Malley said. "You can talk in front of her. Think she already knows what happened. That Carlee didn't make it. Isn't that right, Caity?"

"I...uh didn't mean to eavesdrop," Caity started to explain. "I just happened to overhear Dr. Denizer when she was talking to you on the phone," she added, a bit embarrassed at getting caught.

None of them were buying Caity's explanation, but they figured it didn't really matter any more.

"Afraid we couldn't save her," the doctor said, dejectedly. "Too many internal injuries. Assume you'll want to do an autopsy under the circumstances. We've reached her next of kin. They live out West. Her parents will be coming east to deal with everything. Not sure about the rest of her family."

"Let us know when you make contact with them," O'Malley stated, handing Dr. Denizer yet another card out of habit. "Appreciate the help."

"No worries. Been on a twenty-four-plus, time to get some rest," the doctor responded. "Good luck with all this."

Once the doctor left, Caity made a quick departure, presumably heading back to the city to prep for tonight's show. Then Hank spotted Vito coming out of the men's room.

"Must be something I ate," Vito began. "Hospital food...if you're not sick when you get here, you're gonna be sick before you leave," he added comically.

Hank had a lot on her mind. Her heart was broken, but she owed it to Cary to rally and tell the world what a special person she was. Now that Hank thought about it, she wondered why Eve wanted her on the show tonight if it was supposed to be a tribute to Cary. Hank didn't think Cary had told Eve about their relationship, but she had never been sure. However, Hank figured the way things were, Eve wouldn't ambush her, so she decided to text Caity, accept the offer, and see if she could do her segment remotely.

"I'm going to do the show tonight, Joe," Hank stated.

"What show?" Vito asked. "You mean Eve's?"

"Yeah, they're doing a tribute to Cary," Hank replied.

Then, sensing Vito's uneasiness, Hank added, "Don't worry, Vito. She won't get me to say anything I shouldn't."

Hank knew what Vito feared most was Eve exposing Cary and Hank's relationship. While the revelation could prove embarrassing for the detective personally, the main issue was that she was working the case. The optics weren't good. But Vito decided to let it go.

"You know, guys," Hank began. "The driver's license...bringing Cary here...Carlee...what the hell is going on?"

"We'll sort it all out," O'Malley answered. "I'm heading back to headquarters. See where we're at with forensics. Um, check on the autopsies," he said gently. "Good luck with the show tonight."

"Gonna meet Anna back at Gayle's...the guesthouse. Anna and I will watch from there. We'll get this bastard, I swear to God, if it's the last thing I ever do," Vito declared. And he meant it.

* * *

Crime Watch with Eve Arora was about to begin. Tonight's show would be particularly somber. Brandon sat by the fireplace, filled with anticipation. At the same time, Vito and Anna were finishing their dinner and were glued to the television in the carriage house, while Gayle and Felicia watched from the condo. O'Malley had his set turned on in his office, as he tried to unpack recent events. Meanwhile, Hank sat by her phone waiting for Annie Cline to call. Within minutes, Eve's voice rang out.

"Breaking tonight," Eve announced, "We are truly heartbroken to report that our beloved Cary Mackin has died."

Simultaneously, a picture of Cary with her precious Obelus filled the screen. Then a collage of photos appeared. Eve came back on camera, looking distraught.

"Our first guest tonight will shed some light on Cary Mackin's involvement in the 'Deadly Deranged Driver' case. Detective Hank Nowak, what are your thoughts?" Eve asked.

"Well, thank you, Eve, for having me on," Hank began. "Cary was helping the police track the killer, and she was—" Hank continued, but Eve cut her off.

"Detective Hank Nowak, what can you tell us about Carlee Delgado, the frontline worker at the hospital who also died today?"

Eve had mostly kept her word that the show would focus on paying homage to Cary. But she couldn't help but bring up the recent attack.

The incident with the fawns was now common knowledge, so Hank was mainly focused on not revealing the fact that Cary was the one who had witnessed it. Likewise, the detective was determined that her relationship with Cary be kept under wraps for the time being. She could handle Carlee Delgado.

"Yes, I'm afraid Ms. Delgado was struck by a car this afternoon. We're processing the scene, and her family has been informed," Hank declared.

A montage of interviews with the staff was shown, and then Eve ended the show with one last question for Hank.

"Detective Hank Nowak, if you could sum up Cary Mackin in one word, what would that word be?"

The question confirmed Hank's suspicion that Cary had indeed told Eve about the two of them.

Without hesitation, Hank replied, her voice cracking, "Kind."

TEN

It was fitting that Cary's funeral was to be held on a late fall day, the trees awash with an array of striking colors. Gayle and Felicia planned every detail with Anna's help. Although Felicia insisted that the service be held in a church, Gayle and Anna overruled her. And so, it was decided that as Cary was not a religious person, a memorial would be conducted at her favorite place: the dog park. Then she would be interned in the Mackin family mausoleum in Fairview's Catholic cemetery.

As promised, Eve, Clyde, and Annie had arrived at JFK International Airport in the early morning hours, technically, the day after Cary's death. It would prove to be a busy day. Cary's autopsy was performed, and then funeral preparations made. It was a lot to process. Gene and Eve decided to cancel the show that evening and rerun an evergreen episode on a case that never got old: JonBenét Ramsey.

After the funeral, the plan was for O'Malley, Hank, and Vito to meet up and review the autopsy results as well as all the forensic evidence collected to date. That would include Cary's chopped-up driver's license, both hers and Carlee Delgado's post-mortem findings, and anything of interest from Hank's car, the area where Hank's car was discovered, and the crime scene where Carlee was run down. And then, there was the "Deer Killer." Well, at least it was a start.

* * *

"We have to leave now, Ma," Gayle called out to Felicia. "The car is waiting."

Mrs. Felicia Mackin appeared in the foyer of her condo, impeccably dressed in her most expensive black suit. Gayle had wanted to honor what she believed would have been Cary's wishes, a more informal affair, but far be it for her to interfere with any more decisions her mother made on this awful day. Changing the location from the church to the dog park was victory enough.

"Martin, Jane, Sharon, hurry up. We're leaving. I left the car keys on the table in the front hall. Don't be late, and don't forget to lock up," Gayle admonished her kids.

"We'll be there on time, promise," Jane answered on behalf of her and her siblings.

"Great. Love you guys," Gayle said, and she headed for Vito's car.

Vito and Anna greeted Gayle and her mother as they approached the vehicle. There was dead silence until Vito spoke up.

"We'll be there soon," he began. "Not much traffic today."

Awkward small talk would have to suffice on the ride to the dog park. No one was up for anything else.

When they arrived, Hank and O'Malley were already inside the park, along with a few unis and some obvious undercover cops. Vito knew the sergeant was hoping the killer would crash the service. But Vito couldn't help wondering: even if he did, how would they ever know? Anyway, now wasn't the time. Today was all about Cary. Catching her killer at her memorial would be an unlikely bonus.

"Hank, Joe, glad you're here already," Vito said in a relieved tone. "This isn't gonna be easy."

And then Anna spotted Cliff Danjuma in the distance, the bodyguard who had been unable to protect Cary. He stood watch over her casket, doing in death what he had failed to do in life. At least that's how he saw it. Anna waved to him and, nodding to the others, said, "Excuse me, just going to say hello to Cliff for a minute." Then, without thinking, she added, "I thought Cary wanted to be cremated."

That was too much reality for Hank. Her face turned ashen as she glanced in the direction of the simple pine box. Hank didn't know how she was going to get through the day.

"God, I'm so sorry," Anna said, owning her insensitive remark.

"It's okay," Hank responded. "It's not your fault."

"Be back in a minute," Anna answered, as she headed in Cliff's direction.

"Ma, let's go sit down," Gayle said.

"Good idea," Vito added. "You guys take the front row. We'll be right behind you."

So Gayle walked her mother to the makeshift arrangement of benches and chairs, not likely to be adequate enough to hold the large number of guests expected to attend. Not long afterward, her kids joined them.

"There's something I gotta take care of myself," Vito said to Hank. "Give me a minute."

As Vito walked away, Hank could clearly see that he was texting someone on his phone. But his actions gave Hank the opportunity she needed to pull off something of her own. The detective made her way surreptitiously to Vito's car and retrieved an object from the trunk.

Meanwhile, people were flooding into the park, taking their places for the service. As Vito, Hank, and O'Malley regrouped, they observed Eve and her staff marching in together, a small army of colleagues coming to pay their respects. Next were Kim Hunter, Siobhan Browne, Rebecca and James Caldwell, Richard Riordan, and Tom Cooper. Only Tim Shaw, as usual, appeared to be missing. Otherwise, the "Deer Killer" victims were well represented, mourning who they believed was his latest victim.

When Vito returned, he took O'Malley aside and whispered something in his ear. Then he took Hank's hand and said, "Let's sit down."

As the three of them made their way to the row of benches behind Cary's family, a man was already positioned in the aisle seat. Vito touched him on both shoulders; he stood up, turned around, and gave his daughter a big bear hug. Hank was completely taken aback. Apparently, Vito had taken it upon himself to surprise Hank at Cary's funeral with the company of her dad and his best friend, former Det. Henry Nowak. From the expression on Hank's face, it was evident that Vito had overstepped his bounds. She seemed rattled and discombobulated by her father's presence, and her reaction wasn't lost on Vito. But before he could put two and two together, Hank dragged Vito aside.

"Look, I know there isn't time for this right now, but my dad doesn't know about Cary and me. In fact, he doesn't even know that I've dated...am dating...guess what I'm trying to say is *was* dating a woman: *Cary*," Hank explained.

"Shit, I'm really sorry," Vito began. "Don't know what I was thinking. I should have checked with you. I just thought under the circumstances..." he rambled.

"Can't do anything about this now. Let's just get through this nightmare of a day, and I'll deal later," Hank declared. "I wasn't planning on speaking anyway," Hank continued to explain. "The investigation...better if I don't complicate things right now. You know what the media will do if they get wind of me and Cary," she said in a worried tone.

"It's all good," Vito responded, as he gave Hank her second bear hug of the day.

Then he noticed the small pouch she was carrying.

"What's in the bag?" Vito asked, kicking into detective mode.

"Oh, um...it's nothing. I mean, actually, it's, um, it's Obelus... his ashes.... I know Cary would have wanted..." Hank continued, breaking down.

Vito's eyes welled up with tears as he extended his hand to take Obelus from Hank.

"Here, it's heavy," he began. "Let me hold him."

As Hank entrusted Vito with precious Obelus's remains, she started to shake.

"I'm not gonna make it," Hank said with desperation.

Vito put his arms around her as they took their seats in the crowd. He didn't think he was going to make it either.

A hush settled over the audience as the first of several speakers approached the podium. Vito was to make the introductions, beginning with Eve herself. As the queen of crime took the microphone out of Vito's hands, she started to tremble.

"I am here today," Eve began, "to pay tribute to a very special lady who I have known and worked with for a very long time: Cary Mackin. Cary was, in many ways, my soulmate. We saw things the same way and helped each other out over the years. I have been blessed to call her a friend," Eve concluded, fighting back tears.

Vito came to her rescue, introducing the next person.

"Thank you, Eve. And now we're going to hear from a very special person in Cary's life: her twin sister Dr. Gayle Mackin," Vito declared.

Gayle stood beside Vito looking shaken and pale. He wasn't sure she would be able to address the group in a coherent manner, but he knew she had to try.

"When you're ready," Vito said, turning to Gayle.

"First, I'd like to thank everyone for coming today. Cary would have been truly touched. We're here in this beautiful dog park because it was Cary's favorite place, the place where she found inner peace and spent time with her precious Obelus. Now both Cary and Obi are gone," Gayle said, barely able to breathe. "But we must take solace knowing they are together again. We just don't know where," Gayle said, unable to say anything more.

Vito got all choked up listening to Gayle as she tried to maintain her composure. He thought she did an amazing job under the circumstances. Gayle took her seat next to Felicia, and Vito addressed the throng.

"If there's anyone else who would like to say a few words about Cary, please form a line," he said.

Several *Crime Watch* staffers, including Ellyn Joseph, Lee Snow, and Annie Cline, got up from their seats to honor Cary with their memories of her. Then Vito made an announcement.

"That concludes the service, folks," Vito said. "Thank you all for coming. Those who wish to continue on to Cary's final resting place with us, just pull your cars over to the side of that little road," Vito said, pointing. And then, looking up at the sky, he added, "We love you, Cary," and broke down.

* * *

Brandon observed the impromptu ceremony from the last row, adorned with sunglasses and a fedora. *If Cary's memorial didn't call for a dramatic touch, what in the world possibly could?* he wondered. Brandon was still unsure if this was the best time to expose himself. But in the end, he decided that no one remotely suspected him of anything at the moment, and he was Cary's landlord of sorts, after all. With that in mind, he made his way to the front of the crowd, walking in the opposite direction from everyone else.

When he got near the podium, Vito, Hank, and O'Malley were collecting their things and directing people to the exit. An older gentleman was still sitting right behind Cary's sister and mother, and Anna, of course. Yes, the gang was all here. Brandon cleared his throat, took off his sunglasses so he could look them straight in the eye and, tapping Vito on the shoulder, simply said, "Sorry for your loss."

Cary's inner circle of family and friends didn't recognize the man. Neither did Sergeant O'Malley.

"Vito here," he said to the man. "Are you a friend of Cary's?"

"No, I mean...meant to introduce myself," Brandon began. "I'm Brandon, Cary's landlord. Feel bad about what's been going on in our beautiful community as of late," he added deceitfully.

"Hi, I'm Cary's sister, Dr. Mackin," Gayle said. "Please let us know when we need to get her things. It's just with all that's been going on..." Gayle tried to explain, but Brandon cut her off.

"No rush...no rush at all," Brandon answered. "Wasn't planning on renting out the cottage again any time soon, anyway."

Vito made the rest of the introductions, beginning with Anna, O'Malley, and Hank. Unbeknownst to Vito, Brandon was already familiar with all the players.

"Hank," Vito said, addressing Henry Nowak. "There's someone I'd like you to meet."

Nowak got up and put out his hand. He and Brandon locked eyes, as if they were having a staring contest. After a moment, Brandon reached out and shook Nowak's right hand.

"We usually call him Nowak," Vito interjected. "Because of his daughter and all."

"Yes, Nowak," Henry stated.

"Very nice to meet you," was all Brandon said in response.

* * *

When they got to the cemetery, Vito pulled his car behind the hearse, and the rest of the vehicles formed a line behind him. Then they all made their way to the Mackin family mausoleum. Although it probably wouldn't have been Cary's first choice, the priest from her mother's church was chosen to say a few words. That was the deal Gayle had made with her mother so that the memorial could be held in the park.

"Please gather round," Father Philip McCarthy said. "As we stand here before God, we leave Carole Mackin at her final resting place. May she find eternal peace with the Lord. Amen."

As the doors of the spacious stone structure opened, Cary's casket was brought inside. Vito, O'Malley, Gene, and Zeff were among the pallbearers who carried the heavy box. As they came back outside, Hank approached Vito.

"Vito," Hank said. "Where's Obi?"

"I got him. No worries," Vito answered, taking Hank's hand. "He's in the trunk."

"Please get him," Hank implored Vito. "Cary needs Obi, please."

Vito nodded, a grim expression on his face. He walked to his car, opened the trunk, and gently picked up the small wooden box that held Obelus's ashes. Vito couldn't help but think, *That's where it all leads: to a container.* But as he went to close the trunk, something caught his eye. A piece of paper appeared to be stuck in one of the rear brake lights. As Vito pried it from the plastic to take a closer look, his heart started to race. "Odd Jobs" it read, with nothing on the back.

Sick fuck, Vito said to himself, as he walked back toward Hank. He couldn't let her know what had just happened. She was having a tough enough time as it was. But Hank, always in detective mode, immediately sensed something was terribly wrong.

"Vito, you okay?" Hank asked. "You look white as a ghost."

"Yeah, um, uh..." he began.

"What is it, Vito?" Hank asked. "If you're keeping something from me, I need to know. Please give me Obi's ashes," she pleaded.

Vito knew, best intentions aside, that he had to show Hank the card. So, handing Obelus over, he tried to prepare her for what was to come.

"Hank, I think we better sit down," Vito said. "There's a bench over there."

"No, Vito, what the fuck? Just tell me," Hank insisted, as she held Obi close.

Vito acquiesced, clutched the all-too-familiar card by the edges, and handed it to Hank.

"Oh, my fucking God," Hank shrieked. "Where did you find this?"

"It was stuck on the car...in the brake lights in the rear," Vito explained. Then, glancing at Gayle, her mother, Anna, and the rest, he said to Hank, "Let's keep this quiet for now. Don't want to throw everyone into a panic."

But he and Hank motioned to O'Malley, and the sergeant made his way over to them.

Hank handed him the card.

"Where in the hell did this come from?" O'Malley asked them.

Vito explained again and asked him not to say anything until they got back to police headquarters for the meeting. O'Malley agreed.

And so, Hank, looking drained and anxious, put her head down, trying to hide her tears.

"There's something I've gotta do," she told them. But Vito already knew what it was.

Hank went inside Cary's permanent home and placed Obelus's remains beside her coffin. They would spend eternity there together. Then Hank put one hand on top of each of them and made a solemn promise.

"This isn't over. Not by a long shot," Hank told the woman she loved more than life itself. "We're gonna get him and make him pay... for everything."

And then, between sobs, she added, "See you on the other side."

* * *

Brandon took off his hat, poured his drink of choice, and sank into his favorite chair. He had knowingly tempted fate today. But life wasn't worth living if you didn't take risks. He had decided he would have enough time once they got to the cemetery to discreetly leave his calling card. No one had spotted him—of that he was certain. The meet-and-greet at the dog park was another matter. It was one of his more understated performances but well played. Henry Nowak had a beautiful daughter—one more thing to use against him.

ELEVEN

Hank passed on the scheduled post-funeral meeting. She needed to spend some time with Barry and relax as much as was possible these days. It had been a long, emotional day. So Vito dropped her off at home and headed to Stamford to meet up with O'Malley. But he wasn't alone. Hank's father insisted on coming with him, for old times' sake. As they drove, more or less in silence, Vito couldn't get Cary out of his head. She had been like a daughter to him, and now, she was simply gone. He once saw a meme that summed up life: don't exist, exist, don't exist. *Whoever thought of that one,* Vito contemplated, *was spot on.*

Vito had gotten a weird vibe when he introduced Cary's landlord to Nowak at the memorial. He couldn't put his finger on it, just a gut feeling. *I've been doing this too long,* he said to himself. Being suspicious of everyone and everything was getting old. Vito wondered how much longer he could be a private investigator and stay sane. Maybe it was time to call it quits.

As they pulled into the station parking lot, Vito turned to Nowak, who was sound asleep. He had been so engrossed in his own thoughts that Vito hadn't even noticed that Nowak was in a near coma the whole way down. Vito had a great deal of affection for his best friend. He remembered that they used to call him Nowak-it-all back in the day. Yes, Nowak was a first-class smart ass, but Vito figured that was what had made him such a good detective.

Vito's hand on his shoulder startled the old man. Nowak woke up, a bit disoriented. Vito and he were the same age, but Hank's father didn't seem to be aging as well.

"What the hell?" Nowak said as he tried to get his bearings. "Car rides always put me to sleep. Sorry."

"All good," Vito reassured him.

Vito parked his car in the lot normally reserved for active law enforcement, and they made their way to O'Malley's office. When they arrived, the only other person there was Max Craven, the evidence technician. From O'Malley's expression, it was clear that he wasn't expecting Nowak. Vito didn't think to clear it with him. Trying to do damage control, Vito addressed the sergeant.

"Hank thought it might be...um...useful if he came along," Vito began, hoping the sergeant would give the former detective a break.

"I can wait outside if it's a problem," Nowak said, putting O'Malley on the spot.

If there was one thing Sgt. Joseph O'Malley hated it was being ambushed, even if that wasn't Vito's intention. So he responded the only way he could for the moment.

"Fine, okay. Just everything we say in here, as you know, is confidential," he added, pointedly.

"10-4," Nowak answered.

Vito thought that Nowak resented the young, handsome sergeant and probably didn't even know that he may have been involved with his daughter. At least that was Vito's current theory.

"Why don't we all take a seat?" O'Malley instructed the group. "This is Max Craven, our evidence tech. Max, you know Vito. And this is former Detective Henry Nowak."

"Pleased to meet you," Nowak said. "Bettin' you crack a lot of cases around here," he added, to O'Malley's annoyance.

There appeared to be no love lost between the sergeant and former detective. Vito figured there was no real reason for the animosity, just bad chemistry. He regretted letting Nowak tag along, but it was too late now.

"Max, why don't you bring Vito, I mean, them, I guess, all of us up to date on where we stand evidence-wise," O'Malley said.

Max Craven was one of Hank's most trusted colleagues. She never doubted his work. Not for a minute. In his late twenties and slightly overweight, Craven was a CSI wannabe as much as anything else and had realized his dream. But he was a brilliant young man and principled to boot. So O'Malley and everyone else in the department had come to rely on his findings.

"Afraid I couldn't get prints off the driver's license," Craven began. "Must've been wearing gloves. This guy knows what he's doing," he concluded.

"And the rest?" O'Malley said, trying to move the meeting along.

"Oh, yeah," Craven responded. "Well, only prints we were able to find on Hank's, sorry, Detective Nowak's vehicle, were hers and Cary's. Doesn't appear anything incriminating was left at the scene... the market where the car was discovered. Likewise, looks like whoever left the license fled on foot. Probably had a car hidden somewhere within walking distance, most likely on the street. We're checking security cam footage, but nothing definitive yet."

"What about the young woman from the hospital? Carlee Delgado?" O'Malley asked.

"We're waiting on autopsy results for both Delgado and Cary. But pretty sure we know what they're gonna say." Craven answered his superior. "Thing is there were no skid marks on the street where Delgado was struck. But we're checking security footage and hopefully the guy wasn't in a blind spot when he hit her, so we can catch a break regarding the car."

Craven, flustered as always when it came to dealing with people, had taken things a bit out of order. But he was compulsive when it came to forensic analysis, and if anyone could make sense of recent events, it was him. Nowak sat quietly, taking in all that the young investigator had said. While the former detective understood the importance of concrete evidence, he believed there was always an X factor that blew a case wide open. Maybe Nowak himself would be able to provide it.

"Well, guess that wraps it up for today. As soon as we get the post-mortem reports, I'll let you know, Vito. Same goes for the security footage. Though I can't say I'm optimistic at the moment, expecting a big break. We're dealing with a very devious mind here, thinks through every move. And he's careful. But we'll get him, we will," O'Malley declared.

"If it's the last thing I ever do," Vito answered.

* * *

Vito and Nowak were greeted by a small group of protestors as they drove out of the parking garage. The well-meaning citizens held signs that read, "Justice for Cary" and "Dogs Lives Matter." Vito nodded as they passed by the crowd, honked his horn in solidarity, and headed toward I-95.

"Mind if I give Anna a call?" Vito said. "Been meaning to check in with her."

"Course," Nowak replied.

After one ring, Anna picked up. Vito was about to put the call through on Bluetooth, but something stopped him. Consequently, Nowak could only hear his end of the conversation.

"How ya doing?" Vito asked Anna.

"How do you think?" Anna answered, clearly spent.

Vito was taken aback by her tone, but he understood where she was coming from. For decades, Anna had considered Cary to be her best friend. It had to be an enormous loss for her. Anna likely hadn't even begun to process Cary's death, the long-term effect it would have on her life.

"Sorry, babe," Vito said contritely. "Just wanted to make sure you're hanging in there. How's Gayle and her mother?"

"It's okay, Vito. I shouldn't have snapped like that. Gayle and Felicia are resting at the condo. I ordered them some food. We should follow up with them tomorrow," Anna muttered.

"See you back at the cottage?" Vito asked.

"Yeah, sounds good," Anna affirmed. "I'm going to try to lie down for a few minutes. Wake me when you get here."

"Where are you staying?" Vito asked Nowak. "Can I drop you off somewhere?"

Nowak took a moment and then answered.

"Think I'll head home. Dumped my bags there this morning but didn't leave it in the best shape when I took off for Santa Fe. Looks like I'll be sticking around for a while, though, so might as well get to it," Nowak replied. "It's a bit of a drive from here, Vito," he added. "Can hop a cab from your place if that's easier."

"Wouldn't think of it," Vito replied. "Anyways, I've been staying at Gayle's...um, with Anna, so not that far, really."

"Look at you, you old stud," Nowak said, punching Vito in his upper arm. "Always liked that girl."

Vito wasn't sure what Nowak's plans were. He had just thought it would be a nice thing for Hank if he came to Cary's funeral to support her. But now that Vito thought about it, it was really none of his business. Hank should have been the one to make that decision.

Vito pulled up to Nowak's home, located on the border of Fairview and Bridgewater. The house was old and in need of repair but sat on a bay with a small dock. Nowak had a dilapidated motorboat that was currently covered up with a blue protective shield. It was his pride and joy. Vito said his goodbyes, and Nowak made his way inside.

As always, upon entering, a flood of memories came over him. Flashes of a boy, a car, running into a convenience store, seeped out of his subconscious. He opened the fridge, and a putrid smell emanated from inside it. Nowak put a new liner in the garbage can and filled it with old takeout containers of Chinese and Indian food. *Guess I should have cleaned this motherfucker out before I left,* he said to himself.

The former detective threw some logs in the fireplace, struck a match, and lit up the room. He opened the pantry door and took out a six-pack of Budweiser. Nowak opened one can and put the rest in the fridge. In one gulp, he downed the contents and threw the empty container in the overflowing recycle bin. Then he made his way to the first-floor bedroom.

As Nowak walked toward the dresser, an antique wooden piece adorned with family photos, he steeled himself for what was to come. Nowak grabbed the handle of the top drawer and pulled it toward him. The former detective looked inside, as he had done a thousand times before, and stared down at some newspaper articles, a worn photo of a toddler, and a baby shoe. It never got easier.

* * *

Brandon woke up in a manic mood. Today was the day he would say his final farewell to Cary Mackin. Her sister and Anna Zee would be clearing out the transient home she had made for herself at his guesthouse. He had already met them in person at Cary's memorial at the dog park, and so far, he hadn't raised any red flags. Therefore, Brandon didn't see what harm it would do if he ambushed the pair at the cottage. He felt it incumbent upon himself to treat his latest tenant with a bit of respect.

Gayle pressed the buzzer at the entrance of Brandon's estate and announced herself. She knew the code but thought it was presumptuous to just plug it in like they had done the other day and drive through. Brandon held down the button and released the gate. They parked Gayle's truck right outside the guesthouse front door and paused before exiting the vehicle.

"This is going to be too much," Gayle said anxiously.

"I know, I know," Anna answered her. "None of this seems real. It hasn't registered yet, none of it."

As Gayle took out Cary's key to unlock the door, a voice called out to them.

"Hang on," Brandon yelled. "I'm here to help."

Brandon thought he had helped enough already, but the women were none the wiser. He felt packing up Cary's things would provide him with a well-deserved thrill. After all, none of this would have happened if it weren't for him.

As they entered through the door and glanced around the room, Gayle couldn't help thinking that, knowing her twin, this is exactly what she had never wanted Hank to see: her sad, lonely life. Gayle was relieved that Hank had agreed to let Anna and her handle it.

"Guess we should start with the books," Anna suggested. "I'll go grab some boxes."

Gayle nodded and made her way over to a shelf that held about two dozen of Cary's favorite novels. *The Girl with the Dragon Tattoo* trilogy and first three *Game of Thrones* paperbacks were among them. Next, Gayle opened the closet that held most of Cary's clothes. Her tee shirts, sweatshirts, and anything else that could be folded, were in the dresser. Adjacent to a sink in the corner was a microwave, dorm-sized refrigerator, and toaster oven that comprised Cary's kitchen. Lastly, on another shelf beside Cary's bed, was a photo of Obelus and his favorite ball and pull toy. That's what was left of Cary's life.

Brandon had remained outside while Anna and Gayle boxed up Cary's possessions. He wanted to appear helpful but also considerate. He balanced the two well. As the women exited the guesthouse, boxes in hand, Brandon rushed over to them.

"Please," he began. "Let me."

Brandon took the first box from Gayle, the heavy one containing the books, and placed it in the back of the truck. Before long, all of Cary's things were in the cargo bed, except, of course, her wallet, gun, and distinctive ring. *Everything and everyone end up in a box*, Brandon told himself. He had just hastened Cary's departure.

* * *

Hank was apprehensive as she got ready to meet her dad at the diner for an early lunch. She hadn't gotten much sleep, tossing and turning throughout the night. All she could picture was Cary's coffin next to Obelus's ashes in that cold, secluded place. She spent the night going over and over in her head what, if anything, she could have done so things would have turned out differently. But the answer didn't matter. Nothing could bring them back.

When Hank arrived at the diner, she spotted her father smoking near the entrance. She thought he had quit a long time ago. *So that's why he always has mints on him*, Hank concluded. *What a detective I am*, she scolded herself. Nowak noticed his daughter getting out of her car and quickly dropped the cigarette on the ground, stomping it out with his right foot.

"How's my girl?" Nowak said, greeting his daughter with a hug.

"Dad," Hank started. "I thought you quit..." she continued, but Nowak stopped her.

"Not today, sweetie," he responded. "The lecture can wait. Just worried about you with all the shit that's been flying around here lately."

"Okay, I'll drop it for now. But you know what the doctor said," Hank responded, backing off.

They made their way inside and were shown to a booth in the back by none other than Hank's regular server, Xanthe.

"When you're ready," Xanthe told them, as she handed the pair a couple of menus.

"What do you usually get here?" Nowak asked his daughter. "I'm gonna stick with breakfast. Best meal of the day," he added, trying to lighten the mood.

"I'm not really hungry," Hank answered her father. "Just a hot chocolate, maybe."

Hank was a die-hard coffee drinker, but today, she wanted everything to be about Cary. Her father didn't get it. *Why would he?* she asked herself. Hank hadn't exactly been honest with him when it came to her social life. They just didn't have that kind of relationship. As close as Nowak thought they were, from Hank's point of view, the foundation of their relationship was mainly based on work. But Hank loved her dad and knew he had her back.

Nowak got Xanthe's attention, and they placed their order. As he was about to bring up the "Deer Killer" case, Hank's phone began to vibrate.

"Sorry, gotta take this," Hank said. "It's O'Malley."

"The autopsy results came back," Hank told her dad. "Gotta go."

Nowak's first impulse was to ask his daughter if he could accompany her to the station, but something made him hesitate. *Let her be,* he told himself.

"That's okay. You go ahead. See you later?" Nowak asked Hank.

"We'll see," Hank began. "I mean, let me see what's going on. I'll call you."

Nowak finished his breakfast, drank Hank's hot chocolate, and went to the counter to pay, leaving Xanthe an adequate, if not generous tip, on the table. When he got to the register, she handed him the bill and smiled.

"I'm so sorry about Cary," Xanthe said compassionately. "They made such a lovely couple. Hank must be devastated."

If there was one thing Xanthe was known for, it was putting her foot in her mouth. From Nowak's reaction, she regretted the statement.

Taken aback, Hank's father handed their server thirty dollars and turned toward the door.

"Your change," Xanthe called out to him.

"Keep it," Nowak answered and left.

* * *

Hank drove well over the speed limit on her way to the station. But she was a detective after all, so if a uni pulled her over, she'd talk her way out of it. Hank didn't think the autopsy reports would reveal anything unexpected, but they would be difficult to listen to. With that thought in mind, Hank placed a call to Vito. It went straight to voicemail.

"Hey, Vito," Hank said. "On my way to O'Malley's. Will you be there?"

Hank arrived in record time and parked in her designated spot. When she got to O'Malley's office, she hesitated before entering. Collecting herself, Hank made her way inside.

"Hey, Hank," O'Malley said, uneasily. "Vito will be here in a minute."

Hank figured he must have been driving at the same time she was and had his phone turned off. She was relieved when Vito walked through the door. Following behind him was Craven. They were ready to begin.

"So here's what the ME found," O'Malley said. "Cause of death is what we were more or less expecting. Cary died from internal injuries and a brain hemorrhage, hematoma...a bleed," the sergeant explained, putting it in layman's terms unnecessarily. "She also had a couple of broken ribs...head trauma...bones..." he continued.

Hank stood up abruptly and left the room.

"I'll go after her," Vito said. "Give me a minute."

Vito found Hank pacing around the hall outside O'Malley's office. She looked awful, a look of anguish on her face. He went over to Hank and grabbed her by the shoulders. Hank put her head on Vito's chest and started to shake.

"It'll be all right," Vito said. "Somehow, it'll be all right. It has to be. Come back inside."

Vito took Hank's hand, and they went back into the room. As they returned, O'Malley gave Hank a tender look.

"Okay if we continue?" he asked her.

Hank nodded and O'Malley looked down at the reports.

"The same goes for Carlee Delgado. Cause of death: internal injuries, head trauma. Manner of death, however, for both of them, was inconclusive," O'Malley said dubiously.

"What the hell does that mean?" Vito asked.

"It means the ME is leaving it as undetermined right now, pending more information," O'Malley explained. "Forensics, you know. Max is collecting all the cam footage. We'll take a look at it later. Maybe it'll tell us something. But so far, we haven't been able to lift prints off anything...unidentified prints. Not from Hank's car, the card found at the cemetery, Cary's driver's license. Nothing," he added, clearly frustrated.

Craven had sat quietly by while O'Malley took charge of the meeting. He would play an instrumental role in the investigation, and he knew it, which is why Craven waited until O'Malley had finished and then volunteered the following information.

"As soon as all the footage is organized, I'll let Sergeant O'Malley know, and hopefully, we'll find some kind of connection. But if we can step into the room down the hall, there's something I'd like to show you," Craven added.

O'Malley, already up to date on Craven's findings regarding the "Deer Killer" investigation, nodded to the evidence tech and stood up. The four of them made their way to the conference room at the end of the corridor. As they entered, Vito and Hank took note of a large white board. Next to it was a bulletin board with pictures of the "Deer Killer" victims, grouped in chronological order. Thanks to Cary's confession, they had even added a generic photo of two fawns labeled with the date of the original incident: the night that Hank blamed for destroying hers, Cary's, and Obelus's lives.

Cary's picture was in the center of the board. Under it the word *missing* was crossed out and replaced with *deceased*. Carlee Delgado's photo had been added right under Cary's. The caption also read *deceased*. A dotted red line connected it to a photo of Mickey Shanahan, the old man who happened to be outside the hospital when Delgado was hit. Additional evidence photos pinned to the board included Cary's reassembled driver's license and several "Odd Jobs" cards. The actual items were in the evidence room in the basement for safekeeping. It was clear that all the incidents, including what happened to Cary and Carlee, were being treated as one case, despite the medical examiner's inconclusive findings.

Vito was always impressed by Craven's thoroughness and attention to detail. But that's what the job required. Vito and Cary had conducted a shadow investigation of their own, replete with a white board as well. Just not as comprehensive. And where had all their hard work led? To Cary's murder. Vito had to stop himself from thinking about it: unintended consequences.

"It's a lot to take in," Vito began, glancing at Hank.

He thought it was time to get her out of there. *How much more can Hank take?* Vito asked himself. And so, gentleman that he was, Vito tried to end the meeting.

"Think we can regroup when you've got that footage together?" he asked O'Malley.

"Yeah, we'll be in touch," the sergeant responded.

"Hey Hank, wanna follow me home? Maybe you, me, and Anna, we can all grab an early dinner later," Vito suggested.

O'Malley looked at Hank and made his move.

"If you have a few minutes, Hank," he began. "There's something I need to talk to you about."

Hank wasn't sure what O'Malley was up to, but she decided that now was the best time to get it out of the way. She didn't feel much like having a bite with anyone tonight, anyway, not even Vito and Anna. So Hank acquiesced to O'Malley's request.

"You go ahead, Vito," Hank said. "I'll call you guys later."

Vito wasn't sure what he was in the middle of, but he agreed to give Hank her space and departed. Craven straightened up a few piles of papers and took off as well. That left O'Malley and Hank alone in the cold, sterile room, surrounded by evidence that triggered unwanted memories.

"What's up, Joe?" Hank asked.

"I don't know, it's just been a while. Thought maybe we could get a drink and talk," the sergeant answered.

Hank knew that O'Malley had been crushed when they broke up. And she hadn't been completely honest with him as to the reason why. While Hank identified as bisexual, and had always been attracted to women, Rose was the first one she had ever slept with. Until Rose, she had only been with men. Hank always got the feeling that Cary thought she had been with a lot of women but saw no reason to dispel her illusion. Now that Hank thought about it, she wasn't sure Cary realized that she was the only woman Hank had ever fallen for. Hank's relationship with Rose just validated that there was part of her that needed to be with a woman. That's the purpose it had served. Hank was never in love with her. But she saw no harm in grabbing a quick drink with O'Malley, devastated though she was from Cary's death.

"Sure, that'd be fine," Hank replied. "Where do you wanna go?"

"How about that new place around the corner? We can walk," O'Malley said.

That worked for Hank as the thought of being alone in a car with O'Malley was the last thing she needed right now. When they got to the bar, O'Malley held the door for Hank, and they went inside. The name of the pub was Te-KILL-a. Hank surmised that was the owner's attempt to appeal to the building of cops nearby. She was unaware that a couple of retired officers actually owned the place until O'Malley set her straight.

"Remember Bobby Burns and Chuck Vasiglia?" O'Malley asked. "They took their savings and opened this place up a couple of months ago."

Then, sensing Hank's uneasiness at being spotted with him, O'Malley added, "Don't worry, they won't be here today. The guys play poker every Tuesday afternoon."

"It's fine, Joe, really. I agreed to go out, right?" Hank asked, annoyed.

"Yeah, sorry, just thought..." O'Malley started to explain. "Let's grab those stools over there."

O'Malley went to the bar to get their drinks, while Hank saved their seats. Hank thought consuming alcohol in her current state would likely throw her into a total depression, so she opted for iced tea instead. O'Malley returned holding a beer in one hand and Hank's drink in the other.

"Here we go," he said, handing Hank her glass.

Hank already regretted her decision to accept O'Malley's invitation. She needed to make this quick.

"So, what's up, Joe?" Hank repeated.

"Nothing really, just wanted to make sure you were okay," he answered.

"Look, Joe, I'm most definitely not okay...not sure I ever really will be again. But we need to work together to catch this guy. For Cary and everyone else," Hank declared.

"Speaking of Cary," O'Malley began. "What exactly went on with you two?"

"Are you fucking kidding me?" Hank asked, making no attempt to hide her anger.

"What kind of a reaction is that?" O'Malley challenged her.

Hank started to get up, but O'Malley grabbed her by the arm.

"Please, Hank. I need to know, even now with everything that's going on. I still need to know," he pleaded.

"I can't, Joe. How can you ambush me like this after everything that's happened?" Hank replied.

"Tell me, Goddamn it," O'Malley said, losing all control.

"You fucking asshole. Every time I try to give you a break, this is how it ends. It's none of your fucking business," Hank added, raising her voice.

"I think it is. You ruined my life," O'Malley declared, "And I need to know why."

"You're a cop, figure it out. Why do you think?" Hank asked him. "Cary's dead...dead. Do you fucking get it? I don't know, I discovered something about myself, it's fucking Tuesday, it may rain tomorrow. Who cares why we broke up?" she asked in an incoherent manner.

"I do," O'Malley answered. "I do."

Hank put down her untouched drink and took her keys out of her bag. She looked O'Malley straight in the eye and gave him the brutal honesty he was looking for.

"Cary and I, uh, we were in love," she blurted out.

O'Malley's face turned red. While he understood that Hank and Cary had been involved from the way Hank acted at the farmers market, he assumed it wasn't serious, and the timetable didn't match up either.

"But Cary was after, way after," O'Malley declared. "How many others...other women were there?" he asked.

"Joe, please, not now," Hank answered.

"You think you know a person," O'Malley began. "But you never do. You ruined my life," he repeated.

"And the 'Deer Killer' ruined mine. So I guess we're even," Hank whispered and walked out the door.

TWELVE

While Hank was meeting with O'Malley and Vito, Nowak found himself alone and unsure of the best way to spend the afternoon. Although he knew the most productive way to pass the time was to check out his house for leaks or damage, the former detective loved car rides. So Nowak got into his 2002 Ford Bronco and headed in no particular direction. Fairview County was beautiful this time of year. The drive would do him good.

Nowak's subconscious led him past the reservoir, which would take him to the shoreline. As he drove, Hank's dad tried to process what Xanthe had told him. That his daughter had been involved with a woman: Cary Mackin. Nowak had never even met her. How could he have missed the clues that must have been there right under his nose? The revelation made him question his relationship with his daughter. But he loved Hank more than anything in the world, so what hurt the most was that she obviously didn't trust him.

As Nowak continued along the shoreline, he decided he would have to have a talk with Hank—when she was ready, of course. He noticed several boats already dry-docked near the water. He would have to figure out what to do with his own during the winter. But Nowak didn't have to worry about that right now. As he continued to drive, Nowak felt himself nodding off, so he pulled over in front of the local coffee shop, frequented by beachgoers. It stayed open year-round. He went inside and ordered his usual: coffee black, no cream, no sugar.

Nowak sat on a stool at the counter facing the window, sipping his coffee, looking out at the horizon. The sky was now overcast, and it appeared that a storm might be moving in. He decided to take a short walk along the beach and then head home. There was driftwood along the water's edge, not unusual this time of year. Some of the pieces were eye-catching. In the past, Nowak had collected them and had even made a table or two out of the debris.

The retired detective got back in his car and headed home. He couldn't help thinking about the "Deer Killer" case, Cary's death, and everything Vito had told him. Nowak knew from the way O'Malley had treated him at the meeting after Cary's funeral that he planned to exclude him from the investigation. But Nowak's gut told him this was no ordinary case. And just going through the motions of screening security cam footage, checking for fingerprints, and interrogating potential witnesses wasn't going to solve it. There was something much more nefarious going on. He just didn't know what.

Nowak found retirement boring. While he enjoyed his off-season time in New Mexico, he was getting restless. So, the detective in him didn't see what harm it would do if he poked around, off the grid, of course. Nobody needed to know, not even Vito and Hank. If Nowak discovered anything noteworthy, he would, of course, tell them. He could conduct his own parallel investigation without anyone being the wiser.

With that thought in mind, Nowak decided to take a detour on his way home and drive by Cary's last known residence: Brandon's estate. He didn't know what, if anything, he might find there, but it was a start. Nowak had casually asked Vito where the place was after he met Cary's landlord at the memorial. Vito, thinking nothing of it, provided his friend with the answer. As Nowak approached Brandon's domain, he slowed down, pulled over, and turned off his car.

He reached in the glove compartment and took out a pair of binoculars. Nowak never knew when they might come in handy.

Looking through the lens, he surveyed the grounds, main house, and cottage. Nothing immediately struck him as out of the ordinary. The estate was well kept, the lawn and shrubs impeccably maintained, and the place overall had a pleasant feel about it. *Don't know what the hell I was expecting*, Nowak thought to himself. He turned the key in the ignition and started to drive away. As he made his way down the secluded road looking for the best place to turn around, Nowak spotted the cabin, located toward the rear of the property. Using his binoculars, he zeroed in on the front door. A heavy padlock hung from the handle. *That* struck him as odd. Nowak opened the glove compartment for the second time and took out a little notebook. He started a page titled: *Things to Be Followed Up On* and noted the lock. Then he drove away.

* * *

By the time Hank got back to her place, she was in a near rage, exhausted, drained, depressed, and alone. She hadn't even begun to process Cary's death and didn't know how she ever would. What a mistake it had been to go out with O'Malley. She should have known better. *How could he pull a stunt like that?* Hank asked herself. *And why now?*

As she headed toward the kitchen, Barry got up off the floor and ran toward her. Sensing her anguish, he jumped up and licked Hank's face, then held out his paw. *Dogs*, Hank thought to herself, *how does anyone live without one?*

Hank fed Barry, then opened the refrigerator and got a mango spindrift for herself. She made her way to the couch, as Barry forsook his meal and joined her. They huddled together, comforting each other. Barry always sensed when something was wrong. And Hank feared that he was traumatized from witnessing what happened to Cary. She couldn't even think about it. Although O'Malley had really pissed Hank off, she regretted overreacting. Making a scene like that in public was completely out of character for her. During their entire time together, Hank couldn't remember ever having a blowout fight like that. She was losing it. But they had to work together to solve the case. Hank owed it to Cary to find her killer, and nothing would get in her way. That meant that Hank would have to eat a little shit and text O'Malley to apologize. So she grabbed her phone and sent the following message to the sergeant, her former lover: *Sorry, Joe, really. Just under a lot of stress.... Let's get this guy, together.*

Hank read the text again after she hit the send button. O'Malley knew her well enough to be skeptical of her sincerity, but Hank thought it would smooth things over between them anyway. She couldn't let this kind of bullshit fuck up the investigation. At the end of the day, the sergeant was still a professional and certainly wanted the "Deer Killer" caught as much as she did. Currently, O'Malley had seven open murder cases to deal with, not including the killings of the fawns and three dogs. The pressure was going to get to him. He'd have no choice but to cooperate with Hank to solve the murders.·

* * *

Meanwhile, as Hank was doing damage control with O'Malley, Brandon had an investigation of his own to deal with: the man who had come by his house earlier in the day. As luck would have it, Brandon happened to look out the window as the vehicle came to a stop. The man wasn't the only one who owned a pair of binoculars. But by the time Brandon had retrieved his from the bottom drawer of the desk, the car was driving away, down the road. Brandon hoped that his surveillance cameras would enable him to identify the person who was spying on him; provide him with the *who*. He, however, would have to figure out the *why*.

* * *

Brandon decided to wait until the morning to check the security cam footage. Nothing was going to happen overnight. After going for a run, showering, and having a quick breakfast, he made his way to the monitors in the study. Brandon sat down and watched the footage from the front-lawn camera. Zooming in, he spotted the car: a Ford Bronco. Although the plates were only partially visible from the footage, Brandon was certain he knew *who* the man was. He just didn't know *what* he was up to.

The "Deer Killer" relatives were demanding justice, and with Cary's death and the incident at the hospital, Brandon figured the police were feeling the heat. O'Malley, Detective Hank, and Vito had seven unsolved murders on their hands, not counting Nicole, the annoying tenant he had been forced to dispose of. The investigation would be a priority for the entire force. With that in mind, Brandon decided it would be a good time to move Cary's things from his study to the cabin. He couldn't take any chances. And he was being watched. So Brandon would have to be careful. He'd wait until it was dark.

After having a light dinner, Brandon made his move. He opened the desk drawer where he had hidden Cary's wallet, gun, and ring and placed them in a small bag. He turned off the outside lights and used a flashlight instead to make his way to the cabin. When Brandon got to the door, he opened the padlock with a key. Then he went inside. Pushing aside a rug in the center of the room, he removed several planks that lay beneath it. Brandon picked up a metal box and took out another key to unlock it. He lifted the lid and placed the gun and wallet inside. However, a voice inside him said to hold onto the ring, so Brandon slipped it back in his pocket. He locked the container, but before covering it with the wooden planks, he took out a small envelope from the secret compartment and looked inside. It held some documents and old, yellow-tinged newspaper articles. As Brandon perused them, his eyes filled with rage. He shoved the papers into the envelope, placed it back where it belonged, and put the planks on top.

Then he covered them with the rug. He would get even if it was the last thing he ever did.

* * *

Nowak decided to take his unofficial investigation slow and to stick to one thing at a time. With that thought in mind, he returned to Brandon's estate to see what, if anything, might turn up. Nowak was actually surprised when, just as he was about to bag it for the night, he spotted the glow emanating from Brandon's flashlight. Even with his binoculars, Nowak couldn't make out what Brandon was carrying, but he thought the act itself was suspicious.

Nowak took out his trusty notebook from the glove compartment and added: *Brandon moved something to the cabin at night.* While the officials, led by O'Malley and his own daughter, were following the science, he was doing good old-fashioned police work. It was invigorating. He was competing with the authorities, and they didn't even know it. Nowak decided that discovering what Brandon had hidden in his cabin was of paramount importance. He would, therefore, need to keep a close eye on his comings and goings and then figure out a way to break into the building without getting caught.

* * *

Vito and Anna had taken a couple of days off to decompress and process everything that was going on. They had pretty much holed up in Gayle's guesthouse while Hank and O'Malley were out and about trying to solve the "Deer Killer" case. But after checking up on Gayle and her mother, they decided enough time had passed and that they needed to take charge of the situation. So after breakfast, Vito decided to give Hank a call to see how she was holding up and what, if anything, he could do to help.

Hank and Barry were awakened by the sound of her phone's ringtone. When she saw it was Vito calling, Hank picked up.

"Hey, Vito," she answered. "What's up?"

"Nothing. We just thought it was time to see how you're doing... how things are going. Sorry we've been MIA," Vito added apologetically.

"That's okay," Hank answered. "Afraid O'Malley and I...we had a bit of a blowout the other day. My fault really, overreacted. Haven't heard from him since," Hank declared.

Vito had a feeling he knew what the fight must have been about, but he played dumb. Hank, however, understood and came clean.

"He brought up Cary...and me," Hank explained. "Vito, you get that Joe and I were involved, right? I mean, we kept it quiet given work and all," she added.

"Yeah, I sorta figured that out," Vito said. "The detective in me... but guess you don't have to be Sherlock Holmes to..." he continued.

"Well, anyways, I've got to fix it. Can't have this personal bullshit fucking up the investigation," Hank said emphatically.

"Roger that," Vito agreed. "He'll come around."

"Have you heard from Gayle?" Hank asked, concerned.

"Yeah, she and Felicia are doing about as well as you'd expect," Vito said. "It's gonna be a bumpy road—for all of us."

"Vito," Hank began. "What if O'Malley shuts me out...of the investigation...takes me off the case?" Hank asked in a worried tone.

"Let's not get ahead of ourselves," Vito reassured her. "Sure he'll be in touch soon."

Within minutes, a text popped up on Hank's phone. The sender was O'Malley. The message read: *Sorry too. We need to get past this and catch that prick. Are you with me?* Hank thought for a minute and then wrote back: *In.* O'Malley answered with a thumbs-up and the following: *Max is almost done compiling the security cam footage. We'll meet tomorrow. Tell Vito.*

* * *

It was now late afternoon, and Nowak sat patiently out of sight near the corner of Brandon's estate. With his binoculars, the former detective was able to make out the front door and four-car garage from a particular angle. Nowak had been there since lunchtime and was getting antsy and needed to pee. As he was figuring out the best way to proceed, Nowak noticed Brandon's garage door open. A man in a Tesla drove away from the house and through the front gate.

Nowak had no way of knowing how much time he had to poke around the cabin, so he acted quickly. He got out of his car holding a small tool bag and made his way to the shack. The padlock wasn't enough to keep Nowak out. Using his reliable pick, he jiggled the lock until it opened. *Easy peasy,* he said to himself. *I've still got it.* Nowak wasn't sure what he was looking for, but hopefully, he would find out soon enough. The small bag Brandon had with him the other night couldn't have held much.

As Nowak perused the interior of the cabin, he tried to put himself in Brandon's shoes. *Where would you hide something here?* he asked himself. After looking through a dresser, shelves, and some drawers, Nowak came up empty-handed. Then he noticed the rug. *Not terribly original,* he told himself. But he thought Brandon figured whatever was hidden inside the cabin was protected by the padlock. So Nowak pushed the carpet aside and examined the boards. One was out of alignment. Squatting down he pried it off with his hands, then repeated the process until the metal box was visible.

Nowak picked up the container and put it down on top of the dresser. Then he used his pick to unlock it. He removed the lid and saw the gun and wallet. He opened the faux leather billfold and took out some credit cards and other forms of identification. Of course, there was no driver's license. Brandon had seen to that. But as Nowak looked through the plastic squares, one name stared back at him: Carole Mackin.

"Holy motherfucker," Nowak exclaimed. "It can't be. Sweet Jesus."

It was well past four o'clock now, and the cabin was getting dark. Nowak was afraid to turn the lights on or even use his phone to illuminate the room. But he was able to make out an envelope crammed in the hole of the floor next to where the metal box had been. As he picked up the pouch, headlights from an approaching vehicle lit up the room. Nowak froze, hoping the car would go away. He peeked out the window but saw nothing.

Panicking, Nowak decided the best thing to do was to get the hell out of there. He wasn't sure, however, if he should take the gun and wallet with him. But before he could determine the best course of action to take, the decision was made for him. As Nowak juggled the gun, wallet, and envelope, he heard footsteps outside the door. The interior of the tiny cabin provided no cover. If whoever was outside came in, Nowak was screwed. Suddenly, the door swung open, and he was blinded by a flashlight pointed right at his face. Then the room went dark.

"You didn't think I was going to let you have all the fun," Brandon said, taunting the former cop.

"Who's there?" Nowak asked. "Can't see a damn thing."

Brandon held the flashlight under his chin and turned it on and off frenetically. The light show freaked Nowak out. *This guy's crazy*, he told himself. *Shit.*

"Who's there?" Brandon repeated in a mocking tone.

He flashed the light again and asked Nowak the following question.

"Recognize me yet?"

Nowak took a deep breath and collected himself. He knew exactly who it was: Brandon.

"If you're wondering," Brandon began. "I keep a close eye on the place, my home, my sanctuary. Caught you the other day lurking around. Quite honestly, it didn't really matter to me one way or the other if you were stalking me because I was stalking you. Did you really think you were able to get in here without my knowing, without my help?" he asked Hank's father. "Not in a million years."

Nowak reflected on the hole in the fence he had crawled through to get onto the property. The former detective couldn't believe he fell right into Brandon's trap. He knew Nowak was there the whole time. Brandon left in his car in order to lure Nowak into a false sense of security. He was likely watching Nowak as he made his way toward the cabin, then drove right back through the gate.

How fucking stupid am I? Nowak asked himself. *Pretty fuckin' stupid.*

"If you don't mind," Brandon said, "I'd like my things back."

Nowak looked down at the items he held in his hand and hesitated.

"Let's start with the envelope," Brandon said, extending his hand.

Nowak begrudgingly gave it to him.

"That's good," Brandon said. Then, brandishing his own weapon, he added, "Now the gun."

The envelope was one thing. Nowak didn't even know what was in it. But turning over a likely loaded revolver to this lunatic was another. Still, at the moment, what choice did he really have? At best, it was a standoff.

"Slowly," Brandon ordered the former cop. "And if you're thinking I won't shoot an old man like yourself, think again."

Nowak was in over his head. Before he grasped what he was doing, Cary's gun was back in Brandon's possession.

"Oh, and I'd like the wallet, too, if you don't mind," Brandon declared.

Nowak gave it to him and stood there fully expecting to be shot. Brandon sensed Nowak's anxiety.

"You look like you could use some rest," Brandon said. "Why don't you be my guest for the night, and we'll figure things out in the morning."

"You can't keep me here," Nowak said, raising his voice. "Let me go."

"Oh, really?" Brandon asked. "I can't, can't I? You sure about that, Dad?"

"*Dad?*" Nowak asked, confused.

Brandon had had enough. He walked over to the former detective and hit him over the head with his gun. Then he went through Nowak's pockets until he found his keys and phone.

"Good night, old man," Brandon whispered.

He would always be one step ahead.

THIRTEEN

Hank woke up with the mother of all headaches. *Must be the stress and lack of sleep,* she told herself. She went to the bathroom and splashed cold water on her face, then headed to the kitchen and popped two Anacin tablets in her mouth, washing them down with a tall glass of water. Hank got the coffee going and called out to Barry. She took her beloved canine outside for his morning walk. The cool air felt good. These few minutes with Barry would likely be the only peace Hank would have today. She dreaded what lay ahead.

The meeting with O'Malley wasn't until the afternoon: two o'clock. That gave Hank a little time to herself before she had to face reality. How she missed Cary. She dreamt about her again last night. Hank thought about what her therapist had told her years ago: that the price of love is loss. But the doctor also opined that fantasies give you more time with your loved one. *Small consolation,* Hank noted. She needed Cary back.

Reflecting on last night's dream gave Hank an idea. She needed to spend some time with Cary, to be close to her. Two choices presented themselves: the cemetery or the dog park. Hank went with the second option. She went back inside and got dressed, gulped her coffee down, and grabbed Barry's favorite ball. They got in Hank's car and headed to the one place Cary loved most. Hank wasn't sure how she'd react when she got there. She hadn't been back to the park since Cary's memorial. But this would be the first time Hank would be there under normal circumstances, knowing she could never bump into Cary again. The thought consumed her with sadness.

When they got out of Hank's car, she spotted some of the regulars. This morning, however, she would avoid them. Today's visit was all about Cary. Hank tossed the ball, and Barry ran to fetch it. As they made their way to Cary's favorite bench, Hank was overcome with emotion. What she wouldn't give to go back in time so that they could be together again. *None of this should have happened,* Hank told herself. There must have been a way to stop it. But rehashing the same points over and over again wasn't going to bring Cary back. Nothing ever could. The finality of death: it was impossible to grasp.

Hank thought that spending some time in the dog park would make her feel close to Cary. But being there without her was just depressing. Therefore, she decided to cut the visit short and drop Barry off at home, then head to Stamford. Hank pulled up to her house and went to get Barry out of the car, but she remembered that she had forgotten to tell Vito about the meeting. So she sent him a text: *Sorry, Vito. Forgot to tell you, there's a meeting at O'Malley's at 2 today. Hope you can make it.* Vito answered back with a thumbs-up emoji and: *See you soon.*

Hank hadn't heard from her father in a couple of days. She wasn't worried about him but thought it was time to touch base. So, as she drove, she commanded Siri to send him a text. *Hey Dad...wanna catch up later? Off to a meeting.* When Hank arrived at police headquarters, she parked her car and checked her phone before getting out. No word from her dad. She'd try to reach him again later.

Hank was relieved that Vito would be at the meeting. It was the first time she would be face-to-face with O'Malley since their argument at the bar. She wasn't sure how he would act despite their recent apologetic texts. They decided to meet in the conference room down the hall from the sergeant's office. Hank walked in to find Max Craven juggling four large cups of steaming hot coffee. O'Malley must have sent him to get them as a peace offering. A box of chocolate glazed donuts sat on a table nearby. Hank wasn't going to let herself be guilted out by a bunch of pastries. *Jesus,* she thought to herself. *Let's just move the fuck on.*

"Back in a minute," Craven said, addressing Hank. "Sergeant O'Malley should be here momentarily."

"Sure, no worries," Hank responded.

Hank loved Max. She admired his dedication, professionalism, and found his awkward social skills endearing. His face turned slightly reddish whenever he was alone with her. Hank knew the young evidence tech had a crush on her that he would never act on. *Sometimes wanting something is better than actually having it,* Hank pondered. As she grabbed one of the coffees and a donut, Hank was on edge. *How many more meetings would it take before they caught this guy?* she asked herself.

"Hey, beautiful," Vito called out as he entered the room.

He went over to Hank and gave her a big hug. Vito was worried about her. After all, Hank had always been like a daughter to him, and she was going through hell right now.

"There's coffee and donuts," Hank said.

"Great, I could use some caffeine right about now," Vito answered. "How's your dad, by the way? Haven't heard from him in a while."

"Don't know. Me neither. I texted him on my way down, but he hasn't gotten back to me," Hank declared.

"Why don't we swing by his house after we're done here?" Vito suggested. "He should know what's going on."

"Sounds good, Vito. Thanks," Hank responded.

"Sorry I'm late," O'Malley said as he entered the room, Craven following behind him. "Take a seat...over here."

The four of them sat down at the end of the long table where the monitors were located. But before O'Malley showed them any security cam footage, he asked Craven to review the evidence they had collected to date. It would include all the forensics from the "Deer Killer" victims and crime scenes.

"Go ahead, Max," O'Malley instructed his subordinate.

"Well," Craven began. "Right now, we're going on the assumption that all the cases are related, that we're looking for the same guy. So this is what we have."

As Craven began to list his findings, Hank couldn't help but stare at the wall of photos: the picture of Cary in the middle caught her eye. Then she noticed the one of Obelus from the crime scene, Gayle's house, bloody and still. She had to look away.

"...like I said, despite the ME's report, we're looking at what we consider to be a total of eight crime scene locations, seven human victims, three canines, two fawns...seven 'Odd Jobs' cards..." Craven continued, rambling on and on.

Although that wasn't Craven's intention, it all sounded so clinical the way he laid out the facts—facts that had destroyed so many lives.

"Let's go through the autopsy results," O'Malley suggested. "Why don't you start with the animals, the necropsies?"

"Sure thing," Craven acquiesced. "Well, the only animal—or dog, I should say—that had a necropsy performed on him was Cary's... Obelus. And we know what the results of that were: severe blood loss and um, other injuries."

"And the rest," O'Malley nudged him. "The other victims?"

"Yup, let's take it from the beginning. The Wooster girls, Amanda Caldwell and Emily Browne, the parents finally agreed to autopsies," Craven noted.

"We already know that, Max," O'Malley interrupted, getting impatient.

"Yeah, sorry. Well, they were struck by the same car at more or less the same time, so the injuries were, for all purposes, the same: head and internal," Craven explained. "But just like with Cary and the young woman from the hospital, the ME's report listed the manner of death as undetermined. Doesn't mean..." Craven continued.

"Let me have the reports," O'Malley directed Max.

The evidence tech handed several binders to the sergeant and returned to his seat. O'Malley flipped through them quickly and summarized the contents.

"No autopsy was performed on little Elsie Cooper. Same goes for Blair and Dakota Riordan. Cooper's manner of death, according to the report, is accidental; the Riordans are listed as undetermined. So it appears except for Cooper, and two of the dogs, the victims all died as a result of injuries sustained from being struck by a vehicle at high speed," O'Malley declared.

"Joe, I mean Sergeant O'Malley," Hank added, glancing at Craven. "Don't mean to be difficult here, but don't we know all this already? Where exactly is this getting us anyways?"

"We need to go over everything again and again, or we'll never solve this thing," O'Malley said. "Repetition, extra eyes on it, that's what'll give us our break. Or would you like to take over Detective Nowak?" the sergeant asked sarcastically.

Hank regretted challenging O'Malley. They were on shaky enough terms as it was. But she was beginning to think that he had no idea how to approach the investigation. Vito, picking up on their tension, tried to play peacemaker.

"What about that security cam footage, Max?" he asked.

"We'll get to that in a minute," O'Malley answered. "But first, let's go over the cards again. Max, what have the 'Odd Jobs' cards given us so far?"

"Well, as I said before, we've recovered seven of them. Detective Nowak found one of them in Kimberly Hunter's car. Had partial prints on it and the imprint of a paw, a dog's paw, on the back. We never ran the prints—" Craven continued, but the sergeant cut him off.

"What the hell, Max?" he started. "Why the fuck not?"

"We, um, we decided they were probably from Hunter. Didn't think..." Craven went on, trying to deflect from his negligence.

"Just fucking do it," O'Malley reprimanded him. "I want the results on my desk by tomorrow."

The misstep was uncharacteristic of Craven, whose thoroughness was legendary. Hank, recounting her meeting with the evidence tech, started to blame herself. Craven had seemed a bit flustered that morning when he examined the cards that were found in Hunter's car and at the scene where the fawns were struck and killed. He had clearly been trying to impress her with his skills. Likely, after the meeting ended, he forgot to follow up. While it was sloppy of him, Hank thought she understood how it had happened.

"What about the rest of the cards?" O'Malley stated. "Did we miss anything else?" he asked pointedly.

"Uh, no, don't think so," Craven answered. "The one Cary found where the deer were killed was too degraded to test. None of the others had prints. And the only one that had blood on it, animal blood, well, Obelus's, was the one found by Cary at her sister's house. We should be good."

"Fine, now let's get to that footage," O'Malley declared.

The four of them gathered around the monitors with Craven sitting at the controls. The young CSI sat down and began to scroll through the images.

"Working our way backward," he began. "This is what was taken at the hospital when Delgado was hit."

Vito and Hank looked intently at the screen, hoping to see something that might help identify the killer. A camera recorded Delgado exiting the emergency room and walking on the street. A second camera picked up Mickey Shanahan and his dog behind her. Then a car came into view. It was a black SUV with tinted windows. *This guy thinks of everything,* O'Malley contemplated.

"Can you zoom in? See if we can get a read on the plates?" the sergeant asked Craven.

As the rear license plate filled the screen, they saw that the vehicle had Colorado plates.

"Run them as soon as we're done here," O'Malley directed Craven.

Craven's examination of the license plates would ultimately be pointless as they were expired and stolen. Brandon only put them on his old SUV for moments like this.

The evidence tech continued to scroll through the footage. The four watched intently, expecting to see Delgado get struck, but the car drove out of view. What the security cams failed to detect was Brandon getting out of his vehicle and checking on Delgado. Brandon had scoped out the area and noted the cameras. He made sure to strike her in a blind spot. But just as all seemed lost, a bizarre image popped up on the desktop. The driver pulled over, put down his window about an inch, and stuck out his middle finger. The foursome looked at each other with dismay.

"This guy's a sick son of a bitch," Vito uttered. "Thinks this is funny, huh?"

"Okay, look," O'Malley started. "It's enough. Max and I will go through the rest of the footage. Gonna take another look at the parking lot where Hunter's dog died, also the subdivision where Elsie Cooper lived. Those are our best hope. Maybe we'll see something we missed. Be in touch."

* * *

Vito and Hank left the meeting disgusted and frustrated. They were shattered emotionally and didn't know how they would ever make peace with Cary's death. One way or another, Vito and Hank each blamed themselves for not protecting her. They walked to the parking lot in silence. When they reached their cars, Vito spoke first.

"Any word from your dad yet?" he asked Hank.

She took out her phone and checked the texts and voicemails. But there was nothing from her father.

"Afraid not, Vito," Hank answered. "Let me leave him another message."

As Hank had already texted her dad and got no response, she thought it made more sense to call. Texts didn't always go through. The phone went straight to voicemail.

"Dad, it's me," Hank began. "Starting to get worried. Call me."

Vito could see Hank was getting anxious. The best course of action was to go by Nowak's house like they had planned.

"Wanna follow me to your dad's?" Vito asked.

"Sure," Hank replied. "This isn't like him," she added. "Especially with everything that's been going on."

"He's probably sitting on his boat right now, having a Bud," Vito said reassuringly. "Let's go surprise him."

* * *

When they got to Nowak's house, Vito and Hank parked on the grass beside the driveway. There was no sign of the former detective's car. Hank found the spare key her father kept outside and unlocked the front door. As they entered the home, she called out to him. Vito went upstairs, while Hank headed for the kitchen. There was no one home. They went outside to check the boat: no Nowak. Hank looked at her phone again, but nothing from her dad.

"What the hell, Vito?" she declared. "Where the fuck is he?"

"Don't know. He could be anywhere. Probably just taking one of those drives he loves so much and lost sight of the time. Reception is spotty along some of those roads," Vito added.

"I'm wiped, Vito. Gonna go home and check on Barry," Hank said, clearly exhausted. "Let me know if you hear anything."

"Sure, absolutely, will do," Vito answered. "Maybe we can all have dinner later...if he shows up. I mean, when..." Vito corrected himself.

"It's okay, Vito, really. I know what you meant. Just wish we could catch a break," Hank replied.

"We'll get each other through all this," Vito said. "Gonna check in with Anna, head over to the cottage. Been neglecting her lately. Call you in a bit?" he asked.

"Yeah, thanks, Vito. Don't know what I'd do without you. Work is the only thing keeping me going these days. Work, Barry, and you, I guess. But don't let it go to your head," Hank added jokingly.

"Never," Vito answered, smiling slightly, and gave her a hug.

* * *

Brandon had had a lazy day. It was now late afternoon, however, and time to check on his guest. *He must be hungry by now,* Brandon contemplated. But the former cop looked well fed with his protruding belly and all, so Brandon wasn't worried. Nowak needed to earn his rewards. Brandon had made sure to tie up any loose ends last night before going to bed. Therefore, Nowak's car was now safely hidden in a wooded area behind Brandon's estate. The desk drawer in his study was getting full. He had no choice but to return Cary's wallet and gun to their original place. The ring was already there, waiting. Brandon picked up the envelope and Nowak's phone and headed for the cabin. If the former detective was a good boy, he would get dinner later.

Brandon looked down at the phone as he walked. There was a text from Detective Hank and a couple of missed voicemails. *Minimal effort if you ask me,* Brandon considered. *How worried were these people anyway?* he asked himself. When he arrived at the cabin, Brandon unlocked the padlock and opened the door. The room was dim, but he was able to make out the former detective sitting on the floor in the corner. He looked truly pathetic. Brandon had only tied Nowak's hands, not his feet. He wanted to meet him halfway, after all.

"What took you so long?" Nowak asked.

"Hang on there, old man," Brandon answered, impressed by his audacity. "Heads up," Brandon added, pretending to toss a bottle of water at Nowak.

"Please, I'm starving, thirsty," Nowak said pleadingly.

"One thing at a time," Brandon responded, taking Nowak's phone out of his pocket. "There's something we need to take care of first. Let's listen, shall we?"

"I won't give you the code," Nowak declared. "That's my business."

Brandon looked at Nowak amusingly and punched in five numbers, unlocking the device.

"What the hell? How'd you do that?" Nowak asked, astonished.

"Never mind, we'll get to that in a minute. But first, let's see who's concerned about you," Brandon stated.

As Brandon was about to read Hank's text out loud, another message came in simultaneously from Vito: *Call me as soon as you get this*. Next, Brandon clicked on Nowak's voicemail and hit the play button. When Nowak heard his daughter's voice, he stared Brandon down. *Dad, it's me. Starting to get worried. Call me. Dad, call me, please. Been trying to reach you. Vito and I...we're getting worried.*

"Touching, isn't it? They really do care after all," Brandon said, sarcastically.

But he was fearful that if Vito and Hank didn't hear from Nowak soon, they would start looking for him. He had to throw them off the scent, reassure Nowak's inner circle that he was all right.

"We can do this one of two ways," Brandon stated. He started to text Hank back, muttering the words to himself just loud enough for Nowak to hear: *All good*.

"Or..." Brandon began, but Nowak stopped him.

"Please, I need to speak to my daughter. Please," Nowak begged.

Brandon looked at Nowak with a devilish smile and brandished his weapon. Pointing the gun at the old man, he issued the following warning.

"Just one false move and..." Brandon stated coldly.

"I'm not gonna pull anything. Just need to hear her voice," Nowak assured him.

"Good," Brandon remarked. "That would be wise of you."

Brandon erased the text. He placed the call to Hank, putting the phone on speaker, and held it to Nowak's ear. He nodded to the former cop, all the while holding his gun to Nowak's head. Within seconds, Hank's voice could be heard on the other end: *Hey you, whoever you are, I'm not around right now. So just leave a message or don't—your choice—but I'll get back to you if you do—promise.* Nowak glanced at Brandon and waited for the tone to speak.

"Hey, it's me. Got your messages...see you soon...and, um, don't forget to check on Brady..." he continued.

Brady? Who the hell is Brady? Brandon wondered. He took the phone away from Nowak's head and ended the call.

Brady was Hank and her dad's safe word, named in honor of their favorite family dog: a deceased Alaskan malamute they had rescued. But Brandon didn't know that. He just got a bad feeling.

"If you're fucking around with me..." he scolded Nowak.

"No, no, all good. Can I get out of here now?" he asked his kidnapper.

Brandon was open to letting his captive go under certain conditions. They needed to have a good old-fashioned family talk to clear the air. Brandon would have to lay it out for him.

"I guess I have some explaining to do," Brandon began. "Why I am in possession of Cary's things. And why if I let you go, you won't tell anyone."

But Nowak needed to know the reason Brandon had called him dad. It might mean nothing, just words, but he needed to know. Nowak was emboldened from hearing Hank's voice, even if only for a few seconds, so he decided to confront him.

"Why did you call me dad?" the former detective asked.

"Well, well," Brandon remarked. "I believe I'm the one who'll be asking the questions here, if you don't mind."

Brandon picked up the envelope and waved it in front of Nowak, hoping to pique his interest. The gesture worked. Nowak had no way of knowing what was inside the faded yellow packet, but he knew it had to be important.

"What the hell?" the former cop mumbled.

"Sorry, what was that?" Brandon asked. "Afraid I can't hear you."

"Where's the wallet, the gun?" Nowak asked. "You're not gonna be able..."

"Able to what?" Brandon inquired. "That was an illegal search and seizure you conducted on my property, don't you think? Cops never learn. Suppose I should thank you for fucking up the evidence, not that you'll ever see it again," he added, threateningly.

"What the hell are you doing with Cary's wallet?" Nowak asked in desperation.

"What do you think?" Brandon answered. "Just how would one come into the possession of a dead woman's wallet, I wonder? I am truly stumped, or were you hoping to get an illicit confession out of me as well?"

Nowak's expression revealed his anger and belief that Brandon was involved in Cary's disappearance and murder. Brandon noticed.

"Now, now, let's not go jumping to any conclusions just yet," Brandon said ominously.

He walked closer to Nowak and handed him the envelope.

"Why don't you take a look inside while I go fix dinner?" Brandon said. "Then we'll talk."

"How the hell am I supposed to do that with my hands tied up like this?" Nowak asked him.

"Excellent point. Suppose I'll have to spoon-feed you...the papers that is, and your supper," Brandon said jokingly.

He opened the envelope, took out the contents, and laid them out on a small table. Then Brandon grabbed Nowak by the arm and sat him down in a rickety chair in front of them.

"Better?" he asked.

Nowak nodded and stared down at the papers as Brandon exited the room.

"Hope this doesn't kill your appetite," he said. "I'm an excellent cook."

* * *

As Brandon was preparing a little something for his captive to eat, Nowak perused the articles in front of him. They appeared to be print-outs from a Google search as well as other assorted documents. Using his chin to move the papers around, Nowak read the first one. He was blindsided by the headline and began to feel ill. In bold letters, the words "Three-Year-Old Local Boy Kidnapped" caught Nowak's eye. A photo of the toddler was directly underneath. The article was more than forty years old.

Nowak gasped for breath as images of a car, a little boy, and a store flashed through his head. *It can't be. It just can't,* he said to himself as he went on to the next story. "Tragedy Strikes Missing Boy's Family Again," it read. Nowak skimmed the page until he came to the name— Tessa Nowak—and his deceased wife's photo. *Jesus fucking Christ,* he muttered to himself.

Nowak wasn't sure how much more he could take, but there was one official-looking document he hadn't checked out yet: a DNA report from 23andMe. Next to it was a cover letter from a private detective agency assuring the recipient, Brandon, that all the information included was accurate and had been validated. As Nowak scanned the page the words Biological Father caught his attention. Another familiar name came after them: his own. Nowak couldn't process any of it. His brain raced as he tried to make sense of it all. Brandon would be back any minute. *What a shit show that will be,* Nowak contemplated.

Nowak got up and started pacing around the small room. *Think, think,* he told himself. Then he heard footsteps and the padlock open. Brandon entered holding a small tray with a bowl and some bread. But Nowak couldn't help but think that Brandon had been right. He no longer had any appetite.

"Finish your homework yet?" Brandon asked his father. "Hope you like clam chowder. I believe it's a family favorite," he added provocatively.

"Not hungry. We need to talk," Nowak answered, dazed and confused.

"Look at the lengths I had to go to in order to spend some quality time with my old man," Brandon stated. "And you won't even eat my soup. Rude," he declared.

"Look I don't know what you think...who you think you are, but this isn't funny," Nowak said with desperation in his voice.

"Afraid I know exactly who I am and exactly what happened. Do you?" Brandon inquired.

Nowak was at a loss. This guy was full-on crazy. Could he really be his own son?

"Let's take it from the top," Brandon suggested. "Then, if, or I should say, *once* we see things the same way, I'll let you go."

Nowak thought the odds of this guy releasing him after all he had uncovered were slim to none. Brandon was just messing with him and would likely shoot him in his sleep. Nowak tried to remember what he used to tell people to do if they ever found themselves in this type of situation. Then again, the current predicament Nowak was in appeared to be unique.

"If you don't want my *sister* to find out everything, you'll cooperate and do as I say," Brandon declared.

Nowak felt ill and thought he was going to faint. He needed to have his wits about him or God knows what this maniac would try.

"Look, Brandon, son, I should never have broken into your home, it's none of my business, really," Nowak began. "Just let me go, and we can forget all about it."

"Desperation is not a good look on you. You're not listening. Do I really have to spell it out for you, old man?" Brandon asked, exasperated. "And stop calling me Brandon. We both know my real name," he stated matter-of-factly.

Nowak nodded, put his head down, and began to weep. The show of emotion surprised his son.

"Now, now old man, why the tears? Did you really miss me all these years?" Brandon asked in a Joker-like way. "Your actions, or should I say, the lack of, speak otherwise," Brandon responded.

Besides the DNA results, there was one way Nowak could confirm that the young man standing in front of him, holding him hostage, was indeed his long-lost son. People could have memories lodged in their subconscious dating back to as young as Nowak's son was when he went missing. Hank's dad steadied himself, looked up at Brandon, and asked him one simple question.

"What does Chubbs mean to you?"

Brandon was taken aback, but he knew why Nowak had brought up the name. He decided his father had a good memory after all. *Like father, like son,* Brandon said to himself, mockingly.

"It's the name I had chosen for my first puppy," Brandon answered, clearing his throat.

Nowak's face went white. He looked at his son, unrecognizable from when he last saw him as a toddler, and said one word: "Harry."

"Yes, Harry. Or 4-2-7-7-9, your cell phone code," Brandon said gloatingly.

FOURTEEN

The first thing Nowak did when he got home was grab a beer from the fridge and jump in the shower. He needed to cleanse himself. It was nearly three o'clock in the morning and unlikely that he'd get any sleep. So the former detective put on his long underwear that served as pajamas, lit a fire, and sunk into his favorite easy chair. *What have I gotten myself into?* he asked. Making a deal with the devil: his own son.

Life could change in an instant. That much Nowak had learned. One errand more than forty years ago had destroyed his family. A moment of carelessness had ruined so many lives. And it was all his fault. Nowak remembered that September morning like it was yesterday. They had run out of milk, and Rice Krispies were the only thing Harry would eat. Like so many toddlers, he was fussy. So Nowak volunteered to go to the nearest store and pick up a quart. But his fatal mistake was taking his son with him over his wife's objections. "We'll be back in a couple of minutes," Nowak had assured her. Tessa had had a miscarriage before she got pregnant with their son, and she was overly protective as a result.

That morning, Nowak broke a cardinal rule for parents: never leave your child alone in a car, even for a minute. But those sixty seconds cost Nowak everything. He could still hear the sound of the bottle crashing on the cement sidewalk as he scoured the street for any sign of his little boy. Harry disappeared in an instant and was never found despite years of searching on the part of the police, private detectives, and his own parents. And despite having two more children a few years after the tragedy, Nowak's wife simply couldn't get past the loss of her firstborn, eventually taking her own life.

Nowak had managed to keep his other son, Homer, and Hank from finding out. They never knew they had an older brother who vanished and, likewise, thought that cancer had taken the life of their mother after a prolonged illness. All lies. The former cop had had to go to extraordinary lengths to hide the truth from the people in the world who deserved to know it the most. The only one who knew everything was Vito. Vito the vault, Nowak used to call him, flippantly. But he couldn't find out about Brandon, who he really was. This time, Vito would also need to be kept in the dark.

Nowak agreed not to tell anyone that he had discovered Cary's wallet and gun at Brandon's estate in exchange for his freedom. But Brandon made it clear that the items were now forever out of reach. "Go ahead, tell them," he had said, taunting Nowak. "There goes your credibility with the police." However, Brandon also leveraged his knowledge of the past and used it against his father. That's why he knew Nowak would keep his secrets.

"If you tell anyone who I really am and that you found Cary's wallet and gun on my property, Hank will find out everything," he said, threatening his dad.

Brandon also understood the enormous guilt Nowak must have been carrying around all these years. The toll it had taken. So how in God's name could he turn his son in now when he must have felt responsible for ruining his life? But Nowak extracted a promise out of Brandon as well: that he wouldn't hurt anyone. The two appeared to be at a standoff, except for Brandon's parting shot, an ominous warning: "You'll go home now and wait for further instructions."

* * *

Hank woke up with Barry at her feet; the side of the bed that used to be Cary's was empty. When he saw Hank's eyes open, Barry got on top of his human and buried his head just under her chin. She gave him a big hug and kissed the top of his head. Hank couldn't remember what time she had gone to sleep last night, but Vito never called about dinner. She figured he got caught up with Anna and assumed Hank would have let him know if there was anything to report regarding her dad.

Hank picked up her phone from the nightstand next to the bed to check her messages. There was a text from Vito, time stamp 2:01 a.m. *Sorry about dinner...got waylaid. Let me know when you hear from your father.* As Hank scrolled through the texts, she saw unread ones from O'Malley. They could wait. But there were also three new voice-mails. Hopefully one of them was from her dad. The first two said "Unknown." The next read "Henry Nowak." Weird or not, that's how Hank had her father entered into her cell: by his name, not "Dad."

Hank instinctively got a pit in her stomach when she saw the last message was from him. She should have felt relieved, but these days, anxiety was her predominant emotion. Hank touched the blue arrow and heard her dad's voice.

"Hey it's me. Got your messages...see you soon...and, um, don't forget to check on Brady..." he continued.

What the hell? Hank asked herself. She replayed the message to make sure she had heard right. Although it wasn't the best connection, and the voicemail was a bit garbled, she was certain that he said *Brady.* And so now, Hank was worried. But before she had time to call her father back, her phone rang. The caller: Henry Nowak.

"Dad?" Hank asked. "Is everything okay?"

"Yeah, all good," her father answered.

Before he could say anything more, Hank interrupted.

"Are you at the house? I'm coming over—*now*," Hank said determinedly.

Nowak knew it was useless to try and stop her, so he didn't push back.

"That's fine. Can you just give me an hour?" Nowak asked his daughter. "Got a couple things I need to take care of."

The former detective wished he hadn't added those last words. It would just give his daughter another thing to be suspicious of. But it was the first time he would be seeing her since his abduction. It would also be the first time he would be with Hank since he found out about her and Cary. Knowing she had been in a relationship with Cary made lying to his daughter all the more difficult. He found Cary's wallet and couldn't do a goddamn thing about it.

Nowak needed to get his head on straight before Hank arrived. He had to act completely normal, like it was just another day. But he was kicking himself for breaking into Brandon's house. His son was right. Even if he told the police, they'd never find Cary's things now, and if somehow the wallet and gun miraculously turned up, they were fruit of the poisonous tree: inadmissible in court. Nowak tried desperately to think of any reason Brandon might be in possession of Cary's things other than that he was the one who killed her. However, Brandon hadn't confessed to anything yet, not really. There was still hope.

"I didn't kill Cary, if that's what you're thinking," he had told Nowak. But how could he take Brandon at face value? The detective in him thought otherwise. So Nowak made a plan, one that would hopefully prevent any more murders. He would continue his off-the-record shadow investigation and keep a close eye on his son. Nowak still had so many unanswered questions. He owed it to his dead wife, his surviving son Homer, and Hank to find out the truth about both the past and the present, even if he was forced to keep everything he learned from them. Nowak would just have to be careful because he had no doubt that Brandon was a full-blown psychopath capable of anything.

* * *

Brandon didn't release his father until the wee hours of the morning, so as he went to make breakfast, he was sleep-deprived and irritable. His favorite protein shake and a quick shower, however, would help get him back on track. Today would be challenging. If his dad didn't pull anything over the next twenty-four hours, Brandon felt he'd be safe. And he had ultimately denied having anything to do with Cary's death, whether Nowak believed him or not.

Brandon knew there were several things that would keep his father from betraying his confidence. One was the fact that he didn't want Vito and Hank to know he had fucked up the evidence. And Nowak also knew that he wouldn't be able to produce it any longer any way. Another was that he didn't want Hank to find out about her mother and long-lost brother from Brandon himself. But Brandon believed that the main reason his father would protect him was that he had failed to do so forty-plus years ago and was guilt-ridden as a result. He had a lot to make up for.

Nowak was still in the dark about how Brandon, a.k.a. Harry, had found out about his past, as well as what had happened to him after he was abducted. But there would be time to explain everything. Nowak didn't know it yet, but he would function as his son's conduit for the foreseeable future. Brandon was pulling the strings.

* * *

When Hank arrived at her father's house, she barged through the front door, relieved to see him standing in the kitchen. *Oh my God, I forgot to tell Vito,* she reprimanded herself. But first, she ran over to Nowak and gave him a big hug.

"I've been trying to reach you," Hank said. "Give me a sec.... I need to tell Vito you're okay."

Hank took out her phone and sent Vito the following text: *I'm with my dad. At his house. All good.* It only took a minute for her mobile to ring.

"Vito?" Hank answered. "Yeah, he's fine. Sure."

Nowak could only hear Hank's end of the conversation until she put her cell on speaker. Vito's voice came through loud and clear.

"Where the hell have you been, Nowak?" he asked. "Meet me at the diner for breakfast, both of you. That work?"

"Yup," Nowak answered curtly.

Although Hank had put on a brave front, she had been more worried about her father's whereabouts than she had let on.

"We'll see you in an hour," Hank replied.

As Hank and her dad drove to meet Vito, she started to interrogate him.

"Well, where in God's name have you been?" she inquired.

"Nowhere," Nowak answered, trying to sound nonchalant. "I'll explain everything when we get to the diner. Didn't mean to whip everybody into a frenzy."

When they arrived, Hank parked her car, and they made their way inside. There was no sign of Vito yet, but Xanthe was there to greet them. Her expression reminded Nowak that he still hadn't had *that* talk with his daughter. It could wait, under the circumstances. Hank didn't even know that her favorite server had spilled the beans about her and Cary—to her father no less.

As Xanthe was about to show them to their booth, Vito showed up. The three of them sat down, Vito and Hank, side by side, and Nowak across the table from them. *Jesus, feels like I'm about to face a firing squad,* Nowak said to himself. Looking at his daughter and best friend, the former detective couldn't help but feel like he was betraying them. Nowak knew that if Vito and Hank found out what he had done, they would crucify him. Cary's wallet and gun were now history. They were two key pieces of evidence, whether Brandon was responsible for Cary's death or not. *God did I fuck up bad,* Nowak admonished himself.

Vito's voice brought Nowak back to reality.

"You gonna order?" he asked his friend, nodding to Xanthe.

"Uh, sure. How 'bout some of that great French toast of yours and coffee, black," Nowak answered.

Then Vito got down to business.

"Mind telling us where you've been?" Vito inquired.

"What's with you two?" Nowak asked in return. "Can't a guy take some time for himself?"

Hank and Vito stared back at him. The expressions on their faces demanded a better explanation.

"Jeez, okay. I um...uh...took the boat out for a bit...lost track of time. Ended up spending the night at that little inn on the other side of the cove," Nowak clarified. "There, you guys happy?" he asked caustically.

"We were worried about you. I was worried about you," Hank said, clearly annoyed. "Why didn't you answer my messages?"

"I don't know. Guess I left my phone in the house. Wanted to unplug; isn't that what you younger folks call it? Disconnect from everything. Is that a crime now?" Nowak asked, hoping his story would put an end to their inquest.

"Enough of this," Vito began. "It's your business. That's not the reason I wanted to see you guys. My gun, the one I lent to Cary. It's missing," Vito said in a concerned tone.

Vito had spent the past several days tearing Gayle's guesthouse apart trying to locate the firearm. It hadn't turned up in Hank's car, and he was certain that if Hank herself had found it in her home, she would have told him about it. But he had to ask.

"Unless you have it, Hank," Vito said gently.

Vito wasn't even sure Hank knew about the gun, but it was time to find out.

"Cary told me about it. Well, I, uh, sort of found it, you could say," Hank tried to explain, remembering the revolver she discovered as she felt her way down Cary's back. "But I haven't seen it since the last night, I mean, the last time I saw her," Hank said, rewording her statement so as not to tip her father off as to their relationship.

"Fuckin' A," Vito proclaimed. "This is bad. I gotta find that gun."

Nowak could barely look Vito in the eye, but neither he nor Hank noticed her father's uneasiness. As Nowak was trying to find a way to change the subject without raising suspicion, his daughter's phone rang.

"Sorry, it's O'Malley. I've been ignoring his texts, I'm afraid. Better take this," Hank proclaimed.

She answered the call, walking to a deserted corner of the dining room. When Hank returned to the booth, her father and Vito looked up expectantly, waiting for a report.

"It's nothing. The partial prints on that 'Odd Jobs' card, Max's instincts were right. They belong to Hunter. It's a dead end. We can't seem to catch a break with this guy," Hank declared, frustrated.

"We'll get him. He'll mess up. They always do. Right, Nowak?" Vito asked.

"Uh, yeah, sure, just a matter of time. These things take time," he replied.

Nowak was afraid he was acting weird. But lying to his closest friend and daughter didn't come naturally to him. He couldn't wait to get away from them.

"Guess we're done here," Vito stated. "You guys go along. I'll get the check."

Hank knew from experience that when Vito was in a generous mood, there was no point in arguing with him, so she simply thanked him instead.

"We'll be outside," Hank told Vito.

There was one thing Hank hadn't gotten around to asking her father about yet: *Brady*. It was possible she misheard. The message was somewhat garbled. But she needed to know. So once the two of them were alone outside waiting for Vito, she brought up the subject.

"Dad, were you trying to send me a message? Did you say *check on Brady?*" Hank asked him point-blank.

Nowak cringed inside. The safe word came out of his mouth before he knew what he was saying. At the time, he actually thought he was about to die.

"Brady," he repeated to his daughter. "Don't remember saying that. You must've heard me wrong. These phones are gadgets, junk, not like the old days when you could actually talk to someone..." he continued, rambling on.

Hank thought her father wasn't acting like himself. But he seemed certain that he never uttered the name. *People hear what they want to,* she told herself. *The mind can play tricks on you.*

As Vito exited the diner, he spotted Hank and Nowak standing near the parking lot, engaged in conversation. He walked over and joined them. Normally he might have been curious as to what they were talking about, but today, he had one thing on his mind: the gun.

"Gotta find that gun," he said in an anxious voice. "Don't know what I was thinking giving it to Cary like that. Look where it's gotten us."

"The gun has nothing to do with what happened to Cary or anyone else," Hank declared. "But yes, we need to find it. Don't want it getting into the wrong hands. And God forbid O'Malley finds out."

"Fucking Jesus Christ," Vito responded.

As Nowak was about to weigh in, a text popped up on his phone. The sender was identified as "Your Son." *What the hell...shit,* Nowak said to himself. He remembered Brandon's last words before he let him go: *You'll go home now and wait for further instructions.* At the time, Nowak thought it was just an idle threat. He didn't actually expect to hear from him. This was all becoming too much for the elderly detective. His cat and mouse days were decidedly behind him. He should have left well enough alone, let the professionals handle it and not use the case to prove something to himself—useless hindsight.

Nowak's hands began to twitch a bit. He hoped Vito and Hank hadn't noticed. God knows what they were making of his recent behavior.

"Um, afraid I've gotta take this," he told them. "Answer it."

Vito thought Nowak looked awful. Trying to help his friend out, he intervened.

"Hank, wanna come with me?" Vito asked. "Your dad looks like he could use some rest."

But Hank noticed the tremors as well. When her dad got stressed or forgot to take his meds, his hands trembled. She was getting really worried about him.

"Dad, is that all right with you? You'll be okay? You look kind of pale," Hank continued. "Maybe you should go see your doctor."

"Don't you fret about me. I'm fine, really. Just have to make this call, then I'll be a good boy and go home and take it easy—promise," Nowak said, trying to get them off his back.

Once Hank and Vito were safely out of view, Nowak got into his Bronco and stared down at his phone. The text from Brandon read: *Hope you enjoyed breakfast.* Nowak looked around to see if he could spot his son, but Brandon was nowhere to be found. *Jesus, is he stalking me now?* Nowak asked himself. As Nowak was trying to figure out his next move, another text came in: *?*. Nowak was afraid if he didn't respond, it would set Brandon off. But he wasn't sure how to answer. Then his phone rang: "Your Son" popped up on the screen.

Nowak considered letting the call go to voicemail, but it was entirely possible that Brandon was watching him right now. He knew he had no choice but to pick up.

"How did you...?" Nowak inquired.

Brandon knew what his father was referring to: that someone had entered him into Nowak's phone. That someone, of course, was Brandon.

"Not sure what you mean," Brandon responded, messing with his dad.

"Cut the bullshit," Nowak muttered.

"Woo...let's settle down, shall we? If you're wondering how my contact info got into your phone, think again," Brandon said. "Or do I have to explain everything to you?"

Brandon's words triggered Nowak's memory, and he put it together immediately.

"You took my phone...figured out the passcode...fine...you win..." Nowak uttered, defeated.

"See, you've still got it," Brandon answered, in a menacing tone. "How else are we going to stay in touch?"

"If you're wondering what I was doing with my daughter and Vito..." Nowak said, starting to explain.

"I trust you, old man. I trust that you are too smart to do anything stupid," Brandon declared.

Nowak didn't know how to shake this guy: his own son. But there was one thing he had to tell him: that the gun belonged to Vito, not Cary. And he needed it back.

"Listen, there's something you should know," Nowak began. "It's about the gun. It isn't...I mean wasn't Cary's. That firearm belongs to Vito, and I need to get it back to him before anyone finds out."

"Outstanding," Brandon said caustically. "And why exactly would I do that...give you the gun?"

"Look, I'll just tell Vito that I found it in the guesthouse or at Hank's or in the neighborhood where Cary was hit. But I need that gun, and you're gonna give it to me," Nowak said, losing all control.

"I think you're forgetting who's in charge here," Brandon stated brusquely. "And it's not you."

Nowak couldn't think of anything else to say that might change Brandon's mind and get him to cooperate. There clearly was no upside nor incentive for him to turn over the weapon. And while Nowak knew that Brandon must have put it somewhere that no one would ever find it, if the revolver surfaced, Vito would pay the price.

"I think we're done here. But please do stay in touch, and I will do the same," Brandon said mockingly.

Then the phone went dead. Nowak reached into his pocket and popped two pills in his mouth. He swallowed them dry, without water. When he got home, he would wash any remaining residue down with beer. *Goddamn it,* he said to himself. *What the hell am I going to do?*

* * *

While Nowak was negotiating with Brandon, Hank and Vito headed to her place. They shared a mutual concern for Nowak's well-being.

"Your dad," Vito began. "He's not himself. Not sure what to do about it."

"I know. Did you see his hands? The tremors are back. He's so fucking stubborn...needs to get checked out," Hank responded.

"I'll talk to him...at least try," Vito added. "He's one headstrong SOB, but I'll do what I can. In the meantime, why don't you come by for dinner tonight? I'll see if Gayle's around too. Might be good for all of us if we just tried to have one goddamn normal evening."

"That would be nice," Hank said. "What about my dad? Should I ask him to join us?"

"Don't see why not, as long as he's up to it," Vito answered. "Maybe we can all do a little brainstorming, figure out how to catch this guy. There's something we're missing I know it. I just don't know what that something is...*yet.*"

Hank suddenly had a moment of clarity.

"Vito, my dad said he took the boat across the cove and spent the night. But..." Hank tried to finish her thought as Vito interrupted.

"But the boat was there when we checked his house, and his car wasn't," Vito declared.

"Exactly," Hank said as she gave Vito another worried look.

* * *

While Brandon was talking to his father on the phone, he stayed one car length behind Vito and Hank. Brandon could multitask. *I can walk and chew gum at the same time,* he noted, *unlike half the fucking world.* He would have loved to hear what Vito and Hank were talking about, but right now it was enough that he kept an eye on their whereabouts. When they got to Hank's home, it took a couple of minutes for her to get out of the car. Then Vito drove away. Brandon sat for a moment reflecting on the call with his dad.

It was important for Nowak to know that his son wasn't going anywhere, that he was keeping a close eye on him. But news of the gun had surprised Brandon. *Did it really matter who the firearm technically belonged to?* he asked himself. Of course, it would worry Vito. *Sloppy work,* Brandon told himself. But as far as Brandon was concerned, the weapon, along with Cary's wallet, needed to be disposed of either way. Out of expediency, Brandon had put the items back in his desk drawer after his father left. But now it was time to get rid of them once and for all.

✳ ✳ ✳

Brandon waited until dark and went to the shed near the cabin to grab a shovel. He had Vito's gun and Cary's wallet with him in a small bag. Then, Brandon made his way to a heavily wooded area at the rear of the property. He dug a deep but narrow hole by his favorite tree. Brandon marked the spot with an inconspicuous rock and returned to the main house. *Brandon one, Dad nothing,* he congratulated himself— not that he was keeping score or anything.

FIFTEEN

It was almost dinnertime, and Anna and Vito had really knocked themselves out preparing an unnecessarily elaborate spread for Cary's immediate family and friends. The spontaneous plan, initiated by Vito, was turning into more of a dinner party food-wise, but he thought they all deserved it. As Anna was putting the final touches on her famous lasagna, Vito cleaned up in the kitchen. Then, they heard banging on the front door.

"My dad will be here soon," Hank said, as Vito let her into the guesthouse.

"Great. Glad he was up to it," Vito replied. "Let me take your jacket."

"Thanks. Smells great in here," Hank commented. "Who do I owe for this?"

"I think Vito thinks it was a team effort," Anna began to explain. "And if you're referring to the lasagna, well, I'll collect the IOU for that one," she said jokingly.

Vito was happy to let Anna take the credit even though he had driven all the way to Newtown to pick up Connecticut's best ice cream: the ice cream Cary had always been so fond of. There didn't seem to be any neutral topics left these days. Everything led to pain.

Another knock on the door alerted the three of them to Nowak's arrival. They knew Gayle would be the last to show up, as she was always late. Vito peeked out the window and got up to greet his friend. Nowak looked exhausted, but Vito and Hank wouldn't have understood why. The stress of dealing with Brandon and hiding the truth from the two people he loved most was starting to take a toll on Nowak. He just couldn't handle it.

"Hey there, buddy," Vito said, giving his friend a big bear hug. "Glad you could make it."

"Wouldn't have missed it," Nowak answered. "If there's anything that could get me out of the house, it's one of Anna's meals."

"Who wants wine?" Vito asked. "Or should we wait for Gayle?"

"Think we can go ahead without her," Hank answered. "She shouldn't be too long."

Hank was right, as a vehicle could be heard pulling up just as Vito began to uncork the bottle.

"I'll get it," Hank said, turning to Vito. "Just be a minute."

Hank hadn't seen Gayle in a while, so she took the opportunity to get her alone. She opened the door and stepped outside just as Gayle was getting out of her car.

"Hey, Hank," Gayle started. "It's so good to see you."

"Same here," Hank responded, giving her a hug. "How are you and your mom holding up?"

"Not great. Pretty bad to be honest," Gayle answered. "I still can't believe Cary's gone. It's too much...just too much."

"We're all hurting," Hank replied. "But Vito and I...O'Malley... something will give. We'll figure out who's responsible...for every-thing. And they'll pay, I promise."

Gayle wasn't a vengeful person, but Hank thought she'd make an exception when it came to Cary's killer. "Here, let's go inside. Anna has really made a lovely dinner, went all out."

As they made their way to the cottage, Vito opened the front door.

"There you are," he said. "Thought you two got lost."

"Just catching up," Gayle replied. "So good to see you guys."

"Hope you're hungry. Anna went a bit crazy," Vito said laughingly. "There'll be plenty of leftovers for everyone to take home, I'm betting."

"This was so thoughtful of you, Vito. I could sure use the distraction," Gayle muttered.

"How's your mom doing?" Vito asked. "I mean, considering. I've been meaning to check up on you guys. Sorry if..." he began.

But Cary's sister just gave him a grim look and took his hand. When they got inside, Anna came right over to Gayle and put her arms around her. The embrace provided little comfort for Gayle, who felt lost and alone knowing she would never see her twin again. Vito, sensing the mood had turned somber, decided it was time to eat.

"Why don't you guys grab a plate and take whatever you want," he suggested. "There's plenty more, believe me," Vito repeated.

So Nowak, Hank, and Gayle filled their plates with Anna's lasagna and salad and sat down around the fireplace. Vito and Anna followed suit. For a few minutes, they ate in silence, then Hank had an idea.

"If you guys don't mind, think we could turn on *Crime Watch*?" she asked. "Curious whether they're still paying any attention to the 'Deer Killer' case or Cary's, for that matter. Not that they're unrelated," Hank added, rambling.

Hank's question took the rest of them by surprise, but in the end, they didn't think it was such a bad idea. Anna and Vito were mostly worried about Gayle, but she set them straight.

"Don't worry. I can handle it," she said, looking at the two of them. "We've got to know what's going on. If the story dies, it'll make it even harder to catch this guy."

So Vito stood up, found the remote, and turned on the television. Flipping channels, he stopped when he got to LNN and Eve's show. They were about to take a commercial break, but when Eve returned, she was going to bring everyone up to date on the latest developments in the case. The group was actually surprised that the show hadn't abandoned the story. There really wasn't anything new to report. But Hank in particular knew how much Cary had meant to Eve and the rest of her staff. So, if keeping the case alive in the news could in any way help catch Cary's killer, Hank was certain Eve wouldn't let it go.

The only guests Eve had on for the segment were Todd Zeff and Caity Murphy. As Eve questioned them, a photo of Cary with Obelus by her side appeared on the screen. Then a montage of the other victims popped up. It was difficult to relive the trauma, to be reminded of what had taken place in their own community, no less. Hank started to think it hadn't been such a great idea to watch the show after all.

Gayle was the first one to speak.

"Sorry, I really am, but can we turn it off? I just can't..." she uttered, her voice cracking with emotion.

"Yes, of course," Anna answered, sparing Hank. "Vito, can you...?" she asked.

"On it," Vito responded. "Anyway, good to know they're still paying attention."

Anna gave him a look that screamed: *I know you mean well, but just stop talking*. As an awkward silence settled over the room, Nowak's phone rang. "Your Son" appeared on the screen. If Nowak's ringer had been off, he would have considered ignoring the call, but everyone in the room already heard it. Brandon was never going to leave him alone. *Jesus fucking Christ*, Nowak thought to himself. He had to get him off his back. So, using the call as an excuse to get out of there, Nowak simply said, "Guess it's time for me to leave anyway."

When the former detective was in the privacy of his own car, he looked down to see an alert on his phone that read: *Missed call, one voicemail*. He touched the little blue arrow and held the mobile device to his ear. The message said: *Hey Dad, have a present for you. Hint: it's shot. Meet me in an hour at the entrance to Devil's Den. And don't be late.*

Nowak hesitated before returning the call. Brandon picked up after one ring.

"What the hell do you think you're doing calling me like that? I was with my daughter and Vito," Nowak said in an agitated tone.

"Not my problem," Brandon said commandingly. "Just do as you're told."

"Look, I just want the gun. That's all. Got it?" Nowak asked.

"Who said anything about a gun?" Brandon inquired.

"Stop fucking around with me...please," Nowak begged.

"Guess you got me," Brandon replied. "If you want it, come get it," he laughed, and the call went dead.

Son of a goddamn bitch, Nowak muttered to himself. *This kid's gonna be the death of me.*

* * *

Brandon had been paying attention too. He ended the call, turned off *Crime Watch with Eve Arora,* and put on his jacket. Eve hadn't forgotten about him after all. It was time to meet up with his father again and have it out with him. Brandon picked up his car keys and a small bag he had packed. He locked the front door on his way out, set the alarm remotely, and made his way to the garage, where his reliable smart car waited for him. It would more than suffice for what he had planned for the evening.

* * *

When Nowak pulled up to the entrance of Devil's Den, it was dark and secluded. At this hour, no one would be around, and that was what Brandon was counting on. Nowak sat in his car for a minute, feeling jittery about the meeting. But he needed to get Vito's gun back and then figure out a way to return it to him without involving Brandon. Nowak could tell Vito he went back to the scene where Cary was struck and found it in the brush. He could point out that the location he discovered it in was far enough away from where Hank's car had been parked so that Vito wouldn't be suspicious as to why the authorities hadn't stumbled upon it during their search of the area. That was his best option.

Nowak decided to wait until Brandon got there to get out of his car. Staring out the driver's side window, Nowak was startled by a vehicle inching its way toward his own with the headlights off. *Brandon's attempt at a sneak attack,* Nowak told himself. His son had a flair for the dramatic, Nowak decided. Brandon flashed his headlights to signal to his father that it was time to talk. Nowak steadied himself and got out of his Bronco to meet him.

"That's far enough," Brandon told his dad.

"Where's the gun?" Nowak inquired, anxious to get what he came for and leave.

"You mean this one?" Brandon asked, as he reached into his pocket. "This one's mine," he responded, pointing the revolver at his father.

"Is that really necessary?" Nowak asked, panicking.

"Depends, I guess," Brandon answered. "But first things first, we need to talk. Or have you no curiosity about how I found you...how I discovered where I came from, who I am? Where I've been all this time? I suppose not, since you put the incident behind you rather quickly, I should say."

"That's not true," Nowak shot back at him. "We did everything... *everything.*"

"Rewriting history, are we?" Brandon quipped. "Should I have brought a *Father of the Year* mug with me?" he asked sarcastically.

"Grow up," Nowak shouted back at his son. "None of this gives you the right to..." he continued.

"The right to what exactly?" Brandon questioned his father.

Nowak was starting to feel lightheaded and afraid he had walked into a trap.

"Where's the gun?" he repeated.

"Shut up, old man. You'll get it when I decide it's time. So here's the quick recap of the mess that became my life because of you," Brandon said, starting to explain.

Brandon began at the beginning. The man or woman who snatched him when he was just a toddler abandoned their young captive outside a small town in Pennsylvania and was never caught. Someone discovered Brandon by the side of a road and brought him to the local sheriff's department. After spending time in the foster system, a wealthy, childless, somewhat older couple adopted him, legally, and made Brandon their heir. After they eventually died, he collected his inheritance and hired a private eye who, using DNA and other resources, identified Henry Nowak as his father.

Brandon spent years going over and over the same detailed reports that the man had provided him with. That's how he discovered what had really happened to his mother: that she had finally succumbed to severe depression as the result of the kidnapping and killed herself. He also found out that he was in the custody of his father right before he was abducted. In Brandon's mind, it was all Nowak's fault. And to be honest, his dad more or less agreed with that assessment, having blamed himself for the tragedy all these years.

Brandon hadn't discovered that Hank was his biological sister until recently. He had just wanted to identify his father. Nowak's son had bided his time, moving back to his birthplace and setting up house. Brandon had watched his father on and off for years, waiting for what he considered to be the right time to make his move. Brandon decided the best way to exact his revenge was to terrorize the community: to make everyone pay for what had happened to him and then make sure his father understood he was responsible for all those deaths too. And the time was now.

Brandon wasn't prepared to confess to anything just yet. He planned on savoring his vengeance. Oh, sure, he had had urges dating back as far as he could remember. That's why he started hurting animals when he was just a boy. But he was content to hold his father responsible for all of it.

"I do have one question," Brandon said. "How did you pull off that abomination of an obituary about how my mother died of cancer? How totally unethical and unoriginal to boot," he added.

"I, uh, how did you...things got complicated. I didn't want Hank to know. Nor your brother. Had a friend who owed me a favor," Nowak went on, trying to set the record straight.

"Save it for someone who cares," Brandon responded angrily. "You did the same thing my kidnapper did: abandoned me. Does that make you feel like a man, Dad?"

"I didn't. I swear. We looked everywhere...did everything we could at the time," Nowak said pleadingly.

"Fucking bullshit," Brandon said, cursing at his father, totally out of character. He considered himself to be a gentleman, after all.

"My sister had a normal life. Bet you doted on her, didn't you? Daddy's little girl who grew up to be just like him," Brandon added.

"Look, you need help," Nowak said, carefully. "Let me..." he continued.

"Why do I need help? You're the one who needs help," Brandon responded, interrupting Nowak.

The former detective stood there, trying to figure out a way to bring up the gun again without setting Brandon off any more than he already had.

"We've all suffered, paid a price for that awful day," Nowak said as his hands started to tremble. "If you only knew..." he went on, but Brandon wasn't having it.

"Enough, old man," he shouted. "Here's an idea. Why don't we call my sister and tell her to meet us here?" Brandon asked, picking up his phone.

"No, please, don't," Nowak pleaded. "Just give me the gun, and I'll go. It would kill her if she knew that her own brother was responsible for..." he rambled on.

"Responsible, responsible for what? I haven't done anything. My conscience is clear. Can you say the same?" Brandon asked.

Nowak didn't think his son was even capable of having a conscience. He was a full-on psychopath.

"What do you want from me?" Nowak asked, defeated.

"Ah, now we're getting somewhere," Brandon said as he checked his other pockets. "Appears the only gun I brought with me this evening is my own."

"What the hell is the point of all this?" Nowak asked, exasperated. "I need that gun."

"You'll have to earn it, I'm afraid," Brandon answered.

He handed his father three "Odd Jobs" cards and waited for his reaction.

"What am I supposed to do with these?" Nowak inquired.

"You will keep them in a safe place where no one can find them and wait for further instructions," Brandon said mysteriously. "It'll be fun," he added.

"Fun!? Are you out of your mind?" Nowak uttered before he knew what he was saying.

"I'd watch it, old man, if I were you. Watch how you speak to me," Brandon said, as he continued to point the gun at his father.

Nowak was at his wit's end. He had no leverage. Brandon was calling the shots. *How in God's name am I going to get out of this mess?* Nowak wondered.

"It's a wrap, as they say," Brandon stated, as he made his way back to his car. "Hopefully I will have a nice surprise for you very soon."

Nowak took Brandon's last words as a clear threat, but to whom he wasn't entirely sure. He waited for Brandon to leave, then he sat quietly in his car reassessing what had taken place. Nowak decided the best course of action for the time being was to steer clear of his daughter and Vito. But he wasn't sure how long he'd be able to avoid them. *One step at a time,* he told himself. He'd figure it out because he simply had to.

* * *

When Brandon got home, he poured himself a brandy and started pacing in front of the fireplace. He needed to think. *What better way to lure Nowak to a secluded place than on the pretense of returning Vito's firearm?* he asked himself. And it had worked.

His father left their meeting of sorts frustrated and afraid. But it was time to plan his next murder and test former Det. Henry "Hank" Nowak's loyalties. The thought that his father and sister shared the same nickname struck Brandon as odd. *No one calls him that anyway because it's fucking confusing,* Brandon reflected. He was confounded by his father's arrogance and ego.

But he had more important things to worry about, such as who his next victim would be. Then Brandon had an idea. He needed to get his inspiration from somewhere, so he decided to rewatch Eve's latest shows on the case. Turning on the television, Brandon began with the *Crime Watch* episode about Cary's disappearance before he had dumped her at the emergency room. But nothing about the show excited him. Next, he scanned through the program that had paid tribute to Cary's life and death—again, nothing particularly noteworthy. But the third show, the one aimed at keeping the case alive and in the news, caught his eye for one reason: Caity Murphy. She would do.

Brandon took note of the chyron on the screen that identified Caity and her job title: Field Producer/Intern. *Intern?* Brandon contemplated. *Her parents must be so proud,* he concluded, mockingly. The young woman seemed sincere yet ambitious. That could work in Brandon's favor. He would lure her to his home on the pretext of giving the up-and-coming journalist an exclusive interview with Cary Mackin's landlord. So Brandon Googled the email format for LNN and sent Ms. Murphy an invitation to come to his estate at her earliest convenience. Brandon figured that for a pushy reporter, that would mean ten minutes ago.

Despite the late hour, Murphy returned the email immediately. *When and where?* she answered. *Send me your address.* Brandon saw no reason to play hard to get. *These people are animals.*

* * *

Caity was excited that Brandon had been so impressed with her appearance on *Crime Watch* that he chose her over all the other correspondents that would have killed to get the exclusive. Caity had come a long way in the relatively short amount of time she had worked on Eve's show. Having started as an intern last year and only working intermittently, Caity had finally landed a staff position that required her to go into the field. She was realizing her dream.

Caity stayed up half the night coming up with provocative questions to ask Cary's landlord. The interview had to make a splash. If she handled him right, Brandon could catapult her career to the next level. Caity wanted to look the part, so she thought her new jeans with a black suit jacket would be the appropriate attire for a casual yet important rendezvous with someone who had been close to Cary. God knows what information he might reveal during the sit-down.

* * *

As Caity pulled up to Brandon's estate, she was blown away by the enormity of it. Caity herself came from a modest background, growing up in a small town along the northern border in Upstate New York. But she had come prepared this morning, even stopping to pick up two coffees and some pastries along the way. When she got to the front gate, the young woman pressed the button and waited for someone to answer.

Brandon, of course, was already watching her, courtesy of his security cameras. *This is just too easy,* he told himself. Hopefully, getting away with the eager girl's murder would provide him with more of a challenge. Brandon waited exactly thirty seconds before responding to the buzzer. He used the time to assess his prey's demeanor and appearance. Caity was striking, likely even more so in person, and she appeared to be nervous. Brandon intended to enjoy every minute he spent with her.

"Who's there?" he finally asked.

"Me. I mean, it's Caity Murphy from *Crime Watch*," she answered. "We were supposed to meet this morning. Hope I'm not too early."

"Not at all," Brandon responded. "Just pull your car around to the front, and I'll meet you there. Oh, and thanks for coming."

Caity was conflicted about whether or not to tell Gene and Eve about the interview. But it had all happened so fast she decided to see how the conversation went, and if she felt good about it, she would surprise them with the news. So no one but Brandon even knew that she was there.

The aspiring reporter got out of her car and walked up the elaborate entrance to the front door. When Brandon opened it, he had a big smile on his face. He saw no reason to hide his excitement.

"Come on in," Brandon said invitingly.

"Thanks so much for asking me here," Caity responded.

Then, remembering the coffee and pastries, she added, "So sorry, I left something in the car. Back in a minute."

The misstep on Caity's part would be her first faux pas of the morning, and likely the last of her short life. As she attempted to juggle the coffee, baked goods, and equipment she had brought to record the interview, Brandon stepped in to help.

"Please, let me," he began. "How very thoughtful."

Brandon took the two hot drinks and bag holding several chocolate croissants and brought Caity inside.

"There, that's better, isn't it?" he asked her. "Right this way."

Brandon decided the den would be the best place to record the interview. His study was off limits right now as he had turned it into more or less of a situation room, where Brandon monitored the comings and goings of anyone who might be snooping around these days, invading his privacy, in the hopes of cracking the case. He would let Ms. Murphy conduct the entire interview and then dispose of her. And Brandon knew exactly how he was going to accomplish that.

"What a beautiful fireplace," Caity said upon entering Brandon's beloved room.

The remark reminded him of Cary's similar reaction the first time he met her. *Things are progressing nicely,* he told himself. Everything was in sync. Brandon decided to let Caity take it from there, after all she was the professional. So he waited for her to tell him where to sit and what to do. It didn't take long.

"Why don't I set up the camera on that stool over there, and we can sit opposite each other at an angle in front of the fireplace?" Caity suggested.

"Whatever you think is best," Brandon answered cooperatively.

Brandon was sure that Caity didn't realize he was an actor and had never seen him in anything. *Why would she have?* he asked himself. *Damn that actress who messed up the schedule for the Hulu series. God knows when it will go forward, if ever,* he bemoaned.

"How do I look?" Brandon asked the young woman. "Ready for my close-up?" he joked.

Brandon couldn't resist turning on the charm. He sensed that Caity was warming up to him and was already developing a crush in the short time they had spent together. *Too bad,* he thought. *This will be the shortest relationship in history.*

"Camera ready," she answered, blushing slightly.

What a handsome couple we would have made, Brandon considered. But it was time to focus. They took their seats, and Caity turned on the camera and tested the microphone. They were good to go. Her first question was an easy one.

"Can you tell us how and when you met Ms. Cary Mackin?" Caity asked.

Jesus, really, thought Brandon. He had been expecting more—a lot more. *This girl is a total amateur. What a waste of time.*

"Well, I was looking for a tenant, and my real estate agent brought Cary over to see if she would be interested in renting my guesthouse," Brandon answered, clearly bored.

Brandon let Caity ask several more questions before he put a stop to the interview. It was time. He had given a lot of thought to how he would kill Caity. *No more cars,* Brandon decided. This murder would be up close and personal.

"Can I use your bathroom?" Caity asked, snapping Brandon out of his homicidal thoughts.

"Why, of course. It's the second door on the left," Brandon instructed her, somewhat startled.

The request gave Brandon a few minutes to collect himself. He put on his favorite leather gloves and a ski mask and waited. He could feel his adrenaline pumping. Brandon couldn't help wondering what it was going to feel like this time: snuffing the life out of a beautiful young woman by actually touching her. *How many people got to experience this kind of moment with another human being?* Brandon contemplated. Soon, he would truly understand the unique bond that existed between a murderer and his victim. Sure he had shoved Nicole down a flight of stairs, but it just wasn't the same. Brandon heard the bathroom door open and stood ready. He waited for Caity to enter the room. Brandon had positioned himself facing the window so that his back would be toward Caity when she returned. How dramatic it would be when he turned around and saw her panicked expression.

"Thanks so much for everything," Caity began as she approached Brandon. "I'll let you know when the interview is going to air."

Brandon took a deep breath, turned around, stared directly into Caity's terrified eyes, and waited.

"Oh my God," Caity gasped as she tried to process what was happening.

Brandon thought she looked absolutely frantic; the mask and gloves had served their purpose. As Brandon made his way toward his next victim, he wanted her to understand what was going on. He couldn't help but wonder if Caity realized he was the "Deer Killer" and that he had murdered Cary as well. But Brandon saw no reason to confess. All he wanted was for Caity to grasp that she was about to die. And then, right on cue, the young woman began to beg for her life.

"Please...I'll do anything...anything...whatever you want. I won't tell anyone..." Caity uttered desperately.

So predictable and unoriginal, Brandon told himself. *Let's get this over with.*

"Any last words...requests...other than the one you just mentioned?" Brandon inquired.

Caity glanced around the room, looking for a way to escape. But there was none. Brandon got within an inch of her and placed his hands around her throat.

"Now, now," Brandon muttered. "It will all be over very soon. Say hello to Cary for me when you see her."

And with those words, Brandon started to squeeze Caity's neck as she struggled, futilely, to get away. The young woman passed out after a minute, falling to the floor. But Brandon had learned his lesson from the near fiasco with Cary's murder. So just to be sure, he lifted up his right foot, clad in a heavy boot, and stomped on Caity's throat. He checked her pulse and poured himself a scotch. *Live spelled backward is evil,* Brandon pondered. *That tracks.* Brandon sat on the couch in front of the fireplace, picked up his phone, and sent the following text to his father: *Leave one of the "Odd Jobs" cards at the entrance to Devil's Den tonight at 10 p.m. sharp.*

Brandon had a lot to do while he was waiting for his father to answer. First, he needed to store Caity's body somewhere safe until nightfall. That was easy. He would simply put her in the meat freezer in the basement. And there would be no blood to clean up; strangulation definitely had its perks. Next, he had to get rid of her car. That would be a bit trickier. For now, he would park it in the barn behind the main house. But he would need to figure out a long-term solution.

Brandon stood up and looked down at the dead girl, his latest casualty. *Her only crime had been naivety,* he pondered. Brandon picked up the lifeless body and made his way to the basement, where he laid

Caity on the floor and went through her pockets, looking for car keys. Brandon found them stuffed in her jeans. He opened the oversized metal box and placed her gently inside.

"Rest now," he said to the corpse. "We have a big night ahead of us."

* * *

Nowak was alone at home when he got the text. *What has my son done now?* he asked himself. "Bad, bad," he muttered out loud. Nowak had spent the morning working on his boat. Then he had gone out to pick up lunch from his favorite little seafood place, the one on the water, near the beach. After eating, the former detective had taken a nap that lasted longer than he had planned. So the old man didn't see the text until hours after it was sent and wasn't sure how to respond. Knowing Brandon, however, Nowak assumed he was already pissed at him for what he would perceive as ignoring the message.

Better reply now, he told himself. Nowak thought he'd begin with a text instead of calling. If Brandon failed to answer, then he could try him on his phone. *But the less that's in writing, the better,* Nowak contemplated. However, at this point, he wasn't sure it made any difference. Either way, there would be a trail. So he touched the screen and typed: *What's this all about?* Nowak put his phone down on the kitchen counter and waited. As he opened the fridge to grab a beer, he heard the text tone. The words "*JUST DO IT*" popped up along with the name "Your Son." Nowak knew he had no choice but to obey. "What the fucking hell?" he muttered out loud. Fatherhood was getting way too complicated.

* * *

Nowak allowed himself forty-five minutes to get to Devil's Den. He couldn't risk being late and had no idea what or whom he would find when he got there. The former cop opened the top dresser drawer that contained mementos from his son's kidnapping. He stared down at the three "Odd Jobs" cards Brandon had given him and picked up the one on top. "God help me," he said.

Devil's Den was completely deserted when Nowak pulled up to the entryway. It was 9:45 p.m. and dark. Creepy was the only word that came to mind. He decided to do exactly as he had been told and not get out of his car until 9:55 p.m. That would give him five minutes to decide where to leave the card. Nowak looked out the windshield but saw only brush and trees. His gut told him if Brandon was there, he was hiding and wouldn't show his face.

Nowak looked down at his watch and noted the time: 9:54 p.m. He picked up the "Odd Jobs" card, opened the driver side door, and got out of the vehicle. Using his phone as a flashlight, he made his way to the entrance, looking for the right spot to leave the small rectangular piece of cardboard. The only time Nowak had touched the cards, albeit by the edges, was when Brandon initially gave them to him. Otherwise, being a detective, he had always worn gloves. The same was true tonight.

It was now exactly 10:00 p.m. Nowak bent down and placed the card on the ground, partially covering it with some dead leaves. Brandon hadn't given his father specific instructions, so Nowak prayed he was doing the right thing. Nowak stood up, scoured the area, and returned to his car; then he drove away. At 10:03 p.m., his phone rang. The call was from "Your Son." Nowak was still in the vicinity of Devil's Den, so he pulled over and turned off the car. He touched the green circle on the screen and answered the call.

"Listen," the former detective began, but Brandon cut him off.

"Have we been a good boy tonight?" Brandon asked.

"The card is under some leaves near the entrance, if that's what you mean," Nowak answered nervously. "You didn't..." he added.

"Didn't what? You're a cop. Can't you think of anything on your own?" Brandon inquired disrespectfully.

"Look, I did what you asked. You can check for yourself," Nowak declared.

"For sure," Brandon replied. "That's the plan."

* * *

Brandon was just a ten-minute drive from Devil's Den when he called his dad. He had been acutely aware of the time when he descended to the basement to collect Caity Murphy's body. Although there had been no spilt blood, as a precaution, Brandon lined the trunk of his car with plastic so as to prevent the poor girl's DNA from getting on the vehicle. He had decided to transport Caity's remains in his smart car, which meant that he literally had to stuff her into the back.

Brandon placed the call to his father at exactly 10:03 p.m. He wanted to make sure that Nowak had taken his orders seriously. After ending the call, Brandon waited five minutes before heading toward the "Den." When Brandon arrived, he parked in the brush, got out of his car, and locked it. Combing through the grass and leaves piled near the entrance, it only took him a few minutes to spot the card. *Good,* he told himself. Nowak had done as he was told. The sooner the cops found the card, the better. He was losing patience with all of them.

Brandon needed to decide how close to the card he should leave Caity's body. He settled on ten feet. *That should do it,* he assured himself. Brandon found the perfect place to deposit the cadaver and returned to his car. He opened the door, removed the deceased, and carried her to an isolated area under a tree. *No point playing games,* Brandon reflected. It didn't matter whether the authorities realized he wanted them to find her or not. Brandon knew what he was doing.

* * *

Caity's disappearance and murder were about to play out on all fronts. Her absence wasn't lost on Eve and Gene, nor the rest of the *Crime Watch* staff. She had failed to show up for work yesterday and was uncharacteristically late today. And no one had been able to get in touch with her. Meanwhile, after a sleepless night, Nowak received a text from his daughter asking him to join her and Vito for breakfast. Although he had been trying to avoid them, Nowak decided it was more important to act normal and not raise any red flags. In that vein, he accepted the invitation.

When he got to the diner, Nowak parked his Bronco and took a minute to check himself in the mirror. He looked goddamn awful. Hopefully neither Hank nor Vito would notice. Nowak spotted his friend pulling into the parking lot, followed by his daughter. He prayed his son wouldn't text or call him while he was with them. At some point, they were bound to get suspicious. Nowak got out of his car and waited in front of the diner for the two of them. Suddenly, it occurred to him that he had never spoken to Hank about what Xanthe had told him: that Hank and Cary were involved romantically. But Nowak was keeping an even bigger secret from his daughter: that Brandon was her brother and Nowak suspected he had killed her lover. Vito's booming voice brought him back to reality.

"Hey there, big man," Vito said, making his way over to Nowak.

"Hi, Dad," Hank chimed in, glancing uneasily at Vito.

Nowak got the feeling they had indeed noticed his state of disrepair but controlled themselves from saying anything. Breakfast couldn't end soon enough. The three of them made their way to a booth in the back and sat down. There was no sign of Xanthe today, and the restaurant seemed short-staffed. Nowak feared the meal would take longer than he wanted. A server they had never seen before came over to the table and took their order. Nowak sat in uncomfortable silence, anticipating what the conversation would be. But before each of them could take their first forkful of food, a text came in on Hank's phone. *Please call me, hon,* it read. *Eve.*

"Sorry, it's Eve. Wonder what she wants," Hank contemplated. "Be back in a minute."

Both Nowak and Vito couldn't imagine what Eve would be texting Hank about, unless they wanted her on the show tonight. But Eve rarely, if ever, called the guests herself. That job was left to Annie Cline and her staff of bookers. When Hank returned, their question was soon answered.

"Caity Murphy is missing," Hank began.

Vito had a senior moment and couldn't place the name immediately. Then, before Hank had a chance to explain, he remembered who she was.

"That's right...that's right, the girl on Eve's show, the one who was snooping around the hospital?" Vito asked.

"Yeah, she never showed up for work yesterday, and there hasn't been any sign of her today. They can't get in touch with her either. I'll call O'Malley, but if she doesn't show up by late afternoon, we should probably launch a missing person investigation," Hank declared.

Nowak was getting a very bad feeling that Brandon was behind Caity's disappearance and that that was the reason why he ordered him to leave the "Odd Jobs" card at Devil's Den. It had to all be connected. *What the fucking hell,* Nowak said to himself. *If Brandon has his way, it's only a matter of time before I'll be an accomplice to murder.*

* * *

Brandon spent the better part of the morning in his hot tub, indulging himself. After all, he had put in a long night. He decided lugging bodies around was better than hitting the gym. *Hey, it worked for Dennis Rader,* he noted. After drying himself off, Brandon made his famous protein shake and turned on the television in the kitchen. Changing channels, he settled on News 12, but there was no report yet of a missing woman, much less the discovery of a body. "Step it up," he muttered.

Then it occurred to him that LNN, Caity's home network, might report the news first. So he changed channels. After a while, Brandon got bored as there was no news of Caity, so he decided to go to his exercise room and do a half-hour on the treadmill. As he was working out, he remembered that Caity's personal effects—her pocketbook, wallet, and car keys—were still in the den, along with the GoPro and recording. *This is not the time to get sloppy,* he told himself. But disposing of the items would give him something to do this afternoon while he waited for the discovery of Caity's body to make the news.

Brandon got off the exercise machine, grabbed a towel, and headed for the shower. He got dressed in sweats and a tee shirt and made his way to the den. He turned the television on, lowering the volume. Then Brandon picked up Caity's bag. Her wallet was inside it along with a comb and some makeup. Those were the last items that had been of any use to her.

As Brandon was deciding what to do with them, a *Breaking News* graphic popped up on the screen. Brandon turned up the volume and stared at the television. The daytime anchor made the following announcement and then tossed the story to none other than Eve Arora.

"All of us at LNN are sorry to report the discovery of a body near Devil's Den in Connecticut who authorities believe is that of *Crime Watch* producer Caity Murphy. Eve, what can you tell us?" the talking head added.

"First, I'd like to say that Caity's family has been notified. We waited to break the news until they were informed," Eve began.

Brandon's trick had worked. There was one item he had removed from Caity's wallet and placed on her chest before he put her body on the ground: her driver's license. Only, unlike Cary's, this ID was in one piece. Brandon's reasoning was simple: sometimes cops just needed to be led by the nose. He wanted the story to hit the news as soon as possible. So he spoon-fed the police the victim's identity.

Eve went on and on, theorizing about who might be responsible for Caity's death and whether her murder could be connected to the other presumed "Deer Killer" cases. But she provided no additional details, only teasing that her show this evening would be devoted to Ms. Murphy. Brandon couldn't help wondering if the police had found the "Odd Jobs" card, and if so, would they even tell the public about it? So far, the authorities had released as little information as possible, hoping to trap the "Deer Killer" by making him overconfident. Brandon knew the oldest trick in the book for investigators working murder cases was to hold back one critical piece of information only the killer knew about. In his case, that tidbit was the "Odd Jobs" cards. But Brandon knew as long as they found the one near Caity's body, they would understand who had killed her.

Brandon turned off the television and decided that now was as good a time as any to get rid of Caity's things. He would have to wait until dark to bury her pocketbook and wallet, but for now, he would need to hold onto her car keys. Brandon would dig another hole next to the one containing Cary's wallet and Vito's gun. But he wasn't sure what to do with the camera and recording itself. *What a perfect keepsake*, he told himself. So Brandon picked up the GoPro device and brought it to his study. He opened the cabinet below the drawer that held Cary's ring and placed it inside. There was still Caity's car to deal with, but for now, Brandon would leave it in the barn. Once things cooled off, he would hit up the druggie who owed him, the one who worked at the chop shop. The car would be history soon enough.

* * *

Nowak had gone straight home after breakfast and fell asleep in his favorite chair in front of the television. He was woken up by the ringing of his phone. It was now early afternoon. When Nowak picked up the call, Vito and Hank were on the other end.

"Turn on the TV," they said in unison.

Nowak's television was already on, although the volume was muted.

"Sorry, was just sleeping. What's going on? Which station?" the former detective asked.

"Put on LNN," Hank answered. "Now."

Nowak changed channels until he saw Eve Arora on the screen. Raising the volume, he heard that a young woman's remains were found at Devil's Den. Nowak's brain began to race. *What have I done?* he asked himself. *Jesus fucking Christ.*

"You still there?" Hank inquired.

Nowak was so blindsided by the news that he could barely speak. But in retrospect, the discovery of another body shouldn't have come as any surprise. Why else would Brandon have had him leave the card there? Nowak was overwhelmed with guilt. What a mess he had made of everything.

"Uh, yeah, sure, of course," Nowak answered, trying to sound normal.

"Eve's doing her show on the 'Deer Killer' case tonight and on Caity, in particular, because she worked on the show. You never met her, but she was a sweet girl and good at her job," Hank added. "The thing is we're hoping Eve will suggest, subtly, that the cases may be connected. Keep that narrative alive. Afraid it's all we've got right now."

Nowak didn't know who Caity was until Hank explained. By the time he tuned in, Eve was already teasing her show and the name of the victim didn't resonate with him. Nowak was overcome with emotion, emotions that he needed to hide.

"Hank and I are gonna head over to Devil's Den, see what we can find," Vito said. "We'll keep you posted."

Stupid, stupid, stupid, Nowak muttered as he hit his forehead with his hand. *That goddamn son of a bitch of mine.*

* * *

Brandon had been expecting a call from his father—if he didn't have a heart attack from the news first. He let the phone ring four times before answering.

"Hello, Brandon here," he said cordially.

"What the hell?" his father responded in an agitated tone. "How could you? What in God's name..." Nowak continued, his voice shaking. "You promised me."

"I said you'd have to earn it. The gun," Brandon reminded him. "And there are still two cards left."

"Gun? Do you really think I give a flying fuck about a goddamn gun. You killed someone," Nowak said, accusingly.

"Let's not go jumping to any conclusions just yet, shall we. Life is filled with coincidences," Brandon added, trying to aggravate his father.

"Listen to me and listen good. You're going to turn yourself in and give me back that gun. It's the only proof..." Nowak said, regretting the slip.

"Exactly," Brandon declared. "Thanks for pointing that out. But for now, you will wait for further instructions. One down, two to go."

And with those words, the call dropped.

* * *

It was nearly four o'clock when Hank and Vito arrived at Devil's Den. Caity's body was still where Brandon had left it, only now it was covered with a blanket. There were swarms of cops everywhere. They spotted O'Malley about a hundred yards away and made their way over to him.

"Any news?" Vito asked the sergeant, as O'Malley went to meet them halfway.

"Take a look at this," O'Malley said, holding up Caity Murphy's driver's license.

"Where the hell did you get that?" Hank asked.

"Whoever did this left it lying right on top of the victim's chest. But no sign of her wallet," O'Malley answered.

"So the creep wanted her ID'd right away. Must think we're pretty fucking incompetent," Vito added, annoyed.

"Sure looks that way," O'Malley answered.

"Caity worked for Eve. Maybe whoever did this...the killer... wanted publicity. He must've known that Eve would be all over it," Hank noted.

"Possibly," the sergeant answered.

"I'd like to see her," Hank said.

"Uh, yeah. The preliminary assessment is that she was strangled," O'Malley started to explain. "You're sure you can handle this? I mean, knowing her and all."

Hank nodded, a pained expression on her face. When they got to the yellow crime scene tape, a uniformed police officer raised it over their heads. O'Malley lifted the blanket, exposing Caity's discolored face and neck. Tears welled up in Hank's eyes.

"That fucking bastard," she said.

As the three of them walked away, they noticed several unis squatting on the ground about a dozen feet from them. O'Malley's favorite cop, Brian, motioned to the sergeant.

"Hey, over here," he yelled.

O'Malley, Hank, and Vito exchanged glances and made their way over to the group.

"What's up, Brian?" the sergeant asked.

"Think you better see this," the officer answered.

Wearing gloves, Brian handed O'Malley the "Odd Jobs" card Nowak had left at the scene.

"Well, I'll be goddamned," the sergeant responded.

Then, turning to Hank and Vito, he issued the following warning.

"No one—I mean, *no one*—can know about this. You got it?" O'Malley asked, making his point.

"Roger that," they answered in unison.

SIXTEEN

Hank and Vito left Devil's Den and drove back to Hank's house so that she could check on Barry. There was no doubt that Caity's death was the work of the "Deer Killer." The police would, of course, run prints on the latest "Odd Jobs" card that had surfaced, but it would likely prove to be yet another exercise in futility.

"He killed all of them," Hank said. "If only we had caught him before..." she added.

"Now don't go blaming yourself for any of this," Vito stated adamantly. "It's not like we haven't been trying. You, me, the police, even Cary...we've really really tried," Vito said with sadness in his eyes.

"And look where it's gotten us," Hank declared. "No-fucking-where."

When they got to Hank's place, Vito pulled his car into the driveway and hesitated. He was going to suggest that Hank come back with him to the cottage for dinner and to watch Eve's show, but he wasn't sure she was up to it. Hank sat for a minute and then started to open the door.

"Thanks for the ride, Vito," Hank said as she got out of the car.

"Look," Vito began. "Why don't you go take care of that precious boy of yours and then come over to the cottage? Anna and I will order takeout...catch Eve's show together, all of us. We can ask your dad too. Sound good?"

Although Hank was exhausted, she didn't want to miss Eve's show, nor watch it alone. And she had next to no food left in her house. So, she accepted the invitation.

"Sure, Vito. I'd love that," Hank answered.

"Great. Why don't we call your dad now?" Vito suggested.

And then they both had the same thought: Nowak didn't know about the card.

"I know, the card," Vito said as Hank started to speak.

Hank picked up the phone and called her father.

"Dad," she said, as he answered. "Wanna join us for dinner at Gayle's guesthouse tonight?"

"Put it on speaker," Vito whispered.

"Dad, I'm here with Vito. You're on speaker. There's something we need to tell you, but you can't say anything. Okay?" Hank asked.

Nowak wasn't sure how much more bad news he could handle, but he had to hear them out.

"Go ahead," he responded.

"Nowak, it's me. They found an 'Odd Jobs' card near Caity's body. Testing for prints, but don't think we'll find any. Just wanted you to know. This guy's a piece of work. The goddamn nerve," Vito added.

Since they found the body, Nowak figured it would only take so much time before they also discovered the "Odd Jobs" card he had left at the entrance. *I was just following orders,* Nowak chided himself. His mouth was getting dry, and he couldn't think of the right words to say in response to Vito's revelation.

"You still there?" Vito asked.

"Yeah, I'm here," Nowak mumbled quietly.

"Dad, come by the cottage tonight. We'll have a bite and watch Eve's show together. Okay?" Hank inquired.

"Yeah, sure, I'll try to make it," her father answered, trying to maintain his composure. And then, abruptly, he got off the call.

***

As Hank was leaving to meet her dad, Vito, and Anna at the guest-house, a text came in on her cell. It was from Annie Cline. *We'd love to have you on the show tonight. Any chance? We can send a car.* It was nearly six o'clock, and the last thing Hank felt like doing was going into the city, escorted or not. So she texted Annie back: *Does it have to be tonight?* Annie responded with a sad emoji and an alternative suggestion: *You can always do a phoner.* Hank paused to think for a moment and then answered with a thumbs-up emoji. *Great. I'll send you the details,* Annie messaged her back.

Hank knew how important it was to keep the "Deer Killer" case in the news, so she didn't want to do anything that might dissuade Eve and Gene from continuing to cover it. The show tonight was supposed to be mostly a tribute to Caity, yet another *Crime Watch* staffer whose life had been cut short by a madman. Therefore, Eve would likely just use Hank to set up the case and explain its possible connection to the others. Although Gene knew about the "Odd Jobs" card that was left in Cary's ice cream, he had been sworn to secrecy. Hank understood that if both Eve and Gene were aware that another card had been found near Caity's body, it would be difficult to stop them from telling the world that the "Deer Killer" had, in all likeli-hood, killed Caity. For the time being, the fewer people who knew about the cards, the better. They could prove to be the X factor that breaks the case.

✳ ✳ ✳

When Hank arrived at the guesthouse, she spotted Gayle walking down the path that led from her house to the cottage. Hank wasn't sure if Cary's sister had been planning on joining them for dinner and didn't know where she was staying these days. Gayle spotted Hank getting out of her car and waved to her.

"Hey," Gayle called out. "Wait up."

"So glad you could make it," Hank began. "We weren't sure if you would be..." the detective continued, hesitantly.

"It's okay, Hank. Vito called me. He feels bad that we haven't been in touch lately, so I figured what the hell? I could use a nice meal."

"You're not staying at the house yet, are you?" Hank inquired. "I mean with…" she continued.

"No, it's too soon, if ever. Still at my mom's. Not enough time yet," Gayle continued, disjointedly.

"No worries, I get it," Hank responded. "Tonight will be good for all of us."

* * *

Nowak ignored the dinner request. Frankly, the invitation went right out of his head as soon as he got off the phone. He had spent the hours since the call with his daughter and Vito pacing around the house in a state of total disarray. *How had things gotten this out of control?* the former cop asked himself. Nowak was on his fifth beer since he turned off his cell. *What have I done?*

Images of the day that destroyed his family popped into Nowak's head: a car, a toddler, his wife, a store, and a broken bottle of milk on the pavement. The guilt he had carried around all these years was like a dam about to burst. The final straw: the alliance, albeit forced, with his son: Harry a.k.a. Brandon, the psychopath. Nowak had allowed himself to be manipulated and to be complicit in Brandon's evil plans. No amount of rationalization could lead to the conclusion that his son was innocent, that he hadn't killed Cary and all the others. Her wallet and Vito's gun weren't the only proof of Brandon's involvement. In his own twisted way, Nowak's long-lost son had actually confessed to the killings by denying them.

Nowak went to the bedroom and opened the top dresser drawer that held mementos from that awful day. He removed the photo, newspaper articles, and baby shoe and put them on the kitchen counter. Then he went to get a pad of yellow lined paper. Nowak found a pen in the drawer by the sink, took one last beer out of the fridge, and sat down to say goodbye to Hank, the daughter he had kept in the dark her entire life.

As he started to write, Nowak's hand began to shake. He thought about his wonderful wife, whose life was shattered by his negligence. *Don't be so hard on yourself,* Vito had told him at the time. But there was no way that he couldn't be.

As Nowak continued to write, a thought struck him. He wore gloves when he obeyed Brandon's orders and brought the "Odd Jobs" card to Devil's Den. *Gloves, gloves, gloves,* he repeated to himself. In his mind, that made him more of an accomplice. Random notions raced through Nowak's head as he wrote on and on. *We never had that talk about you and Cary,* he said. *Your mother didn't die of cancer, she killed herself...because of me. Brandon is your brother. He threatened me... got me involved...gave me the cards...I messed up the evidence.* Nowak explained everything. He wondered if Hank could ever forgive him. He would, of course, never get the chance to find out.

Nowak collected the photo, articles, and shoe, and placed them on the kitchen table. He told Hank to talk to Vito, that he knew about the kidnapping, her mother's suicide, all of it, except that Brandon was his son. Nowak wrote that her brother had to be the "Deer Killer" and that he had Cary's wallet and Vito's gun. *Get him,* were the last words Nowak penned, before ending the letter with *I love you more than you could ever know, Dad.* He folded the note in half, wrote Hank's name on the front of it, and put the paper next to the other items on the table. Nowak got up, walked to his bedroom, opened the trunk at the foot of the bed, and took out a .45 caliber handgun. He released the safety, placed the pistol to his right temple, and pulled the trigger.

* * *

Hank tried calling her father one more time to see if he was going to join them for the evening. Dinner was almost ready, but Nowak was nowhere to be found.

"Okay," Anna called from the kitchen. "Hope you're all hungry."

"Should we wait for your dad?" Vito asked, turning to Hank.

"I can't reach him. Guess we should go ahead and eat. If he shows up, he shows up," Hank declared.

Everyone took a plate and dug in. Hank was hungrier than she realized as she hadn't been eating well since Cary had died.

"Everything looks delicious," Gayle chimed in. "Thanks, guys. This is really nice."

Vito was paying particular attention to the time, as he didn't want to miss even a minute of Eve's show tonight.

"Can I take those for you?" Vito asked Hank and Gayle, once he saw their plates were empty.

"Sure," the two answered in unison.

"I'll put the coffee on, and then it should just about be time for the show," Vito stated.

Hank was getting concerned that her father hadn't called back. His absence in and of itself wasn't what was worrying her. But he rarely failed to return her calls. *Unless he forgot to charge his phone again or decided to "unplug" for the night,* Hank told herself. She'd catch up with him in the morning.

"Eve's on," Vito announced. "Come quick."

Anna and Gayle began making their way to the dirty dishes by the sink, but they aborted their cleaning mission and joined Vito and Hank around the television. Hank had almost forgotten that she was supposed to be on the show tonight.

"Shit. Where's my phone?" Hank asked. "Annie called me this afternoon about doing a phoner. It went right out of my head. Can someone call it? Call my number?"

Anna picked up her phone and placed the call. Hank heard the ringtone immediately and spotted her cell on a stool in the kitchen. When she picked up her phone, she saw that there were two missed calls from Annie.

"Damn," she reprimanded herself. "Give me a second."

Hank called Eve's head booker prepared to apologize for her forgetfulness. When Annie picked up, however, she couldn't have been kinder.

"No worries. We moved you to the 'D' block. I'll call you five minutes before you're supposed to go on," Annie said.

Hank chalked the lack of hysteria on Annie's part up to her recent loss: Cary's death. By now, she assumed everyone on the show probably suspected that she and Cary had been involved romantically. But none of that mattered any more. All that counted was that they catch the "Deer Killer" and make him pay, *legally*, of course.

In addition to paying tribute to Caity Murphy, the show was more or less a repetitive display of the victims and timeline of the killings that had taken place over the past several months. There, of course, could be no mention of the cards, so tying the cases together, including the deaths of Cary, Carlee Delgado, and Caity Murphy was a bit of a stretch, evidence-wise. But somehow, Eve managed to pull it off.

Hank held her phone as she watched the show, prepared to go on air at a moment's notice. When Annie called, she picked up instantly.

"Ready?" Annie asked Hank.

"Yeah, let me find a place with some privacy. I'm with Vito and some other people. Just be a minute," Hank explained.

She decided the bathroom would suffice for the interview. Hank motioned to Vito and the rest that she was heading toward the restroom.

"All set," Hank told Annie.

Eve was thrilled to have Hank on the show tonight. They had developed a close relationship and thought the world of each other. As Hank responded to Eve's questions about the "Deer Killer" case, Vito, Anna, and Gayle watched from the other room. Hank, as always, rose to the occasion, giving concise and insightful answers. The picture they used of her as cover for the phoner was beautiful. As Vito looked at the screen, he understood why Cary had fallen in love with her.

It was ten o'clock when the show ended, and they were all exhausted. Gayle went back to her mother's, and Anna, having insisted on cleaning up solo, got to work on the dishes. But Vito wanted a moment alone with Hank, so he took the opportunity to escort her outside.

"I'm worried about your dad," Vito began. "He hasn't been himself lately...acting weird, and this no-show tonight, well, guess I might be overreacting, but where the hell is he?"

"Home...I'm sure he's home...just probably didn't feel up to it," Hank said, hiding her own concerns.

"Look, I've known your dad for as long as I can remember, and something just isn't right." Vito added.

"I have an idea. Why don't we both get a good night's sleep, and I'll text you in the morning if I haven't heard from him. If he hasn't surfaced by then, I'll meet you over at his place, and we can check up on him. Sound good?" Hank asked.

"That's fine," Vito answered and gave Hank a kiss on the cheek. "Get some rest," he said, as he went back inside to join Anna. Then, looking over his shoulder, Vito left Hank with the following words: "Stay safe."

＊ ＊ ＊

Hank woke up to find Barry sitting next to her on the bed, staring down at his human. When he saw her eyes open, Hank's loyal companion got on top of her and started licking her face.

"Hey, my good boy," Hank said, hugging him.

She looked at the clock on her nightstand: 6:04 a.m. Hank grabbed the phone and checked her messages. No text, no call from her dad, no word from him at all. It was still early, but her father tended to get up at the crack of dawn, so Hank decided to try him one more time before getting in touch with Vito. The call went straight to voicemail.

"Shit," Hank said out loud.

She didn't want to start the day like this: assuming something was wrong and worrying Vito unnecessarily. Therefore, despite what Hank told Vito last night, she decided to get showered and dressed, take care of Barry, and then head over to her dad's, alone.

* * *

When Hank pulled up to her father's house everything seemed to be in order. His boat was at its usual place off the dock, rocking to the waves, and his beloved Bronco was in the driveway. *Vito and I have got to stop feeding off each other, working ourselves up into a frenzy over nothing,* Hank told herself. She walked up to the front door and knocked out of courtesy. Hank hoped her father was already awake, that she wasn't disturbing him. She waited a couple of minutes for him to answer the door. But there was no sign of her dad. So Hank let herself in using the spare key her father kept on a ledge by the window.

As Hank made her way inside, the room was dark, so she pulled the curtains aside to let in some light. Hank decided her father had become domesticated as the house appeared to be clean and tidy. Hank continued to walk until she reached the kitchen. Looking around, she noticed the table where Nowak had left the items and suicide note. As Hank got closer, the first thing that caught her eye was her name in her father's handwriting on top of a folded piece of yellow paper. There were several objects next to it.

Hank picked up the baby shoe and photo. Then she flipped through the stack of old newspaper articles Nowak had left for her to find. *What the hell?* Hank wondered. She stared down at the note that had her name on it. A sick feeling came over the detective. Hank sat down at the table and unfolded the paper. As she continued to read, her head started to spin. Did her mother commit suicide? Was Brandon really her brother? And was he also the "Deer Killer?" It was too much to process all at once. *Talk to Vito,* the note read.

But where was her father? Hank took a deep breath and stood up. She clutched her hands and headed toward the bedroom. As she made her way inside, the room was pitch black. Nowak cherished his naps these days and had blackout drapes installed so he'd be able to sleep any time, day or night. Hank braced herself as she opened the curtains. Sunlight flooded the room. Hank turned and looked around for any sign of her dad. Nothing. Then she walked toward the bed, past the trunk, and around the corner. Lying on the floor with half his head blown off was her father, the gun beside him. There was blood everywhere.

Hank's entire body shook as she fell to the ground. She cried out, but there was no one to hear her. "Oh my God. Oh my God. How will I ever..." she sobbed. Although Hank was shocked by the discovery of her father's body, she nevertheless had the presence of mind to call Vito. Reaching for her cell in the rear pocket of her jeans, Hank placed the call.

"Hank?" Vito asked, as he picked up the phone.

"Come...come now...to my dad's...please," Hank implored him.

"What's going on? You sound..." Vito asked in a worried voice.

"You'll know soon enough," Hank responded, in a state of shock.

* * *

Vito drove as quickly as possible without risking an accident. If he got pulled over, he would explain that he was a private detective rushing to the aid of a real one. Vito didn't know exactly what Hank had found at her father's house, but he knew it couldn't be good. Upon arriving at Nowak's, Vito pulled in behind Hank's car and got out of his own. He paused for a moment to collect himself and made his way to the front door: it was wide open. Once Vito got inside, he called out to Hank, but got no response. He started pacing around the living room, then went into the kitchen, but there was still no sign of Hank.

Vito knew the next place he needed to check was Nowak's bedroom.

"Hank?" he yelled again.

As Vito made his way inside the room, he saw Hank sitting on the floor, bent over her father. Then Vito spotted the gun lying in a pool of blood. Hank's hands were covered in the red liquid. Vito stopped in his tracks trying to make sense of the macabre scene before him. As he approached Hank, she spoke.

"You knew," Hank said to Vito. "You knew."

"Knew? Knew what?" Vito responded. "What's going on here, Hank?" Vito continued as he knelt down. "I mean, Jesus," he sighed.

"Talk to Vito...talk to Vito...I...uh..." Hank began but couldn't formulate the words.

Vito touched Hank on the shoulder and tried to get her to stand up. She resisted at first but acquiesced to his request.

"Let's go to the kitchen," Vito suggested. "We're gonna have to call this in."

"Water...I need water," Hank muttered, holding her head.

As Vito brought her a glass, he noticed that Hank's forehead and hair were now smeared with her father's blood, as well.

"Here ya go," Vito said, trying to comfort Hank. "Let me..." he continued, using a wet napkin to remove the red mark on her face. "There that's better."

"I have to call my brother," Hank said in a fog.

Vito hadn't seen Homer in a couple of years, as he was stationed in the Philippines and rarely came home. But Hank stayed in touch with him through FaceTime and email. Nowak was proud of Homer, who he thought was his only living son, for enlisting in the marines, hoping to serve his country and make the world a better place. His other son, Brandon, hardly had the same goal.

"Why don't we deal with the police first, and then we'll give him a call. Sound good?" Vito asked.

Hank nodded, clearly struggling to keep it together. Vito reached for his phone and called O'Malley directly.

"Joe?" Vito asked.

"Yeah, what's up?" the sergeant responded.

"Give me a minute. Just gonna step outside," Vito stated, motioning to Hank.

Vito didn't say any more until he got to his car. He didn't want Hank to hear a word of it.

"Joe, I'm here. Listen, we uh...Hank and I, we're at Nowak's house. No easy way to say this, but from the looks of it...what I'm trying to say is looks like he shot himself. He's dead," Vito declared, overcome with emotion.

"What?" O'Malley answered, stunned. "Stay put both of you. We'll send a couple of cars. And don't touch anything till I get there."

"Roger that. And hurry," Vito added, anxiously.

When Vito squatted down next to his best friend and checked his pulse, he already knew Nowak was gone. If there was one thing Vito could smell from a mile away it was a dead body. He was sure from the blood all over Hank's hands that she had examined her father's vitals, as well, before he got there. Vito went back into the house only to find Hank sitting in her dad's favorite recliner clutching the glass of water he had given her. She looked like a ghost.

"Spoke to O'Malley. They'll be here any minute," Vito said with a pained expression on his face.

The sound of Vito's voice startled Hank, who stood up suddenly and grabbed his hand.

"I need to..." she began. "The note...the police are going to want it, right? But..." Hank continued.

When Vito first entered the house, he was single-mindedly focused on finding Hank, so he hadn't noticed the letter or any of the other items on the kitchen table.

"He left a note?" Vito asked. "Where is it?"

"On the kitchen table," Hank answered. "He left it for me," she explained, her voice cracking.

Vito went over to the table and looked down at the yellow paper.

"What's all this?" he asked Hank, confused.

"I don't want the cops...the police...O'Malley touching it...taking the rest," Hank declared.

Vito looked at the shoe, photo, and old newspaper articles and saw enough to understand that his friend's suicide had something to do with his firstborn son's kidnapping more than forty years ago.

"Hank," Vito started. "I don't know what your father was trying to tell you..."

"There's no time for that now," Hank said, definitively. "I just don't want them to take any of it."

Vito knew they were crossing a line, but he saw no harm, for the time being, in keeping Nowak's personal effects from the authorities. If the items became relevant to the impending investigation, Hank and he could always turn them in.

Vito made the most of the time before the authorities arrived to move Nowak's memorabilia to the trunk of his car. When O'Malley and the unis showed up, the first thing they did was put up crime scene tape at the entrance to Nowak's property. Then the sergeant made his way inside. Hank was still sitting in her dad's recliner, while Vito paced around the room in a circle.

"Vito, Hank...what the hell...where is he?" O'Malley asked, trying not to exacerbate the already tense situation.

"Thank God you're here," Vito answered.

"Let's step outside," the sergeant said to Vito, tilting his head in the direction of the front door.

Vito touched Hank on the shoulder, as if to reassure her.

"We'll just be a minute, okay?" he declared.

O'Malley and Vito walked until they got close to Nowak's prize possession: his boat. The sergeant spoke first.

"Where is he?" O'Malley asked.

"In the bedroom. It's bad...really bad...half his face...head...it's a fucking mess," Vito stated, distraught.

"Jesus. Okay, look, we got to get Hank out of there," the sergeant declared.

Vito knew O'Malley was right, but he wasn't sure how to approach her.

"Listen...is Max here yet?" Vito asked, looking around. "He's probably the only one who can coax Hank out of the house at the moment. Explain that it would help the forensic guys if there were fewer people around. Something like that."

"Yeah, actually," O'Malley responded. "Craven's here with the rest of the CSI team. Let me find him."

O'Malley spotted Max Craven, ace investigator and one of Hank's most trusted colleagues, near one of the police cars, removing a bag from the trunk. The sergeant called out to him.

"Hey, Max, over here," he shouted.

Craven made his way around the yellow tape and approached the two of them.

"What's up?" Craven asked his superior.

"Think you could tell Hank...um get her out of the house while you process the scene. She's in a fog...doing about as well as you could expect...in shock," Vito stated.

Craven looked at O'Malley, who nodded his head as if to say: *Just do it.*

"Of course...anything for Hank," Craven responded. "Absolutely anything."

The three of them went inside and walked right over to the detective. When she saw Max, Hank stood up and fell into his arms.

"It'll be okay," Craven began. "It will. You'll see," he added awkwardly. "Here come here with me and Officer Rooney will keep you company on the porch while we..." he continued.

Even in her disoriented state, Hank understood that they wanted her out of the way while they went through the house, processing the scene.

"Sure, anything to help," Hank answered.

Craven escorted Hank out of the house and signaled to Officer Elizabeth Rooney to come over.

"Liz, think you can hang out with Hank for a few minutes?" Craven asked her pointedly.

"Absolutely," the rookie officer responded. "Nice to see you again Detective Nowak," she added, awkwardly.

"Great," Craven said. "Not sure how long we'll be. Keep you posted."

Craven went back inside the house and headed straight toward where Vito and O'Malley were standing.

"All good," he reported.

The three of them looked around the living room and kitchen. Several crime scene investigators were already at work, processing the area. Nothing unusual stood out in either room except for the kitchen table. But Vito didn't think anyone had noticed the note Nowak had left for his daughter yet. He thought it was time, however, to be proactive. So Vito touched O'Malley on the elbow to get his attention.

"Joe, got a minute? Hope you don't mind, Max," Vito uttered discreetly.

"Do what you gotta do," Craven answered.

Vito took O'Malley out the rear door, and they stepped on to the back porch. Once they were safely out of earshot, Vito took the opportunity to bring the sergeant up to date on what they were dealing with.

"Look, Joe, before we go into the bedroom, there's something I gotta tell you," Vito said.

"Spit it out, please," O'Malley muttered.

"Nowak left a note, addressed to Hank. It's on the table in the kitchen. At least that's where she found it," Vito said, trying to clarify the situation without giving too much away just yet.

"You mean a suicide note, right?" the sergeant responded.

"Yeah...but there's more. It's um...it's complicated...really complicated. A lotta shit from the past that went down Hank didn't know about," Vito declared.

"What the hell? I need to see it...now," O'Malley snapped back.

Vito's full disclosure plan wasn't working quite the way he had hoped. The letter wasn't just your run-of-the-mill I-killed-myself-and-this-is-why note. It was a fucking shitstorm in writing.

"Okay...okay...just give me a minute, and I'll go find it. Wanna check on Hank, too, while I'm at it," Vito stated. "But Joe, this is personal...real personal stuff that's gonna take Hank a long time to wrap her head around. Let's keep it between the three of us for the time being. Can we do that, please? Does that work?"

"It might, and it might not. What part of I have to see it now didn't you understand?" O'Malley said sarcastically and somewhat out of character, considering he was talking to Vito, who he liked and respected.

"Give me a fucking break, Joe. Come on," Vito answered, surprised by O'Malley's attitude.

"Just get me the goddamn note," O'Malley shouted. "And now."

The sergeant lit a cigarette while Vito walked back inside and headed straight for the kitchen table. The forensic guys were still in the living room, so the yellow piece of paper was right where Hank had left it: in plain sight on top of the kitchen table. Vito went through his pockets searching for a pair of gloves. He came up empty-handed, so the private eye had no choice but to ask the CSI guys if they had any extras. The investigators pointed to a box on the mantle. Vito thanked them, took two, put them on his hands, and carefully picked up the letter. Then he stuffed the note in his inside jacket pocket. Vito made his way to the front entrance to make sure Hank was all right. As he observed her from the doorway, she appeared shaken and in shock. Hank clearly wouldn't be all right for a very long time.

"Let me see it," O'Malley said to Vito, as he turned around and came back inside.

Vito, reluctantly, took out the letter and handed it to the sergeant. The side with Hank's name on it was facing up. O'Malley already had his blue-rubber, latex-free, police-issued gloves on. He stared at Hank's name and unfolded the note. It took him a couple of minutes to read the entire message. When he had finished, the sergeant looked up at Vito.

"We don't have time for this now," O'Malley began. "But when we get back to the station, I'd like an explanation," he added.

"Yup, you'll get one," Vito responded bluntly. "But I haven't read the note yet," he added, wondering what else it contained.

"Now I need to see him," O'Malley stated. "Come on."

Vito and the sergeant walked toward Nowak's bedroom, passing a couple of forensic investigators who were currently in the kitchen dusting for fingerprints and searching for clues. It was too early for any official findings yet, but from the look of things, Vito knew the consensus among the police had to be that they were dealing with a suicide, not homicide. Still, they had to go through the motions. When they entered the room, Vito directed O'Malley to the far side of the bed where his friend lay on the floor. The carpet had turned a deep shade of brownish red.

"Jesus," O'Malley uttered as he surveyed the scene. "That's a lot of goddamn blood."

Vito knew that Nowak and O'Malley weren't particularly fond of each other, but he expected a bit more respect under the circumstances.

"Max, get in here now," O'Malley yelled.

The obedient evidence technician entered the room within seconds.

"Sorry, I was just..." Craven started to explain.

"Don't care...get to it...now...and I want a full report by the end of the day: the gun...all of it," the sergeant ordered, losing patience.

"10-4," Craven responded. "I'm on it."

Vito saw no point in sticking around while the investigators went through Nowak's house and things, collecting evidence. He knew Hank, even in her current state, wanted to talk to him about Nowak's cryptic remark in his suicide note: *Talk to Vito*. He figured now was as good a time as any to get his tongue-lashing. Then they could meet up with O'Malley at the station if Hank was up to it.

* * *

Hank was nowhere near up to driving, so Vito gave her a ride back home. They sat in silence. Vito had kept Nowak's secret son from Hank and her brother all these years. He had acquiesced to his friend's demands at the time and decided, no matter how you looked at it, that it had never been his place to tell them that they had an older brother who had been kidnapped and never found. When Tessa took her own life, Nowak was so riddled with guilt and overwhelmed at the thought of being a single parent, that he once again hid the truth. Telling his two young children that their mother had been sick was a lot easier than explaining what suicide was. But that was all Vito knew. He hadn't even read Nowak's suicide note yet. Only Hank and O'Malley had. But from Hank's *you knew* comment, Vito understood that Nowak had mentioned him in the letter and inferred that he had known the truth all along, as far as her mother and long-lost brother were concerned.

When they pulled up in front of Hank's, Vito turned off his car and waited for her to speak. As he anticipated, despite her grief and disoriented condition, Hank wanted to confront him: to find out everything.

"I need to know. I need to know now. Can you come inside, Vito? We need to talk," Hank muttered.

The truth always comes out, Vito thought to himself. The conversation he was about to have with Hank was the one talk he had hoped he would never have to have.

"Are you sure you're up to all this right now?" Vito asked Hank, concerned.

"I don't know what I can handle any more," Hank began. "But if what my father wrote in that letter was enough to make him kill himself, then yeah, I'm up to it...for his sake."

They went inside Hank's house and found Barry lying by the fireplace. Hank excused herself and took him outside for a minute, then returned. She gave her beloved dog some water and a treat and went back into the den where Vito stood by the window, staring at nothing in particular.

"I never even got to read it...the note," Vito began.

Hank took out her phone and held it up for him to see.

"We can fix that. I took a picture," Hank stated matter-of-factly. "It's all here. Read it. Read it now."

"Hank...look...we don't even know what happened. Think it's time to slow down and get the facts," Vito suggested.

"My father's suicide note is full of facts, unless he has...*had* full blown dementia or is...was just a fucking liar," Hank said, raising her voice.

Hank was becoming hysterical and understandably so. Processing the certitude that both parents took their own lives would surely be enough to push anyone over the edge. And Hank had just lost the love of her life as well. *How much more could she take?* Vito wondered. His heart ached for the woman he had always considered to be the daughter he never had.

"Give it here," Vito instructed Hank. "The phone. I'll read it."

The private eye sat down on the couch, hunched over Hank's phone, as he scrolled through the snapshots of Nowak's letter. His friend had spilled it all. But he had saved the best part for last, the part they never knew about: that Brandon was Harry and, in all likelihood, the "Deer Killer." *Get him,* Nowak implored his daughter. *Get him.*

Vito didn't know where to begin: with the revelation about Brandon or that, according to Nowak, his son had Cary's wallet and Vito's gun in his possession. It was all too much: trying to explain years of deception, triggered by a family tragedy, in only a few minutes.

"Hank," Vito began. "I didn't know...didn't know about Brandon. I swear."

"But you knew, you knew I had a brother...a brother that went missing...all these years," Hank continued, in a discombobulated manner.

"Can't fucking believe it. We assumed...I mean, after so much time...we thought Harry...your brother was dead," Vito declared. "Your father must have been shocked out of his mind when Brandon told him."

"Why did my father hide all this from me? And you?" Hank said, accusingly.

Vito stood up, still clutching Hank's phone and handed it back to her.

"Look, Hank, it wasn't my place. In the end, I'm not family, just a friend. He made me promise...swear that I'd never say anything about your brother or the way your mother died. What the hell was I supposed to do?" Vito asked exasperatedly.

Hank took the phone from Vito and went to the kitchen to get some water. She came back, Barry walking behind her, and sat down on the couch next to Vito.

"I'm so sorry," Hank began, her shoulders starting to shake. "I can't live without them...Cary...my dad. How could he do this? Without even talking to me," she added.

Vito took Hank's hand and put his arm around her shoulder.

"Look, kid, your father was the best friend I ever had. But he blamed himself for what happened to your brother...to Harry. I think Caity's death pushed him over the edge. That he felt responsible. Everyone has a breaking point. And that bastard son of his got him so goddamn mixed up, well, he just couldn't handle it all any more," Vito added, getting agitated.

"My mother, Vito. How well did you know her?" Hank asked.

"Tessa was something else," Vito began, smiling slightly. "That woman was one smart lady. Probably the only one who could handle your dad," he continued, laughing through his tears. "It became too much for her to live with. She tried she really did, but depression took over. It was a very difficult time...she needed help...didn't get it. But this...Brandon...just can't fucking believe it. He's Harry. What the hell happened to that boy that turned him into such a monster?" Vito contemplated. "I mean, the kidnapping...but Jesus."

"Vito, you really think he's Harry, my brother?" Hank asked, confused. "I mean, my dad's note said he found documents with DNA proof at Brandon's, but we haven't seen anything. Maybe he got it wrong. Is that even a possibility? That this is all one big misunderstanding?" Hank asked, praying.

"It's him, Hank. Your father's letter was very detailed. No reason not to believe him. That son of a bitch Brandon took it all away from him: the gun, wallet, documents, everything. We gotta find them. Must be at his place somewhere," Vito stated. "Yup, Brandon's Harry and he's also the 'Deer Killer,'" he continued. "Gotta be, how the hell else would he have Cary's wallet...and my gun for Christ's sake. What a goddamn mess."

And then Hank had a thought.

"Vito, didn't my dad say there were three cards? That Brandon gave him three cards, and he only left one where Caity was killed?" Hank inquired.

Vito knew what she was thinking: that Brandon, a.k.a., the "Deer Killer," had other plans.

"He's gonna kill someone else...do it again, if that's what you're getting at," Vito answered. "I'd bet my bottom dollar on it."

"Unless we stop him first," Hank said, with a glimmer of hope in her eyes.

* * *

Brandon didn't hear about his father until early afternoon when he turned on the news. "Holy fucking shit," he called out. "Well, I'll be damned." It was always the unexpected. The old man cracked sooner than Brandon had anticipated. *Some big tough guy, huh*, he pondered. Nowak's sudden death threw a monkey wrench into his son's murderous scheme. But Brandon saw no reason why he couldn't proceed with his agenda alone. Sure, it wouldn't be as much fun, but the whole father/son routine had gotten a bit old anyway.

Brandon changed channels until he got to LNN. He didn't have to wait long before a *Breaking News* banner appeared on the screen. "*We bring you the latest...*" the talking head began. The network had obviously decided to play it safe for the time being, only announcing that former Det. Henry Nowak had been shot in the head and died. As of yet, there was no mention of suicide. Of course, at this point, Brandon had no direct knowledge about what had happened to his father, but his instincts never failed him. Brandon's gut told him that Nowak had killed himself. *If you can't handle the heat, get out of the kitchen,* and that's exactly what the former detective had done.

Of course, Brandon didn't know about the suicide note and its contents. So he had no idea that his sister and Vito knew everything. But it was time to map out his next moves. Brandon wanted to commit two more murders, one for each card he had given his father. He needed to select his next victims. But he thought it best to lay low for a while to see what fallout, if any, came from his father's death. Then he would know the right way to proceed.

* * *

Hank and Vito had gone their separate ways after they talked. But there was still a lot more to say. So they decided to meet up at the diner and continue the conversation. The meeting with O'Malley got postponed until early evening. That would give Vito and Hank plenty of time to finish what they had started. Vito was impressed by Hank's resilience considering the circumstances. Hell, he was impressed with his own. The death of a loved one, family or friend, was a heavy burden to bear. But a suicide was a whole other matter. The whys, the how could you do this to me, all the doubts and blame would be never-ending.

Vito spotted Hank getting out of her car as he waited by the front entrance for her to arrive. She looked uncharacteristically unkempt.

He was worried sick about her. Vito thought she needed professional help. He would try to bring up the subject if the opportunity presented itself. How much could one person take, after all?

"Hey, beautiful," Vito greeted Hank, trying to raise her spirits.

"Not these days," Hank began.

"I was gonna take you to get your car after we ate, but looks like you beat me to it," Vito said."

"Yeah, I took an Uber," Hank explained.

"You need to eat something. It'll help. We'll figure it all out. Lot to deal with here, but we'll solve this thing, we will," Vito declared.

"I've been having nightmares, Vito. About Cary, the way she died. It's awful," Hank confessed.

"Let's go inside. You can tell me all about it. I'm here Hank, not going anywhere," Vito added, sincerely.

When their food came, Vito began to eat, but Hank seemed to have no interest in partaking. The Italian in Vito sprung into action.

"Listen, Hank, you've got to keep your strength up. Otherwise, it's just gonna be a vicious circle. You need to stay strong for Cary...for your father. We've got to get him. Brandon can't get away with all of this. Shit, how many lives he's ruined...destroyed whole families. It's got to stop," Vito stated adamantly.

Hank picked up her fork and took a few bites. It was a start. The pause in conversation gave Vito the opportunity he was looking for to bring up therapy.

"That's better. You know, Hank, I've been thinking. Might not be such a bad idea if you saw someone, professionally I mean. Dr. Langhorne, hear she's really good. Hell, who couldn't use a little help these days, right?" Vito asked.

"Vito, look, not now, not right now. I need to...I don't know...need to process all of this. Maybe later...after we've figured out what the hell we're doing. Time's running out. I'm afraid he's gonna bolt. Brandon, I mean. And then we'll never get him," Hank added, frantically.

"It's okay, whenever you're ready. Just worried about the night-mares. What can I do?" Vito asked, concerned. "I mean it's not every night, is it?"

Hank seemed reluctant to say anything more, but she knew Vito was worried about her, so she tried to explain.

"No, not every night. I'd say two, maybe three times a week. It's always the same. Cary gets out of the car. Barry starts barking. And then there's a crash, and she falls to the ground," Hank continued, shakily.

"Jesus. Goddamn. We don't have to talk about it anymore. Not right now. Let's focus on your dad...Cary...getting you better," Vito said, taking Hank's hand.

"We need to confront Brandon," Hank said, changing the subject abruptly.

"Before we do, let me poke around and see what I can find out. Maybe if we get lucky, something will turn up. I'll look into those ancestry companies, figure out which one Brandon might have used to find his father, to find your dad," Vito said.

"He'll hear about it on the news. Probably already has," Hank declared. "I mean O'Malley has the note, and they're not releasing details just yet. He doesn't know it was a...that he killed himself," Hank rambled on. "But, Vito, he has a heads up. He's not stupid. Brandon's gonna cover his bases. Protect himself."

"You mean get rid of the evidence, the gun, wallet," Vito responded. "But listen he doesn't know that Nowak told us everything. I think that could work to our advantage. The prick thinks he's smarter than every fucking one of us. It's time to set him straight."

"Vito," Hank said, as she fidgeted with her car keys. "Why did he have to kill Cary? Why?"

"You know why," Vito answered, with sadness in his eyes. "We both know why. He saw her as a threat, a fucking loose end. That's all."

And then it occurred to Hank that Brandon must have been spying on them, on her and Cary, all along and that when he murdered her, he probably knew that Hank was his sister. *How could anyone be so cruel?* Hank asked herself.

After they finished eating, Vito took care of the bill. The meeting with O'Malley wasn't for several hours. So Hank went home to rest, while Vito began his investigation. They would meet up at police headquarters in Stamford later. Vito knew Hank was right, that the death alone of his father could set Brandon off. At a minimum, he would likely destroy anything he thought could link him to the murders; he probably already had. But years of experience told Vito that most killers eventually mess up; they talk too much, brag about their crimes to friends or cellmates even once they're behind bars or taunt the police. Brandon would do something to cause his own demise, whether he wanted to be caught, subconsciously or not. They couldn't wait for that to happen, however, because somebody else might die.

Vito returned to the guesthouse and took out his laptop to do a little research and put out a few feelers. Anna wasn't home, so he had the place to himself and the privacy he needed. The first Google search he did was 23andMe. *Why not start with the obvious?* Vito asked himself. After reviewing the site, Vito concluded that he would need to call in a favor or two to access the information he was looking for. But Vito read every word of Nowak's suicide note and knew that he was telling them the truth, so he didn't really need official confirmation from a DNA company that Brandon was his friend's son. It would just be nice to have it in writing for the record.

Vito killed the rest of the time before he had to leave for the meeting, strategizing about the best way to approach Brandon. They couldn't just drive up to his home and accuse him of a bunch of murders while also revealing everything Nowak had told them: namely that he was Harry and, therefore, Hank's brother. And it was better if Brandon didn't know that Nowak had told them that he had Cary's wallet and Vito's gun. *Knowledge is power,* Vito reflected.

* * *

Hank woke up refreshed from her nap and got dressed for the meeting with O'Malley and company. While she wasn't sure she was up to it, Hank needed to be there and to do everything she could to move the investigation along. As she got into her car, Hank remembered she had forgotten to call Homer to tell him the news about their father. But she didn't know what time it was in Manila right now, so Hank decided to put the call off until after she got back.

I wonder if Vito's having any luck tracing Brandon's ancestry, Hank pondered. Like Vito, however, Hank didn't think for their immediate purposes they needed further confirmation. What concerned Hank the most, at the moment, however, was how O'Malley would handle the news that Nowak thought Brandon was the "Deer Killer." Vito and she hadn't really discussed that part yet, but there was no doubt it would come up at the meeting. Hank hoped that O'Malley would give her a chance to figure out the best way to proceed with the case. She didn't want any errors in judgment nor mistakes on the part of the police to compromise the investigation.

* * *

Vito was the first to arrive at police headquarters, followed by Hank. They met in O'Malley's office as usual. The atmosphere in the room was grim. Today it would be the four of them: the sergeant, Vito, Hank, and Max Craven, the evidence technician. Nowak's suicide note was the most concrete piece of evidence they had so far. It was riddled with critical information, assumptions, and accusations. Vito and Hank believed every word of it. They would soon find out if O'Malley agreed with them. The sergeant kicked off the meeting by acknowledging former Det. Henry Nowak's contributions to the force despite the strained relationship between them. And O'Malley knew Hank was hurting and still cared about her in spite of himself, so he put his personal feelings aside for her sake and for the sake of justice.

"I know you've been through a lot lately," the sergeant began. "More than anyone should ever have to. But this note...the letter your father left...we've gotta act on it. Use it to get him, get Brandon. Assuming, of course, that everything in it is true," he added cautiously.

"Look, Joe," Vito began. "It's true. I can feel it in my gut. It all makes sense in a crazy way. Guess I'm one of the only ones who knew about Harry. It made a stir at the time, but over the years, people forgot about it, moved on. This was the way Nowak decided to handle it. Keep his new kids in the dark, protect them. But lesson learned too late, the truth always comes out," Vito concluded.

"Cutting to the chase here," O'Malley said, interrupting him. "What matters is the wallet and the gun; *your* gun, Vito, but we'll get to that later. They're the only reason Nowak thinks...thought Brandon... Harry...whatever his name is killed everyone. What I'm trying to say is," the sergeant added, turning toward Hank. "Your dad concluded that Brandon is the 'Deer Killer' based on what he found in the cabin. So if we can't find them...the gun, wallet, where in God's name does that leave us?"

"I honestly don't know," Hank said, despondently. "But he... Brandon doesn't know about any of this...he doesn't even know about the note...that it was a suicide. Joe, you're not planning on releasing..." Hank continued, but O'Malley cut her off.

"Not yet," the sergeant answered. "The note...cards...hell, even the potential discovery of Cary's wallet and Vito's gun...we'll keep it all under wraps for now...on a need-to-know basis and see where it all leads. If Brandon is our man, I wanna get him as much as you do."

Hank looked at Vito and tried to convey with her eyes the next topic they needed to address: the three cards Brandon had given to her father.

"Joe, there's something else," Hank began. "You already know my dad's part in Brandon's scheme, the 'Odd Jobs' card he ordered him to leave at Devil's Den before he dumped Caity's body there. And you also know Brandon gave him a total of three cards. Do you understand what I'm trying to say?" Hank asked inquisitively.

"You mean Brandon has more work to do," O'Malley responded. "He's gonna kill more people, likely two, if we don't put an end to this. So find that gun and Cary's wallet. That'll be a good start."

As the meeting wrapped up O'Malley made a request of Vito and Craven, both of whom had been mostly quiet during the conversation.

"Guess we're done here for the time being. You guys mind stepping outside? I need to talk to Hank alone," he added.

O'Malley was still in love with Hank, and although she may not have been fully aware of the depth of his feelings toward her, Hank knew he wanted her back. So any attempt on the sergeant's part to get her alone rattled Hank. Once Vito and Craven left the room, O'Malley made his case.

"Hank, I'm worried about you. Sure you're up to this..." he began.

"I'm fine, Joe, really," Hank answered disingenuously.

"How can you be, not after everything that's happened. Not sure it's such a good idea for you to stay on the case," O'Malley said, finally getting around to the point.

Hank was taken aback by his remark. She wasn't sure if O'Malley was just feeling her out or if he really wanted her off the investigation. It was time to find out.

"I have to do this, Joe. Have to work the case. I owe it to my father and to Cary," she added, in a quiet tone, afraid of his reaction to the mention of the name.

O'Malley paused for a moment and just stared at Hank. She was beautiful, radiant, even under the current circumstances. *How did I let her get away?* the sergeant asked himself. Even though O'Malley believed Cary wasn't the first woman Hank had been with after they broke up, he somehow blamed her for everything. Maybe it was because he understood, painful as it was, that Hank had been in love with her, that Cary had shared something with Hank that he never would.

"Fine," O'Malley finally answered. "You can stay on the case. But if you lose your objectivity or it becomes too much, you let me know, okay? We need to catch this guy. More people are going to die."

"I can handle it, really, Joe. Vito and I, we're going to figure out the best way to get to Brandon without raising any red flags. He's smart. But we'll find the gun and Cary's wallet and prove he's responsible for all of it," Hank said determinedly.

"Go for it," were O'Malley's final words.

SEVENTEEN

Former Det. Henry "Hank" Nowak's funeral was to be held in the afternoon. His body had been released to Hank after the autopsy was performed and other forensic evidence collected. Given that the detective was also a former marine and police officer, the proceedings promised to be well attended. Hank had finally reached her brother to deliver the awful news. Homer, of course, was unable to attend on such short notice. He promised Hank, however, that he would visit as soon as possible. She held off telling him anything more regarding their mother and Brandon for the time being. Hank would have to explain their bizarre family history in person.

Vito and Anna picked Hank up to drive her to the church. The detective would need all the support she could get today. Losing your last parent under any circumstances was traumatic. But what Hank was going through was a million times worse. As a young girl, Hank idolized her father. She thought he could do anything. As it turned out, Nowak died a broken man, at his own hand no less. Life had destroyed the once-invincible cop. Everyone had a breaking point. Nowak had reached his.

As these thoughts raced through Hank's mind on the way to the funeral, it occurred to her that her father was in actuality Brandon's latest victim just as much as if he had pulled the trigger himself. She didn't doubt for a second that Brandon's plan all along had been to push her father over the edge, to make him pay. Hank thought she knew her father better than anyone in the world. As it turned out, she couldn't have been more wrong. He had lived with demons all his life, blaming himself for the loss of his firstborn son, and she had had absolutely no clue.

When they pulled up to the church, there was already a long line of attendees waiting to get in. A sea of uniformed cops lined the sidewalk. The first person Hank recognized was Max Craven.

"I'll get out here," Hank said to Vito as he started to pull into the parking lot.

"Anna, why don't you go with her?" Vito said.

"Sure. Is that okay, Hank?" Anna asked.

"Yes, of course, don't know what I'd do without you guys today," Hank responded gratefully.

As Vito parked the car, Hank and Anna walked over to Craven. He greeted his colleague with outstretched arms and a kiss on the cheek.

"I'm so sorry," Craven began.

That was a phrase Hank was prepared to hear often today.

"I'm okay, Max," Hank started. "You don't have to worry about me, really."

"O'Malley's inside," Craven said. "He wanted to be up near the front," the evidence tech explained.

Hank thought O'Malley was getting ahead of himself as far as she was concerned. But his intentions toward her were the least of Hank's worries at the moment. Vito startled Hank by coming up behind her and Anna as they were conversing with Craven.

"Sorry didn't mean to..." Vito began, apologizing to Hank.

"That's all right. Just a little jumpy, that's all," Hank declared.

"Why don't we go inside? Service should start soon. Hank, sure you're up to speaking?" Vito asked, concerned.

"Probably not, but it's something I've got to do," she answered uncertainly. "I've gotten through worse. That's what alcohol is for, right?" Hank added, trying to lighten the mood.

"Look, no one's expecting anything from you...not today. If it gets to be too much...you feel overwhelmed...cut it short. Everyone will understand," Vito stated adamantly.

"Got it. Thanks, Vito. Time to go inside," Hank responded.

They made their way to the front of the church and sat in the first pew. Hank looked around at the audience. She spotted Gayle sitting by herself a few rows back. However, O'Malley was in a seat directly behind Hank. *Jesus,* the detective said to herself. *No boundaries.* As the church filled up, Father Patrick O'Reilly made his way to the podium to address the crowd. After paying tribute to his parishioner and friend, the priest introduced Hank.

Nowak's daughter stood up and walked to the stand to deliver the eulogy. As Hank adjusted the microphone, her hands started to shake. The detective took out the notes she had brought with her and spread them out on the easel in front of her. The next ten minutes would be some of the most difficult of her life. As she spoke to the audience, many of whom were in tears, Hank became emotional.

"My father was a good man, an honest man, a devoted father, husband, and friend. He dedicated his life to helping anyone and everyone. I loved him," Hank continued, breaking down.

Then, just as Hank was about to wrap up her speech, a man in the back caught her eye: Brandon. The sight of him threw Hank off balance and she completely lost her train of thought. *What the fuck,* she mumbled to herself. Vito noticed the change in Hank's demeanor immediately. He just didn't know what had caused it. When Hank returned to her seat, she enlightened him.

"He's here, in the back," Hank whispered to Vito. "Fuck."

Vito knew who Hank had spotted. He looked over his shoulder, trying to locate Brandon. But he was nowhere in sight.

"I don't see him," Vito said. "You're sure you didn't confuse Brandon with someone else?"

"It was him. He was looking right at me. Oh my God, Vito. How are we ever going to get him?" Hank asked despondently.

"Forget about him. We'll make a plan...figure it out...just like we told O'Malley. But for now...today...it's all about your father. We still have to...have to um...bury him," Vito added, awkwardly.

Father O'Reilly concluded the service with an inside joke he had shared with the deceased, then blew a kiss at the enlarged photo of Nowak that was positioned on an easel to the left of the casket. Hank noticed the gesture and decided the priest, as she had suspected, was probably gay. *God knows if he's been crushing on my dad all these years,* Hank contemplated. The thought was a welcome distraction from the events of the day, which included Brandon crashing the funeral. He wouldn't dare show up at the cemetery, however, Hank decided.

As the memorial ended, Vito and O'Malley joined the other pall-bearers who surrounded Nowak's remains. The crowd waited until the men carried Nowak's coffin out of the church to leave. A smaller group would now head over to the cemetery to say their final good-byes to the former detective. Once Nowak's casket was securely in the back of the hearse, Vito joined Hank and Anna. They got back into his car to make the trip across town to the cemetery.

When the threesome arrived at the memorial park, a group of about twenty people, comprised mostly of police officials, awaited them. Hank couldn't help thinking that except for Vito, her father didn't really have any close friends. His circle had included mostly former colleagues who he rarely, if ever, hung out with. Hank found the thought depressing. Then she spotted Father O'Reilly standing in front of the coffin and made her way over to the opening in the ground. Vito and Anna followed suit. There was no sign of Gayle. *She probably couldn't stand the thought of being in another graveyard so soon after losing Cary,* Hank deduced. However, Hank had no choice but to confront another round of pain.

The priest made a few brief remarks as Nowak's coffin was lowered into the ground. Hank stared blankly ahead, avoiding the sight. *This is why people drink and do drugs,* she told herself. A psych professor Hank had in college once told the class that after a child learns about death, they're never really happy again. Hank understood her point. As the dirt was shoveled on top of the wooden box, Hank looked down at the ground. Vito, wearing sunglasses, took her hand and squeezed it. Hank's father had meant the world to him.

As Hank stood in front of the mound of dirt, preparing to leave her dad behind, someone tapped her on the shoulder. She spun around, only to find Brandon in her personal space, extending his hand. Vito removed his shades and stood beside Hank. They were totally blind-sided by his appearance.

"Just wanted to express my condolences," Nowak's long-lost son said duplicitously.

Hank didn't know how to interact with her brother or what to say. So Vito stepped in to save her.

"Nice of you to come," Vito responded matter-of-factly, trying to hide his surprise.

Hank put on her sunglasses and grabbed Vito's arm.

"Thanks, but afraid we're in a bit of a hurry," Hank declared. "Excuse us."

Vito, Hank, and Anna walked away briskly and headed back to the car. When they got inside, Hank started to shake.

"What the hell?" she shouted. "What the goddamn hell."

"Calm down, Hank. He's gone," Vito said, trying to comfort her. "Remember he doesn't know about the letter, that we know every-thing. He's just messing with us, trying to rattle us, for yucks."

"Well, it worked," Hank answered bluntly.

"Look, we've gotta find a way to get to him, get him to trust us, I mean, let his guard down. Then maybe we can find the wallet and gun and prove he's the one," Vito added. "It's important, Hank. How we handle him, respond to all his bullshit; it matters. It could end up being the difference between someone's life and death."

As they drove away, Hank thought about everything Vito had just said. It was true that Brandon had no clue that they knew he was Harry, that is, her brother and Nowak's kidnapped son; nor that he had Cary's wallet and Vito's gun hidden God knows where. But most importantly, Brandon had no idea that they knew about the three "Odd Jobs" cards he had given their father. In other words, that Hank and Vito were aware that Brandon was probably planning to commit two more murders. They had to think through the current situation and use it to their advantage.

When Vito pulled up to Hank's house, he turned off the car and waited for her to speak. After a minute of silence, Hank uttered the following words.

"Thanks for everything today, both of you. Let me sleep on it tonight, Vito, everything you said. I know you're right. I'll just have to put my emotions aside and focus on what we're trying to do here, which is stop Brandon before he does anything crazy again. Then we have to find Cary's wallet and your gun and nail him for all of it," Hank declared.

"That's more like it," Vito began. "Now get some rest."

And Anna and he drove off to do the same.

* * *

Brandon was in a rage when he got back to his house. *How dare that fucking bitch treat me like that,* he muttered to himself. He would show her a thing or two about sibling rivalry soon enough. As soon as he got into the den, Brandon headed straight for the scotch and poured himself a tall glass. He swallowed the drink in one gulp and immediately made another. After he had his third cup, Brandon decided to forego the glass and drink directly from the bottle. *That's better,* he told himself.

Brandon thought it would be wise when it got dark to go to his beloved tree and make sure nothing and no one had disturbed the items he had buried beside it. He needed to stay focused. Brandon couldn't let his emotions get the best of him, not now. His father's untimely death had screwed up his plans, but he had other options. *Resilience is the most important trait a person can have,* Brandon pondered. Tomorrow he would decide who to kill next. But first, Brandon had something else he needed to take care of.

* * *

Hank slept a bit longer than she had planned. She thought visiting Cary and Obelus now that her father had been laid to rest would help her deal with the loss. But it was too late in the day to go to the cemetery. Maybe over the weekend. Hank got out of bed and found Barry lying by his bowls in the kitchen. When he saw her, his tail wagged frenetically. Hank had forgotten to give him water when she got home. She took Barry outside and then gave him his dinner. After he was finished eating, the lovable English sheepdog curled up on the couch, pressed against his human.

Hank put her right arm around Barry and reached for the phone. As she had expected, there were a crazy number of texts, voicemails, and emails wishing her the best and expressing sorrow at the loss of her father. Perusing them quickly Hank gleaned that many of the well-wishers referred to her dad as *such a great man.* Hank wasn't up to going through them all now. She'd do that over the weekend too.

As Hank was about to put down her phone a text popped up and caught her eye. *Think we got off on the wrong foot at the cemetery today. I'd love to take you out to lunch. B.* Hank almost dropped the phone. "What the fuck?" she cried out. How presumptuous to reach out to her, no less to sign the text B. While Hank was processing the import of the message, another text came through. *Sorry, it's me, Brandon.* Hank startled Barry by suddenly jumping off the couch. After pacing around the room for a couple of minutes, she picked up her phone and called Vito. The call went straight to voicemail. *Fuck,* thought Hank. So she left the following message: *Vito, call me. It's about Brandon.* Hank had a very bad feeling about the text and the meaning behind it. She had to get in touch with Vito right away. But Hank couldn't just sit around waiting for Vito to check his phone, so she got in her car and headed straight for the guesthouse.

* * *

Brandon didn't expect his sister to answer the text immediately. She would, naturally, have to take a step back, pause, and think about it. At least he had made the first move. Knowing his father, Brandon was fairly certain that he hadn't told Hank that he was her long-lost brother, nor that he was in possession of Cary's wallet and Vito's gun. But it was entirely possible that the police might be hiding something from the public that could connect Brandon to the murders. Authorities hadn't even released information about the "Odd Jobs" cards yet. *No, that was their little secret,* Brandon contemplated.

Brandon figured it could take a day or so for Hank to respond to his message. But he saw no reason to put off his other plans. So Brandon decided to swing by Nowak's house later tonight and leave a token for Hank to find when she cleared out her father's premises: Cary's ring. Brandon believed he knew more about Hank than she knew about him, so the discovery of her dead girlfriend's prized possession at her father's house would certainly rattle her. And if Hank accepted his lunch invitation before she found the ring, so be it. Either way, he would win.

* * *

Hank pulled up to the guesthouse, unannounced, got out of her car, and pounded on the front door. It appeared that no one was home, as the lights were off, and Vito's car was nowhere in sight. *Damn,* thought Hank. She had no choice but to return to her vehicle and wait. After half an hour, she was getting restless. So Hank texted Vito: *I'm outside the cottage. When will you guys be back?* There was no response. Hank tilted her seat just enough to put her head back comfortably and promptly fell asleep. A pounding of a different kind woke her up: Vito's fist on the driver's side window.

"What the hell are you doing, Hank?" he asked, confused.

Apparently, Vito had forgotten to take his phone with him when Anna and he left to run a couple of errands and pick up dinner. So he wasn't aware that Hank had been trying to reach him. She put her seat back in its upright position and got out of the car.

"Let's go inside, guys. There's something I've got to show you," Hank said, with urgency in her voice.

The three of them made their way inside the guesthouse, and Hank filled Vito in on Brandon's latest stunt by holding up her phone so he could read the text.

"Jesus," Vito remarked. "Betcha he thinks we're clueless about who he is and what he's done."

"Am I supposed to respond to this?" Hank asked, rhetorically. "I mean, really."

Vito thought for a moment and then gave her his answer.

"Look, you're not gonna like what I have to say, but this could be just the opportunity we've been looking for to..." Vito continued.

"I can't, Vito. I just can't," Hank said.

Vito took Hank's hands and pointed to the couch.

"Let's sit down for a minute," he suggested.

They sat down next to each other on the sofa, and Anna went into the kitchen area to fix dinner.

"We got Indian, Hank, plenty for all of us. Does that work?" Anna asked.

"I'm not hungry, but thanks anyway," Hank replied. "Food is the last thing on my mind right now."

"This is what we gotta do, Hank," Vito interjected, taking charge. "You text him back...doesn't have to be tonight it can wait till the morning...tell him you'd love to meet up with him and see what he does," Vito advised. "It's the only way."

Hank knew Vito was right, that Brandon's invitation was an opportunity they couldn't pass up.

"I'll do it, text him back in the morning. But God knows what he's up to," Hank added, concerned.

"Don't matter much," Vito answered. "We got him in our cross-hairs, and he doesn't even know it."

"There's one more thing, Vito," Hank said. "My father's house...I'm going to have to go through it...maybe we'll find something else that will help. Don't think I can deal with throwing his things away just yet though. I'll talk to Homer and see what he thinks about putting the house up...selling it. Not that anyone would buy it under the current circumstances...at least not just yet."

"No rush...I mean you don't have to make any decisions so soon...so soon after...you know," Vito began. "Best to let some time pass, but if you're up to it, let's go over to the house and see what we can find there. You never know what might turn up."

"You mean, you'll come with me?" Hank asked, relieved.

"Of course...be right by your side every step of the way," Vito reassured her. "Now go home and get some sleep. I'll be in touch in the morning."

* * *

Brandon stared at the clock that sat atop the mantle in the den until it struck ten o'clock; it was time to head over to his father's house. He stood up, grabbed his jacket, and walked to the study to collect Cary's ring. Brandon put it in his pocket and headed for the garage. He got into his smart car that had become an accomplice to his crimes and drove to Nowak's residence. Brandon could feel his adrenaline pumping. He was getting excited, anticipating how Hank would react when she found Cary's ring there. Brandon wasn't exactly sure how he would break into the house, but he didn't think it was an insurmountable problem.

As Brandon approached the house, he stepped on the brakes to slow his car down. There didn't appear to be anyone in sight. The place was pitch black; no lights were visible. Brandon parked his car underneath a tree on the darkest part of the street. He opened the glove compartment and took out a pair of rubber gloves, put them on, and got out of the vehicle. Brandon walked up the stairs to the front porch, ducking carefully under the still present yellow crime scene tape. He reached for the handle of the door and tried turning it to the right. It gave way immediately. *Cops are stupid and incompetent to boot,* Brandon muttered. *Guess I should be grateful.*

Brandon found himself in the living room, trying to decide where to leave Cary's antique ring. The location was important. If Brandon placed it in too obvious a spot, it would look suspicious. The ring had to appear to have been deliberately hidden, but some place Hank would look. With that thought in mind, Brandon decided the best place to deposit the ring was in Nowak's bedroom. Glancing around, he noticed the dresser. Brandon opened the top drawer that had once held so many secrets and placed Cary's ring inside it. As he did so, Hank's brother picked up the two remaining "Odd Jobs" cards he had given to his father. The police had clearly overlooked them. *Fair trade,* he joked to himself. *Check,* Brandon muttered and left.

* * *

Hank had a restless night's sleep, anticipating lunch with her father's killer. But Brandon had also snuffed out the lives of so many other people, including Cary. The strongest evidence tying her brother to Cary's death was the wallet, gun, and "Odd Jobs" card that was left at the scene of Cary's memorial. In Hank's estimation, the card amounted to a confession. But it was time to text Brandon back and accept his invitation. Hank thought she'd be able to put lunch off until tomorrow. Today, Vito and she would comb through her father's things and see what they could dig up.

Hank picked up her phone and sent the following message to her brother: *Lunch sounds great. How about tomorrow?* It was the hardest text Hank had ever had to write. Brandon answered immediately. *Meet me at the diner at noon. Looking forward. B. Fucking psychopath,* Hank muttered. She was surprised at the choice of a restaurant. Hank had been expecting some place a bit more upscale. The thought of meeting Brandon at the diner just felt wrong. God knows what Xanthe would make of it. But there was no point in pushing back, Hank had to go along with whatever Brandon wanted to do and wherever he wanted to do it.

Then Hank had a thought. Brandon knew that he was her brother. And she knew that he was her brother. Brandon just didn't know that she knew. *What a fucked-up mess,* Hank contemplated. Her next text of the morning went to Vito. Hank couldn't wait for him to call. *Meet me at my dad's in an hour?* Vito wrote back: *Roger that.* It was going to be another rough couple of days.

* * *

Vito and Hank got to Nowak's home just a couple of minutes apart. Vito was the last to arrive as he decided to make a pit stop at the Coffee An' Donut Shop, a local favorite. Word is that Bill Clinton used to have their donuts flown into D.C. for cabinet meetings. Vito got out of his car and walked over to Hank who was standing with her back toward him, facing her father's boat.

"Hey, beautiful," Vito called out, as he juggled two cups of coffee and a bag of coconut twists and chocolate glazed pastries. "This should help us get a jump on the day," he added.

Hank's appetite was nowhere to be found these days, but Cary had successfully introduced her to the wonders of sugar, so her face lit up at the sight of the white bag.

"Thanks, Vito. That was really sweet of you. Can't remember the last time I had one of these. Must've been when Cary and I..." Hank continued, then stopped herself before saying anything more.

"Why don't we go over there and eat?" Vito said, pointing to the porch. "Then we can go inside. Sound good?" Vito asked, trying to distract her.

"Yes, that'll be perfect," Hank answered, smiling slightly.

They made their way to the stoop and divided up the baked goods. Vito was happy to see Hank eat an entire donut while downing her cup of coffee. He was worried sick about her. When they finished their makeshift breakfast, Vito took the bag, crumpled it into a ball, and threw it in the garbage can situated on the grass to the left of the front steps.

"Let's do it," he said, as Hank wiped her mouth with a napkin.

Vito held the front door open for Hank, and they entered Nowak's house, careful not to disturb the yellow crime scene tape. Once they were inside, Vito reached into his pocket and took out two pairs of blue latex gloves. He put one set on and handed the other to Hank. *Everything by the book,* Vito told himself.

"I'll look around in here," Vito said. "Why don't you check out the kitchen? Then we can both go through your father's things in his bedroom."

"Sure," Hank answered.

As Vito and Hank looked around, she knew that they were trying to accomplish two things with the search: first, see if there was anything lying around that might provide further clues about Brandon's involvement in the killings; and second, Hank wanted to assess how time-consuming it would be to close her father's house down and eventually sell it. But that could wait; catching Brandon was the clear priority.

Vito found nothing of note in the living room and Hank came up more or less empty-handed as well. In general, her father had never been the best housekeeper, but he wasn't a hoarder. That would make her life easier when it came time to deal with closing down the house.

"Let's go into the bedroom," Vito announced. "Ready, Hank?"

The last time Hank had been in her dad's room was when she found his body. It had been a bloody scene she would never forget. However, Hank had to stay strong, she could fall apart later, after Brandon was behind bars, paying for everything he had done.

"Yeah, I'm good," Hank answered. "Let's do it."

As they entered her father's bedroom, Hank's eyes were immediately drawn to the area by the bed where he had died. The carpet was still stained with Nowak's blood. This wasn't going to be easy. Vito noticed Hank's expression and spoke up.

"Listen, you don't have to do this, Hank. Why don't you wait outside, and I'll handle it," Vito suggested.

"Look, Vito, I'm still on the case. O'Malley gave in...left it to me to decide if I could handle all of this. I don't want to let him down, let Cary and my dad down. There'll be time...time to heal...but the time's not now," Hank explained.

"I hear ya...got it," Vito answered. "Just worried about you is all."

"I know you are, and I appreciate it. My dad would too," Hank said, giving Vito a loving look. "You've always been like an uncle to me...or a second father. You know that, right?"

Vito nodded, becoming emotional, then he began to look around the room. Nowak's bed was unmade, and his clothes lay on the floor. Nothing had been moved yet; everything was just as Hank had found it. The only thing missing from the original scene was Nowak's body, but there was still the chalky outline of it on the floor.

"Mind if I look in the dresser?" Vito asked Hank, knowing he might come across more personal family stuff.

"Yeah, go right ahead. Maybe we'll find something," Hank replied.

Vito walked over to Nowak's dresser and started to open the drawers, working his way up from the bottom. When he got to the top drawer, he hesitated, understanding that it was the last place left to look. As Vito slid the drawer open, a shiny object caught his eye: Cary's ring.

"What the fuck?" Vito uttered in disbelief. "What in the goddamn hell is this doing here?"

Hank didn't know what Vito had found, but whatever it was obviously threw him. She walked over to the private eye and looked in the drawer.

"Oh my God," Hank uttered. "What the hell?"

Hank reached in the open drawer and took out Cary's ring. It was the only piece of jewelry she ever wore. As Hank clutched it in her hands, she suddenly started to sob. Vito closed the drawer and hugged her.

"It'll be all right. You'll see. We're here for you. I'm here for you. I made a promise to your father way back, and I intend to keep it," Vito stated adamantly.

"I don't understand," Hank began. "What's Cary's ring doing in my father's dresser?"

Vito thought for a minute before answering.

"Don't think I'm crazy or anything, but I think there's only one explanation. That Brandon...your brother...put it there," Vito said.

Vito's theory made sense to Hank, as according to her father's letter, he was already in possession of Cary's wallet and Vito's gun. *Why wouldn't Brandon also take Cary's prized possession?* Hank asked herself.

"But why leave it here?" Hank asked. "And when?"

"I'm guessing must've been some time last night...definitely after your dad...um...after it happened," Vito declared. "Not sure exactly when, but it's just another one of his sick pranks."

"To what end? I mean why even bother?" Hank inquired.

"Look, Brandon may not know for sure that it was a...well, that your dad took his own life and left a note. But he's not stupid. He would expect us...you and me...to look into...investigate what happened... and why. So for his own amusement, why not get us thinking that your dad did something weird or underhanded? Again, he doesn't know that we know who he is and what your dad told us. It's just his way of saying fuck you, I'd bet anything," Vito concluded.

Hank listened to Vito's premise and decided he was probably right. Brandon took any and every opportunity to mess with them. But Hank had forgotten to tell Vito that her lunch date with Brandon was set for tomorrow.

"Why don't you hold onto the ring?" Vito said, interrupting Hank's thoughts.

Then Hank got an idea.

"Vito what do you think about this...I'm supposed to meet up with Brandon for lunch tomorrow. I sent him a text this morning like you suggested, and he got right back to me. How 'bout we mess with him for a change?" Hank proposed.

"Whatcha mean?" Vito inquired.

"What if I wear Cary's ring; see how he reacts. Catch him off guard," Hank stated.

"I don't know, Hank. It could set him off. This guy's a nut, a manipulative nut at that. Don't want you getting hurt," Vito answered in a worried tone.

"I'll be in a public place: the diner no less. What could he pull? After all, Brandon left it for us to find." Hank declared, confident in her plans.

"Okay, do it," Vito said, in agreement. "Let's see what makes him tick. But, Hank, be careful. He has two cards left to play."

EIGHTEEN

Hank's stomach was in knots as she got ready to meet her brother. After showering and taking Barry out for his morning walk, she made herself a strong cup of coffee and sat on the couch waiting. It was now 11:02 a.m., and Hank had another forty minutes or so to kill before she had to leave. She didn't want to be late. Hank was startled by Barry's wet nose on her face. She had fallen asleep if only for a few minutes. Glancing at her phone, Hank saw that it was now 11:42 a.m. *Jesus, thank God for Barry,* Hank thought to herself. Playing shrink, Hank decided that, subconsciously, she would have been more than happy to have slept through lunch. She stood up reluctantly and headed for the door.

After pulling out of the driveway, Hank realized that she had forgotten to put on Cary's ring. Maybe it wasn't such a great idea after all to wear it. *Why provoke a maniac?* Hank asked herself. But it had been her bright idea, so Hank decided to turn around and go back and get it. Holding Cary's jewelry in her hand, Hank realized that she had only seen the ring on Cary, that she herself had never even tried it on. Hank looked down at the antique piece and decided it would fit best on her left-hand index finger. When she slid it on, the ring glistened in the sunlight. Hank was overcome with emotion.

When Hank arrived at the diner, she parked her car in the usual place and paused to collect herself. If things started to get creepy,

Hank could always excuse herself and cut the lunch short. She'd think of something. How Hank wished Vito would be there by her side to get her through the next couple of hours. But she would have to do this alone. As Hank was about to get out of her car, she spotted Brandon, wearing sunglasses, making his way to the front entrance of the building. *Fuck,* Hank muttered to herself. *Family.*

Brandon waited patiently in the foyer of the restaurant for Hank to arrive. Mania was starting to set in. *If she only knew,* he thought to himself. What an inspiring afternoon it promised to be. Maybe if things went well, they could follow their meal with a visit to the dog park. How thoughtful it would be of him to suggest collecting that beast of an English sheepdog and frolicking around, just the three of them. He'd see how it went and if he and Hank connected. After all, they were bonded by blood.

As Brandon was about to grab Xanthe and ask to be seated, he saw Hank getting out of her car. He watched closely as the detective made her way to the door. Hank looked radiant, even in her grief. *If only you weren't my sister,* Brandon contemplated. *Who knew what might happen?* When Hank got within a foot of her brother, she reached out her hand to greet him. A chill went up her spine.

"So nice to see you again," Hank said, hiding her anxiety.

"The pleasure is all mine," Brandon answered, predictably. Then, turning toward Xanthe, he added, "Could we please have a booth in the back? We'd like a little privacy."

The presumptuous comment took Hank by surprise. *What exactly is he up to?* she asked herself. Once they were seated, Brandon took off his sunglasses and stared directly into Hank's eyes. She couldn't help thinking that Brandon intended to make her feel as uncomfortable as possible during the time they would spend together. Hank's only move was to pick up the menu she knew by heart and pretend she was trying to figure out what to order.

"Come here often?" Brandon inquired, knowing the answer.

"I guess you could say I'm a regular," Hank responded. "Best breakfast in town and served all day."

What a stupid thing to say, she reprimanded herself. But did Hank really give a shit what her brother thought of her conversational skills? Then, Brandon spotted Cary's ring, right where Hank had placed it, on her left-hand index finger. *Touché,* he said to himself. Brandon considered why Hank had decided to wear it to lunch. It could just be a coincidence and have nothing to do with him. Brandon had no reason to think Hank even knew he was her brother, much less suspect him of being the "Deer Killer." Yet she had obviously found the ring where he had left it: in her father's dresser drawer. Brandon couldn't help wondering what Hank must have made of the discovery. He decided to play dumb and just admire the piece without giving anything else away.

"That's an unusual ring," Brandon began, touching Hank's hand.

The contact startled Hank, and her brother noticed.

"Yes...um...it belonged to someone special," Hank started to explain awkwardly.

"Well, they certainly have good taste," Brandon declared.

Hank was starting to get light-headed. She felt nauseous. She had to get away from him—*now.*

"Can you excuse me for a minute? Just need to use the restroom," Hank said suddenly, making her escape.

"Why, certainly," Brandon answered. "Hope you're feeling all right."

Brandon was starting to get suspicious: he thought Hank was acting strangely. Then he noticed her phone across the table from him, screen face down. Brandon looked around to make sure no one was watching him and picked up the mobile device. It was locked so he had to think quickly. Brandon had a knack for figuring out people's passcodes. His father's had been easy: the numerical equivalent of the name Harry. *What would his sister have chosen to protect her information?* he wondered. And then it came to him: *Tessa.* Brandon punched in the numbers that matched each letter and the device unlocked immediately. *I'm a fucking genius,* Brandon thought, congratulating himself. "Who knows you like your family?" he whispered, sneeringly.

But Hank could return any minute, so he had to act fast. Brandon scanned through her emails and texts, but nothing caught his attention. Then he decided on a whim, to look at Hank's photo albums. Screenshots of a letter from their father popped up. Brandon skimmed the images closely enough to understand that his dad had committed suicide and that Hank, and likely Vito, knew everything. Knowledge is power. Who was playing who at this absurd lunch he had arranged?

Brandon returned the phone to its original position on the table and waited for his sister to return. Only now he knew that she knew he was her brother. At the moment, however, Hank thought she had the advantage, as she was unaware of his discovery. Once again, Brandon found himself one step ahead. In light of the revelation, Brandon deduced that Hank had intentionally worn Cary's ring to lunch to get a rise out of him. But he had played it cool. So far, he had given her nothing.

Hank came back to their booth looking pale. She obviously wasn't well. Brandon decided to cut the afternoon short and release Hank from any further obligation. Their meeting had served its purpose. Brandon had gotten more out of it than he could have possibly imagined. *What kind of cop leaves their phone, password protected or not, for the world to see?* Brandon asked himself. Of course, Hank wasn't herself these days and Brandon supposed he would have to take some responsibility for that.

"Sorry, not feeling well," Hank said, snapping Brandon out of his thoughts. "Mind if we reschedule?"

They hadn't even had a chance to order yet, so Brandon saw no reason to prolong the misery. He had had enough of Hank's company for one day.

"Not a problem. Are you up to driving...? I mean, do you need a ride home?" Brandon asked, hoping the answer would be no.

"No, no, that's not necessary. I'll be fine once I get outside...get some air," Hank reassured him. *I'll be fine once I get away from you,* she told herself. Hank was beginning to think it wasn't such a bad idea for her to see the cop shrink. She was struggling with everything these days.

When Hank got back into her car, she let out a deep breath and started to relax. *Did I just have a panic attack?* she asked herself. Hank waited for Brandon to exit the parking lot and then picked up her phone to call Vito. He needed to know what a mess she had made out of the meeting. After one ring, he picked up.

"Hank, are you alone?" Vito asked, whispering. "It's only 12:30 p.m. Thought you wouldn't be done for a while."

"Yeah, I'm alone. What a fucking shitshow I made out of it, Vito. I really fucked it up," Hank said, dejectedly.

"It's okay, it's okay, where are you? I can be there in ten...twenty minutes tops," Vito declared.

"Still in the parking lot. Wanna meet me at the house?" Hank asked.

"Roger that. And Hank, drive carefully. See you in a bit," Vito stated.

"Thanks, Vito. I'm so sorry...thought I could get through it...but..." Hank added, trying to explain.

"We'll figure it out. We're smarter than that son of a bitch any day of the week," Vito said, assuredly.

* * *

As Vito drove to Hank's place, he felt bad that he had pushed her to do something she clearly couldn't handle. They needed a do-over; he would have to come up with another plan. Vito got to Hank's and parked out front. Her car was nowhere to be seen. As he sat in his car waiting, memories started racing through his mind. He'd never forget the day of the kidnapping, and the days, weeks, and years that followed. Whoever was responsible had never been caught. Vito couldn't help wondering if the monster that destroyed an entire family was still alive, and if so, did they ever even think about the consequences of their actions, the pain they had caused?

The sound of Hank's car pulling into the driveway disrupted Vito's morose thoughts. He sat up straight and got out of the vehicle. The first thing on his agenda was to convince Hank that she hadn't done anything wrong, that she had tried her best and failed, but only temporarily.

"Hey, gorgeous," Vito called out.

Hank thought Vito's terms of endearment were getting old. But she knew it was his way of trying to raise her spirits and keep her on track. He meant the world to her.

"Hey, Vito. I'll put on some coffee, and we can talk," Hank answered.

They went inside and were greeted with kisses from Barry. He loved Vito and stood up on his hind legs to greet him.

"Good boy," Vito said to the rambunctious animal as he patted him on the head.

"Make yourself comfortable on the couch, Vito. I'll just be a minute," Hank announced.

When the coffee was ready, Hank poured two mugs and carried them over to the private eye.

"Sorry, I'm out of milk," Hank said, forgetting Vito took it black.

"I'm not a milk kinda guy," Vito responded, giving Hank an affectionate glance.

"Well, let's get to it," Hank said meekly.

"Look, it's my fault. I shoulda known you weren't ready for this, shoulda found another way," Vito began.

"Vito, he touched my hand, pretended he'd never seen Cary's ring before. That's what set me off. I had to get away from him," Hank declared.

"Jesus, that goddamn prick. We need to try again. Any thoughts?" Vito asked.

"I asked him if we could reschedule, so guess I should text him and see how he responds. Should I do it now?" Hank asked, hesitantly.

"No time like the present. He could do something crazy any minute. We can't risk any more lives," Vito said in a worried voice.

So Hank picked up her phone and sent the following text: *Sorry about today. When's good for you?* It took less than thirty seconds for Brandon to respond. *Tomorrow, my place, same time.* Upon hearing the text tone, Hank looked at her phone then turned the screen to Vito.

"Tomorrow it is," he stated matter-of-factly. "Sure you're up to this?"

"I don't know, really, I don't. Think it's okay to be alone with him at his house no less?" Hank asked.

"Can't say I like it. But if you'll feel more comfortable, I can meet you there. And the second anything gets dicey, just text me, okay?" Vito suggested.

Hank considered Vito's proposal and decided this was no time to be a martyr.

"That's fine, as long as he doesn't see you. Can that work?" Hank inquired.

"I'll be like a ghost," Vito promised and gulped down the rest of his coffee.

* * *

Brandon didn't like the way things had gone this afternoon. But he had managed to turn the fiasco into another victory. Their next meetup would be on his terms, on his turf. Brandon doubted he would get much sleep tonight, anticipating what might transpire the following day. For God's sake, Hank couldn't even handle lunch at the diner. Being alone with her long-lost brother in his home would likely rattle her even more. Of course, Hank didn't know that Brandon had violated her privacy and read their father's suicide note. Consequently, he would have the clear advantage.

* * *

Hank and Brandon woke up at more or less the same time. But neither of them had gotten much sleep, albeit for different reasons. They would spend the morning apart, each preparing for their next meeting. They had dissimilar agendas but the same determination. While Brandon decided to stick to his usual routine, which included a run, shower, and protein shake, Hank made herself a cappuccino and took Barry to the dog park. There was plenty of time to kill before she needed to get ready to meet her brother.

It was a beautiful but chilly day, so the park was filled with mostly regulars. Hank stayed to herself, avoiding them. She found a deserted area and let Barry off his leash. Hank let him blow off some steam for about a half hour, then called to him. They got back to the house in time for Hank to take a quick shower and change her clothes. She checked herself in the mirror and decided that the past few weeks had taken a major toll on her. Hank thought she looked absolutely awful. Not that it mattered any more; she had lost everything.

Hank took the scenic route to Brandon's estate, trying to delay the inevitable. But in spite of herself, she arrived a bit early. Hank pulled over and turned off the engine. Then she noticed a car parked a little bit down the road, flashing its lights. It was Vito. Hank responded by doing the same so that Vito would know she had seen him. She checked the time on her phone repeatedly. When it turned exactly 11:55 a.m., Hank put the key back in the ignition and started the vehicle. She drove to the entrance and pressed the button. Brandon's voice greeted her.

"Who's there?" he asked, wasting no time fucking around with her.

"It's me, Hank," she responded, already annoyed.

Brandon pressed the buzzer, and the gate swung open. Hank parked her car as close to the main house as possible and made her way to the front door. Before she had the chance to knock or ring the bell, Brandon appeared before her.

"Such a pleasure to see you again," her brother said, attempting to catch Hank off guard.

"Sorry about yesterday. I...uh..." Hank began, but Brandon interrupted her.

"No worries, please, come in," he said. "This way, follow me."

Brandon decided the best place to corner his sister was in the same room where he had first met Cary: the den. He had already lit the fireplace and poured two glasses of his best wine for the occasion. As they entered the room, Brandon took note of Hank's reaction. She looked around, taking in her surroundings. Brandon reached for Hank's coat and laid it on a chair in the corner. Then he picked up both glasses of wine and handed one to her.

"Oh, um...I don't...can't drink while I'm on duty," Hank began.

On duty? Brandon asked himself. *What kind of hours do cops keep these days?* He assumed she had taken the day off.

"Sorry, I didn't realize you were working today," Brandon said rather stiffly.

Hank thought for a minute before answering him. She was actually working right now, but she would play it smart.

"I go in later this afternoon. We're in the middle of a big investiga—" she began, explaining, then caught herself. *The less said the better.*

Brandon wasn't about to let his guard down any time soon. He knew they were after him. Yet this cat and mouse game he was playing with his sister was beginning to bore him.

"Can you excuse me for a minute? Have to run to the kitchen. I took the liberty of ordering in lunch," Brandon announced. "It should be here shortly."

Hank was relieved to be left alone if only for a few minutes. She didn't see where any of this was getting her. But Hank decided that Brandon's abrupt departure might be the only chance she would have to snoop around and try to find something that might incriminate him. With that thought in mind, Hank began to move around the room looking for anything out of the ordinary. There was a large bookcase filled with all sorts of novels, mostly crime thrillers. *No surprise there,* Hank told herself.

As she started to go through the books, looking behind them on the shelves, Hank found a yellow-tinged envelope. She peeked inside only to see the documents her father had referred to in his letter. As Hank rifled through them, she heard a voice: Brandon's.

"Looking for something?" he asked coldly. "Why don't you give me those?" he instructed her.

Brandon had decided to keep the paperwork that documented his past close by. So he hid the folder behind his favorite book, *The History of Serial Killers in America.* He considered it an accomplishment that he wasn't included in the contents as only murderers who had been caught filled the pages. Brandon walked over to Hank and took the envelope away from her.

"I think it's time we all stop pretending, *sis,*" he declared.

Hank was busted, but she wasn't entirely sure from Brandon's comment how much he actually knew.

"I was just..." Hank began uneasily.

"You were just what exactly?" Brandon shot back.

Hank didn't want to fall into a trap and reveal something by mistake that Brandon didn't already know. But he had just called her *sis,* so for whatever reason he was ready to have it out with her. The statement didn't mean, however, that he knew about the suicide note nor that she already knew he was her brother.

"People shouldn't leave their phones lying around," Brandon remarked.

What the hell? Hank said to herself. *Shit, I left it on the table at the diner when I went to the bathroom. But how did he get into it?* Hank asked herself, bewildered.

Brandon knew what Hank was thinking. He could read her every thought.

"If you're wondering how I bypassed the code, think again," Brandon said, staring at his sister. "Or what I saw," he added.

This wasn't how Hank expected the afternoon to go. She was almost ready to send out an SOS to Vito but controlled herself.

"Look, Brandon. I don't know how you got into my phone. And I have no idea what you think you know, but you had no right..." Hank continued, carefully reprimanding him.

"Let's take it from the top. A cop, no less a detective, one would think, would choose a more secure password than their mother's name," Brandon blurted out, surprising Hank with his accuracy.

"Oh my God," Hank answered, taken aback.

"Tessa...8-3-7-7-2," Brandon explained. "Our family needs to step it up in the security department, don't you think?" he asked her sarcastically.

Hank needed to extricate herself from the current situation she found herself in. She just didn't know how.

"So correct me if I'm wrong," Brandon began, pacing around the room. "But looks like both our parents offed themselves," he stated callously.

Hank understood at once that Brandon had seen the screen-shots of her father's suicide note. He now knew everything. Hank no longer had the advantage she had hoped for. They were on an even playing field.

"How dare you..." Hank yelled back at him.

"Now, now, dear sister, I'd lose that attitude of yours if I were you," Brandon said, indifferently.

Before Hank knew what she was saying, the following words came out of her mouth.

"You think you're invincible, don't you? But we know everything. Give me the gun and wallet now, and maybe we can cut a deal," Hank said desperately.

Brandon looked at her and let out a laugh.

"Give you what gun? Whose wallet?" he asked, trying to appear clueless.

"You know whose," Hank said indignantly.

Brandon walked over to a small cabinet in a corner of the room. He removed a gun from the top shelf, then closed the door. Then he reached into his back pocket and took out his wallet.

"Is this what you mean?" he asked Hank mockingly.

"What did you do with them? Where's Cary's wallet?" Hank answered, angrily.

"This is my gun, my wallet. We both know the old man was losing it," Brandon declared. "I never had what you're looking for. Swear," Brandon concluded.

"This isn't over...not by a long shot," Hank uttered furiously.

"I think our lunch is over. Please leave...now," Brandon directed her.

Hank put on her coat, took out her keys, and started to walk toward the door, Brandon right beside her. He took her arm and literally dragged Hank to the front entryway. As Brandon opened the door, he issued the following warning.

"I'd leave it alone, not rock the boat. Not sure you get what or rather whom you're dealing with. Do you really want to have another thing on your conscience...to blame yourself for?" Brandon asked tauntingly.

"You prick," Hank yelled back at him as she walked out of the house.

"Can't pick your relatives," Brandon muttered loud enough for Hank to hear.

"Unfortunately," Hank responded, red-faced.

* * *

Hank got back in her car and fell apart, shaking from head to toe. She couldn't believe she let things escalate like that, get completely out of control. *How can I tell Vito Brandon caught me snooping around and that it all went to shit?* she asked herself. And then Hank remembered that Vito was just half a block up the road, waiting for her. *Fuck,* she thought. Hank flashed her headlights, and Vito responded in kind.

Then a text came in on her phone. *Follow me to the diner. V.* Hank waited for him to drive away and then started her car. *Fucking shit-show of an afternoon,* she contemplated.

When they arrived at the diner, Xanthe seated the pair at a booth in the back, and they settled in for what would undoubtedly be an unpleasant conversation, at least from Hank's point of view. As much as she dreaded telling him, Vito needed to know what had transpired between her and her brother. Bracing herself for Vito's disapproval, Hank got right to the point.

"It got all fucked up. He…um…Brandon, well, he caught me going through his things…his books," Hank began to explain.

"Jesus, Hank, what were you thinking?" Vito asked, exasperated.

"Let me finish, please, Vito. He left me alone…I thought it would be my only chance to find something…get somewhere…else what was the point of me going over there…to his house?" Hank asked, bewildered.

"I get that, Hank, but you need to be more careful. Look what we're dealing with here…a total psycho," Vito answered, concerned.

"That doesn't matter, Vito, listen. I found the documents, the ones my dad mentioned in his letter," Hank said, revealing what had happened at Brandon's.

"Now we're getting somewhere," Vito answered, hopefully.

"Not really," Hank began. "He took them away from me. We had a big fight. He called me *sis*. We had it out," Hank continued.

"So he knows everything, right? Damn," Vito declared.

"Yes, he knows everything," Hank answered.

"What about my gun? Cary's wallet?" Vito asked, afraid to hear the answer.

"Oh my God, you can't believe what he pulled," Hank said, forget-ting the most important part. "When I brought it up, he had the nerve to show me *his* wallet and *his* gun and tell me my dad…our dad was losing it," Hank said, frustrated.

"Goddamn son of a bitch. How the fuck are we ever gonna catch this guy?" Vito inquired, at his wits end.

"There's one more thing, Vito. As I was leaving, he...well, he sort of threatened me, warned me that I shouldn't want anything else on my conscience. That I should leave well enough alone," Hank expounded.

"All right, look. He's gonna have his guard up at least for the time being because he knows we suspect him of killing Cary and driving your dad to...well to do what he did," Vito added uncomfortably. "But that doesn't mean we're giving up. Can't give into his threats... demands...or God knows what will happen."

"Vito, I have a really bad feeling about all of this. He's crazy but smart. And he's out for blood. The way he looked at me...with such disdain.... What are we going to do?" Hank asked despondently.

"Don't you worry," Vito began. "We'll get him...for Cary and all the others. He'll mess up. Like I've said before, they always do."

* * *

Hank returned home exhausted and depressed. Barry greeted her at the door, and she took him outside for a quick walk. After feeding her loyal friend, Hank jumped in the shower, then dried her hair and curled up on the couch. It was nearly dinnertime, but she wasn't hungry. Barry finished his supper and joined Hank, snuggling beside her. Hank looked around the room and was overcome with sadness. Since Cary was killed, she had had almost no time to herself. It had been a whirlwind of craziness, the latest being her dad's suicide and the discovery that Brandon was her long-lost brother. Then there was the revelation that her mother had done the same thing: taken her own life. What Hank wouldn't have given to have Cary back, to have her old life back, before all these terrible things had happened. And there was one person to blame for all of it: Brandon.

Hank's thoughts were interrupted by a text tone. Looking down at her phone, she read the following: *Might be a good idea for you to check up on Dr. Gayle. B.* Upon reading the message, Hank nearly dropped her cell. Without thinking, she called Brandon. He picked up instantly.

"Yes?" Brandon asked, answering the call.

"What is that text supposed to mean? What the hell?" Hank yelled through the phone.

"You can play it safe, or you can play it sorry," Brandon responded and hung up.

"Shit," Hank whispered under her breath.

She jumped off the couch, got dressed, grabbed her keys, and headed for Gayle's. As Hank raced across town, she realized she wasn't entirely sure where Gayle was staying these days, if she had moved back home. So Hank tried reaching Cary's sister, but the call went straight to voicemail. The next person Hank called was Vito. When he answered, Hank sounded hysterical.

"You all right? What's up?" Vito asked in a worried tone.

"Where are you?" Hank inquired.

"Out, Anna and I were just about to grab a bite," Vito answered.

"Brandon's after Gayle," Hank blurted out. "Do you know where she's living? Is she still at the condo or the house?"

"She's back home now...has been for about a week or so not exactly sure maybe less...sorry if I forgot to mention it with everything that's been going on," Vito said apologetically.

"Go home...now...I'll meet you there...Gayle's in trouble. Vito hurry," Hank yelled through her cell.

"I'm on it," Vito said and ended the call.

Hank thought it was a miracle that she didn't have an accident on the way to Gayle's. She had driven well over the speed limit the entire way. When she got there, Hank decided to leave her car out front on the street and then stealthily make her way toward the house. Vito's car was nowhere in sight, so Hank figured he had obeyed the law better than she had. Hank creeped up the driveway slowly, looking around for any sign of Brandon. As she made her way to the back of the house, Hank was terrified at the thought of what she might find inside.

Hank took out her gun and released the safety. She had muted her phone as a precaution, but as Hank got closer to the side door her cell began to vibrate. Checking the incoming text, she saw it was from Vito. *We're here, Anna will stay in the car,* it read. Hank texted back: *I'm almost at the side door...meet me...I'll wait.* It only took a minute before Vito was right behind her. He touched Hank on the shoulder and nodded toward the window by the side of the door. They crouched below the glass and looked inside. Gayle was standing by the stove making herself something to eat. Hank stuck her gun back between her jeans and back and turned to Vito.

"What the fuck is going on?" she asked, infuriated.

"Afraid he's having a good laugh at our expense," Vito answered, relieved.

"Should we go in?" Hank asked, unsure of their next move.

"Gayle needs to know about this, but I don't think she's in any real danger. Not yet, anyway. Let's hold off...don't wanna scare her until we have to. That goddamn sick son of a bitch," Vito added.

As they walked away from Gayle's house and toward their vehicles, Hank tripped on a small branch about five feet from where they had been standing. It was sticking up at an odd angle. Hank bent down to pick the stick up and toss it into the bushes when she noticed something stuck to it: an "Odd Jobs" card.

"Vito, look," Hank said, pointing to the ground.

Vito extended his arm and removed the card from the tip of the branch. He flipped it over to see what, if anything, might be on the back of it this time, but the other side was blank.

"That bastard believes we have nothing to tie him to the murders...to prove that he's the 'Deer Killer' so pulling a stunt like this...well, he thinks can't hurt him," Vito concluded.

"What do we do next, Vito? We need to tell O'Malley about this. I'll call him when I get home. But Brandon always seems to be one step ahead. We'll never find Cary's wallet...your gun...what else can we do?" Hank asked desperately.

"Wait...wait for your brother to hang himself," Vito answered flatly.

* * *

Brandon had ordered a pizza from Pepe's for dinner. He felt like celebrating, so he washed it down with one of his most expensive bottles of wine. *If only I could have been a fly on the wall when Hank got to Gayle's,* Brandon pondered. He had spent the better part of the evening picturing her reaction when she saw that her would-be sister-in-law was just fine. Brandon's main concern was whether or not Hank had found the card. He would likely know soon enough. Brandon waited patiently, expecting a call or at least a text from his sister, questioning his motives, but a message never came. Clearly, Hank had decided to play her cards differently this time.

Brandon lay in bed contemplating why the average victim thought they could talk their way out of their destiny: being murdered. As if anyone could reason with—much less win an argument with—a narcissistic madman. How boring and predictable. He wondered if his sister would step it up, take it like a man. Brandon didn't think his antics tonight should count toward his total number of victims, after all no harm had come to Cary's sister. But he had used up another card. So in the interest of playing fair, Brandon decided he had one card left and, therefore, one more murder to commit. He would have to choose wisely.

NINETEEN

It was late by the time Hank got home, so she decided there was no point in waking O'Malley up in the middle of the night over something that had turned out to be a false alarm. Hank took tonight's stunt as some kind of a warning, a heads-up that there would be more to come. Brandon had one card left to play, literally. Therefore, what worried Hank the most was who would be his next victim.

* * *

The first thing Hank did when she woke up the following morning was to check the time. It was approaching 8:00 a.m. Hank had forgotten to set the alarm and slept longer than she had expected. Barry lay at the foot of the bed, sound asleep. Hank supposed they had both needed the rest. She decided to try O'Malley right away, but the call went straight to voicemail. *You have reached Sergeant Joseph O'Malley. Please leave a message.* Hank hung up immediately. She needed to think. So Hank took Barry out for a quick run, then jumped in the shower and got dressed. She thought it would be better to deliver the news in person. Hank grabbed a yogurt from the fridge and headed for her car.

As Hank drove to Stamford to tell the sergeant what happened last night, her nerves were frayed. The police weren't getting anywhere: the investigation was stalling out. They needed to come up with another plan, to strategize. Hank would fill O'Malley in on everything. She realized he didn't even know about her meeting with Brandon and that her brother had accessed her phone. Hank didn't think O'Malley would be impressed by her sloppiness—both at the diner and at Brandon's house. She braced herself for a verbal beating.

Upon arriving at the station, Hank parked in her usual spot and took the elevator to the lobby. When she got to the sergeant's office, the door was closed, so she knocked. O'Malley opened it and invited Hank inside.

"What are you doing here at this hour?" O'Malley asked her. "I thought..." he continued.

"Joe, there's something I've got to tell you. Actually, there are a few things you need to know," Hank began.

"Sit down, Hank. I'm all ears," O'Malley responded.

As Hank settled into her chair, she decided it was best to start from the beginning.

"Afraid I've done a couple of stupid things that you're not going to like," Hank said, beginning to explain.

"Exactly how stupid?" the sergeant asked.

"Pretty fucking stupid," Hank answered, embarrassed.

"Go on," O'Malley nudged her.

"Well, Vito and I sort of came up with this plan for me to meet with Brandon. Actually, he reached out to me, but we...well, Vito thought it might not be such a bad idea if I went along with it and met him. So we did...at the diner. But I got sick...couldn't handle it...left my phone on the table," Hank continued.

"Jesus, Hank. What were you thinking?" O'Malley reprimanded her.

"Guess I wasn't. He...Brandon looked through my phone...saw the screenshots of my dad's suicide note. He found out we...I know about him. And he knows what my father did...killed himself and told me everything in the letter," Hank went on, rambling a bit incoherently.

"What else, Hank. I need to know everything," O'Malley said sternly.

"We cut the lunch short because I wasn't feeling well and rescheduled for the following day. He wanted me to meet him at his house. So Vito met me there in case things went south," Hank continued.

"And?" O'Malley asked, getting impatient.

"And when Brandon left me alone, I started going through his things, his books, and I found the documents my father referred to in his letter. But..." Hank said, fearing O'Malley's reaction to what she would say next.

"But, what?" the sergeant queried.

"But he caught me. We had a fight, a big one. He called me sis...laid his cards on the table. I didn't mean for things to get so out of hand. It just went to shit quickly," Hank said, trying to defend her actions.

"So where does that leave us?" O'Malley asked, pissed.

"Not sure, we need to figure out another way to catch him. We'll never find the gun, we'll never find Cary's wallet either, but there's something else, Joe. It's the main reason I came down here this morning. Felt it needed to be delivered in person. Last night, Brandon texted me. He said to go check on Gayle. I asked Vito to meet me there...at the house...but when we got there everything was fine. She was in the kitchen, oblivious," Hank declared.

Then she paused for a second before revealing the following.

"One more thing, Joe. We found this stuck to a branch on the ground," Hank said, handing the latest "Odd Jobs" card to the sergeant.

"What the fuck, Hank? Jesus Christ. What the hell is next?" O'Malley asked, exasperated.

"Look, Joe, Brandon gave my dad three cards. Now there's only one left. I think he's going to do something really crazy—and soon," Hank added.

"You can count on it," O'Malley answered, infuriated.

* * *

Brandon woke up with his mind racing in all directions. He still hadn't heard from Hank. Clearly, she was giving him the silent treatment.

Brandon got out of bed, clad only in his underwear, and went straight to the kitchen to make himself a shake. He took the tall glass to his study, where he situated himself in front of the row of computer screens. But today, there would be nothing remarkable to monitor. Of that, Brandon was sure. However, he had no doubt that the police, led by Detective Hank and Sergeant O'Malley, were scheming, with Vito's help, of course.

Then Brandon had a thought. Before he made his next move—that is, kill again—there were a few loose ends he needed to take care of. The authorities would be closing in on him, watching his every move, hoping to catch him through an unforced error. Brandon decided he had to dispose of Cary's wallet and the gun once and for all. He couldn't leave the incriminating items buried on his property. And then, there was Nicole, the model he had had no choice but to eliminate. *One thing at a time,* he told himself. Brandon would make his move tonight.

*** * ***

Brandon waited until it was well after dark and changed into a pair of black sweats. Somehow that struck him as an appropriate outfit to wear for the task at hand. Brandon made himself a cheese sandwich, ate it quickly, and grabbed a frozen Snickers bar from the freezer. He stuffed it into his pocket. Digging was hard work; he would need his energy. Taking every foreseeable precaution, Brandon made his way to the shed near the cabin to collect a shovel and the other supplies he would need to dispose of the evidence. Then he made his way to his favorite tree adjacent to the spot where the items were buried.

Brandon arrived at his destination at exactly 10:00 p.m. He found the rock that marked the spot where he had hidden Cary's wallet and Vito's gun and began to dig. After approximately ten minutes, the shovel hit an object. Brandon dropped the tool, lowered himself onto the ground, and reached down into the hole, brushing the dirt aside with his hands. He grabbed the wallet and gun and stood up. The bag he had buried them in had more or less disintegrated. While Brandon thought he could just burn the objects in his fireplace, there was still the issue of Nicole to take care of. He saw no point in making two trips. So Brandon picked up the shovel, wallet, and gun and walked to his next stop.

Brandon hadn't visited Nicole in several years. But he remembered the precise location where he had left her body. Unearthing the ambitious model's remains would undoubtedly be grisly work, but he couldn't exactly delegate the job. He had never been the squeamish type, *so might as well get on with it,* he told himself. When Brandon reached the area where he had disposed of Nicole's body, he began to scoop the earth frenetically. He expected a putrid smell to emanate from the ground, but as he looked down into the hole, all that was visible were bones. *That works,* he pondered.

Brandon had the foresight to bring several large plastic bags with him for the occasion, as well as a pair of latex gloves. He proceeded to place the unfortunate girl's remains into the bags and then tied the ends into a knot. Taking stock of his surroundings, Brandon decided that he would have to make two trips after all. So he began with Nicole. There was an incinerator near the cabin that would work nicely to eliminate the skeleton. Then he would go get the other items. Before long, everything that could come back to haunt him would be consumed by flames.

Once Nicole, the wallet, and the gun were disposed of, Brandon took off his gloves and fed them to the fire. *Can never be too careful,* he told himself. Then he had a revelation: Caity's things were still buried underground next to where Cary's wallet and Vito's gun had been. *Shit. I'm getting old.* So Brandon made one more trip to dispose of the remaining evidence. Then he returned the shovel to the shed near the cabin and went back to the house. Brandon rewarded himself with a glass of his best scotch and curled up on the couch in front of the fireplace. He had one more task to take care of: selecting his next victim.

* * *

Hank spent the better part of the evening in front of a muted television, thinking. She was convinced there had to be other incidents in Brandon's past that no one had ever found out about—not necessarily another murder, but something. Hank remembered the scene in *Ozark* where Esai Morales asks what should happen to a female employee who is caught stealing. Jason Bateman provides him with the correct answer: fire her, because it isn't the first time she stole; it's the first time she got caught. Hank would have to do some digging, look into Brandon's past.

Hank knew she wasn't going to be able to sleep tonight, so she took out her laptop and started researching missing person cases in Connecticut over the past two years. Although several popped up, none involved a female victim. If there was one thing Hank was certain of it was that Brandon only killed women and the occasional animal.

Hank expanded her search to include cold cases from the last five years. A more promising set of results came up. One missing woman, in particular, caught her eye: a model named Nicole Schmidt. The twenty-three-year-old woman had vanished four years ago. Nicole was last seen alive at a gas station in Fairview, filling her car. Security footage from the Mobil station documented her last known location. Hank clicked on the Images icon, and several photos of the young woman filled the screen. Some were candid pictures from Instagram and Facebook, while others appeared to be professional modeling pictures. Nicole was beautiful. Hank wondered whether she was still alive and what might have happened to her.

Hank needed to find out exactly where Nicole had been living at the time of her disappearance. So, although the hour was late, she picked up the phone and called Vito.

"Hank," he answered, groggily. "What's up? It's late."

"Sorry to bother you at this hour, but I need to find out about a woman—friends, job, last-known address. Can you help me?" Hank asked urgently.

"Can't it wait till the morning? I'll do it first thing, promise," Vito assured her.

Although Hank was anxious to get the answers, she figured there really wasn't much Vito could accomplish in the middle of the night. So she acquiesced to his request.

"Sure, Vito, sorry, I shouldn't have woken you up. The morning's fine. Her name is Nicole Schmidt. She went missing about four years ago, right in this area. I have a hunch..." Hank continued.

Vito knew instinctively that Hank thought there might be a connection between the young woman and her brother. He hoped her theory wouldn't turn out to be a bust.

"Hank, we have no idea what happened to this girl. She might have just moved...been on drugs...who knows. Don't be disappointed if this turns out to be a dead end...a stretch. But I'll look into it and let you know as soon as I find out anything," Vito declared.

"Thanks, Vito. Maybe I'll actually be able to get some sleep now," Hank said warmly.

"You do that," Vito answered. "We're both gonna need it."

* * *

Brandon had had an exhausting evening covering his tracks. So he had slept well and was ready to face the day. Brandon was a creature of habit, so he stuck with his usual routine and began the morning with a run. He could feel the adrenaline coursing through his body as he jogged along the path that ran parallel to the sound. Brandon found the smell of the water invigorating. Tonight, he would decide on his next move: that is, choose a victim. The thought of holding another person's life in his hands excited him.

When Brandon got home, he made himself a shake and jumped in the shower. Reflecting on his actions last night, he decided he had covered all his bases. There was nothing left to tie him to the local killing spree, nor specifically to the deaths of Cary, the girl from the hospital, and Caity. The "Odd Jobs" cards he had left at Cary's funeral and Gayle's house, as well as the one his father had so cooperatively deposited at Devil's Den, only proved there was a homicidal maniac on the loose. The authorities still couldn't pin even one of the murders on him. *This is too easy,* Brandon concluded.

For a moment, Brandon considered texting his sister. He hadn't heard from Hank since he tricked her into believing he was going to harm Gayle. *Wonder what she's up to?* he contemplated. However, Brandon decided it was best not to stir the pot, at least not until he committed his next murder. Because this one really mattered: it was his final *F U* to Hank and his father, albeit posthumously.

* * *

Vito woke up early, cognizant of the heavy burden he now carried, courtesy of Hank's suspicions. If they could find a connection between the missing young woman Hank had stumbled upon during her web search last night and Brandon, they might be able to trap him. Nicole Schmidt was their only hope at the moment of potentially discovering something sinister in Brandon's past that they could use to take him down. Vito snuck out of bed, careful not to disturb Anna. He washed up, got dressed, and headed to his car, but not before leaving Anna a note. *There's something I gotta take care of. Call ya later. V.*

Vito took his tablet with him so he could poke around and see what, if anything, he might find out about Nicole. He drove to the local donut and coffee shop and picked up a strong cup of black coffee and two chocolate glazed pastries. *Caffeine and sugar should help,* Vito told himself. The private detective in him decided he needed privacy, so instead of grabbing a seat inside, Vito opted to get his sustenance to go and work from his car. So he drove a couple of miles up the road and parked along the street across from the beach. He'd be able to think there.

Vito's initial search of Nicole mainly brought up articles of her disappearance. The twenty-three-year-old woman was an aspiring model who Vito assumed probably took random jobs to support herself while she chased her dreams. He would have to run a full background check on her to see where she might have worked. But for now, Vito's priority was to find out where Nicole was living at the time of her disappearance and the names of her parents or friends. He wondered if the average person had any clue how easy it was to find out personal information about them.

But Vito didn't need to be crafty to locate Nicole's parents; their names and the state they resided in were in the first article he found. Helen and Robert Schmidt lived in a small town in Wyoming; they were forty-nine and fifty-five, respectively. Nicole's best friend was also from her hometown out West: Bonnie Holton. Vito wasn't sure he would even need to track them down, but at least he was making progress.

Although Nicole Schmidt was referred to in the articles as a local girl, none of them mentioned her address, just that she had been living in Fairview County at the time she went missing. Nicole's driver's license, which Vito had no difficulty accessing, only had her Wyoming address on it. So he had a thought. Vito knew that what Hank really wanted to find out was whether Nicole could have been one of the girls who had rented Brandon's cottage. That meant the next step was to track down the real estate agent who helped Brandon get his tenants.

Vito's next Google search brought up the top three real estate agents in Fairview County, only one of whom was a woman: Antoinette "Toni" Moretti. His gut told him to start with her. Vito looked up the phone number of the agency Moretti worked for and picked up his phone. When the receptionist answered, Vito asked to speak to the woman he hoped could provide him with some answers.

"I'm sorry, but she's not in the office at the moment," the woman on the other end informed Vito.

"When will Ms. Moretti be returning?" Vito asked, trying to sound casual.

"Not sure, but I can give you her cell number. Feel free to try her while she's out and about. I'm sure she'll get back to you as soon as she can," the girl assured Vito.

So he wrote down Moretti's phone number and punched in the digits, but the call went straight to voicemail. So Vito left the following message: *Vito Loggia calling. I need to talk to you about something. Hope to hear from you soon.* If they were lucky, Moretti could turn out to be the big break they'd been looking for.

As Vito was debating whether or not to fill Hank in on his progress so far, his phone rang. It was Hank. Vito picked up immediately.

"Hey, beautiful," he began.

"Any news?" Hank asked hopefully.

"Sort of. Actually, I was just about to call you," Vito said. "I got the names of the parents...Nicole's...and her best friend. They were mentioned in one of the articles. She hails from Wyoming. Not sure we'll need to track them down. Guess it depends on whether we hit pay dirt with something I'm working on," Vito explained.

"Working on?" Hank asked curiously. "Working on what, exactly?"

"Didn't wanna get your hopes up. Nicole's driver's license still has her Wyoming address," Vito began. "But it dawned on me that if we can figure out who the real estate agent is that rents out Brandon's cottage, we just might be able to finally get somewhere."

"Vito, you're a genius," Hank stated ecstatically.

"Well, I wouldn't go quite that far, but..." Vito said modestly, as he started to respond. "Hold on, Hank. I'm getting another call. I'll get right back to you."

Vito touched the circle that gave him the option to end the call with Hank and connect with the next.

"Hello, Vito Loggia. How can I help you?" he answered.

"Toni Moretti here, returning your call," the real estate agent said matter-of-factly.

Fuck yeah, Vito thought to himself.

"Thanks for getting back to me," Vito said cordially. "I need to ask you something. Think we could meet up?" he asked bluntly. Then, deciding to come clean, Vito added, "I'm a private investigator."

Moretti was somewhat taken aback by Vito's admission, but the words private investigator also intrigued the real estate agent. So she promptly agreed to the meeting.

"You busy this afternoon?" Vito inquired. "How's three o'clock at the diner?"

"Yes, that will work," Moretti answered. "How will I recognize you?"

"Don't worry, I'll find you," Vito responded cagily and ended the call.

As Vito sat in his car, he remembered that he had promised Hank that he would call her right back. So he did just that. Hank picked up after one ring.

"Vito? What's up?" Hank asked.

"I set up a meeting with an agent for this afternoon, Toni Moretti," Vito began to explain. "Have a good feeling about her. Maybe...if we get really lucky..." he continued.

"Oh, Vito, we've gotta catch a break. If Nicole..." Hank began, about to expound on her theory.

"Look, Hank, I know what you're thinking. But this could turn out to be another dead end. I'd temper your expectations. But yes, our guts are telling us we just may be on to something here," Vito said conclusively.

"What are the odds, I mean," Hank said, "that a girl goes missing right in this area and Brandon's not involved?"

"I agree, it's suspicious. We'll just have to see what this lady says, assuming I can get her to say anything," Vito laughed.

"Call me as soon as you're finished with her," Hank declared and hung up.

* * *

As Vito drove to the diner to meet with Moretti, he tried to decide the best way to approach her. In preparation for the encounter, Vito printed out the clearest picture of Nicole Schmidt he was able to find on the internet. If all went well, hopefully, the agent would recognize the young woman. But that assumed she even knew her. When Vito arrived at the diner, he parked in the rear of the lot and paused for a moment to collect his thoughts. *Please, please, please,* he muttered to himself. *We need a goddamn break.*

Vito got out of his car clutching the manila envelope that held Nicole's picture and walked toward the entrance. He kept a lookout for Moretti. Vito already knew what she looked like from the website of the agency she worked for. Each agent had their photo prominently displayed on the page. Vito guessed Moretti was in her early sixties by now but used an outdated image of herself on the site. *Deception was the mainstay of websites and dating apps,* Vito concluded.

As Vito waited in the foyer of the restaurant, he spotted Moretti through the glass door, getting out of her car. She drove a white BMW, the go-to car of choice for many real estate types. When Moretti got inside, Vito greeted her with a forced smile.

"Ms. Moretti? I'm Vito...Vito Loggia. Glad to meet ya," he said in a friendly tone.

"The pleasure is all mine," Moretti answered flirtatiously.

Although seeing the woman up close confirmed Vito's suspicion that Moretti was using an older photo of herself on the web, he had been wrong about her appearance in general. If Moretti was indeed in her sixties, she looked pretty damn good for her age.

"How 'bout we grab a booth in the back, so we'll have some privacy, Ms. Moretti," Vito suggested.

"Please, call me Toni," she answered.

"Toni," Vito said obediently.

Xanthe came over to the duo and escorted them to their table. She handed them a couple of menus and gave Vito a suspicious look.

"Thanks, Xanthe," Vito began. "We'll let you know when we're ready to order."

Xanthe got the hint and walked away.

"So Vito...I can call you Vito, right?" Moretti asked, knowing the answer.

"Sure, of course," Vito responded.

"So what do you want with me?" Moretti inquired.

"Let's get some coffee first, then we can talk. Sound good?" Vito suggested.

He motioned to Xanthe to bring them two cups and turned his attention to the woman sitting across the booth from him. She was striking. Vito hadn't been expecting that. *Focus,* he told himself.

"Not sure where to begin," Vito said hesitantly. "Guess you've heard about the murders...well, unusual bunch of deaths around here recently."

"I don't live in a cave," Moretti retorted.

"Well, see we're looking into old cases...trying to find a link, something that could lead us to the killer," Vito explained.

"So how do I come into the picture?" Moretti asked.

Vito didn't want to give too much away and let Moretti know that they suspected Brandon. He had to choose his words carefully.

"There's a girl...a young woman, twenty-three years old, who went missing in this area around three, actually four years ago," Vito said. "We're trying to find out where she lived at the time of her disappearance. So figured who better to ask than a real estate agent," Vito said, blushing slightly.

Toni Moretti's mere presence was rattling Vito. He was surprised at the effect she was having on him. But Vito had come here to do a job, and he wouldn't leave until he got an answer. So he took out the photo he had brought with him and laid it on the table.

"Nicole Schmidt, an aspiring model...last seen at a gas station in Fairview. No one's heard from her since," Vito declared.

Moretti studied the image in front of her but said nothing. However, Vito, ever so perceptive, couldn't help but notice the immediate change in Moretti's expression the second she saw the photo. You didn't need to be a body language expert to see that the picture elicited an involuntary response from the woman.

"Recognize her?" Vito prodded.

"I can't say that I do," Moretti began, also choosing her words carefully. "No, don't think I've ever seen her. Sorry."

Vito's gut told him she was lying. But he had no proof.

"Please, look carefully. It's important," Vito added.

Moretti paused, then checked her watch.

"My God, look at the time. You'll have to excuse me. I've got a house to show across town. Can't be late," Moretti stated.

Vito picked up the photograph and gulped down the rest of his coffee.

"Here's my card. If you remember anything, give me a call. People's lives are at stake," Vito said, emphasizing the importance of the matter.

"Certainly. It was a pleasure to meet you, Mr. Loggia, I mean Vito," Moretti said and left abruptly.

Vito went to the cashier to pay, then headed to his car, frustrated by the lack of progress he had been hoping for. *What is she hiding, afraid of?* Vito asked himself. He had to report back to Hank, but she would be as disappointed as he was. Still, there had to be another way. Vito got into his car, picked up his phone, and called Hank.

"Vito? What happened? Tell me," Hank said excitedly.

"I'd bring it down a notch, detective. She didn't say anything... recognize her...but I'd bet my bottom dollar she was lying," Vito concluded.

"What makes you think that?" Hank asked hopefully.

"Don't know...just a feeling. As soon as she saw the picture, there was a visceral reaction she couldn't hide. She's lying, I know it," Vito repeated.

"So what do we do now?" Hank asked.

"Keep an eye on Brandon. Like white on rice," Vito declared.

TWENTY

Toni Moretti drove away from the diner and went straight home. The appointment she had used as an excuse to leave was a lie, just like her answer. Moretti had recognized Nicole Schmidt immediately from the photograph. She remembered the day she brought the young woman to Brandon's estate to check out the cottage. Moretti could still see the expression on Brandon's face when he met Nicole. It was a combination of contempt and lust. She had sensed an instant attraction between the two.

Moretti also remembered the day Nicole Schmidt went missing. Like most unsolved cases, however, news of the girl fizzled, and the real estate agent put it out of her head. Looking back, Moretti decided at the time Brandon was more concerned about finding a new tenant than about Nicole's well-being. Truth be told, Moretti had never been able to warm up to Brandon, but he was a good, reliable, steady client, so she decided his personal affairs were none of her business.

The dilemma Moretti now found herself in had to be dealt with. She had lied to a private investigator who had ties to and was likely working with law enforcement. But for whatever reason, Moretti felt it incumbent upon herself to give Brandon a heads-up that officials were reopening Nicole's case. So she picked up her phone and called Brandon's cell. The call went to voicemail. *Brandon, it's Toni Moretti. I need to speak with you.* That was as detailed a message as Moretti felt comfortable leaving. Within a minute, a text popped up on her phone. It was, of course, from Brandon. *Did you just call?* he asked. *Try again.*

Moretti knew asking her to call back instead of returning the call himself was Brandon's way of taking control. But she'd let it go.

"Toni, what an unexpected pleasure," Brandon said, as he answered the phone. "How are you? It's been ages."

Moretti took Brandon's last three words as an underhanded dig at the fact she never contacted him after Cary was killed.

"I'm good. Been meaning to send my condolences about what happened to Cary Mackin," Moretti said, trying to get ahead of the situation. "But I decided you'd reach out when you were ready.... I mean, if you needed to find a new tenant," Moretti added thoughtlessly.

Typical fucking real estate agent, Brandon contemplated, *always putting business above everything else, including an apparent murder. What about my feelings?*

"I'm good for the time being. Replacing Cary so soon would appear callous, don't you think?" Brandon asked, putting Moretti on the spot.

"Yes, certainly, I didn't mean..." she began.

"No worries," Brandon answered, taking the high road. "So what did you call me about?"

"A man contacted me...a private investigator. He's looking into Nicole Schmidt's disappearance, snooping around. I just thought you should know," Moretti explained.

"What did he say, want, exactly?" Brandon asked.

"Don't worry, I didn't tell him anything. He showed me a picture of Nicole, but I wasn't sure what to do, so I said I didn't recognize her. Not sure why I wasn't honest with him. Guess I thought, in all fairness, it would be better if you knew about it first, seeing as she was living on your property at the time," Moretti added. "They're trying to connect other unsolved cases to what's been going on...to see if they can catch the killer by finding more women who've gone missing in the area."

Brandon had to think fast. He couldn't risk raising any red flags or saying something that would make Moretti suspicious. But it could be problematic if the authorities reopened the case.

"Nicole Schmidt's disappearance is a tragedy," Brandon began. "Such a shame a beautiful young woman like that could simply vanish without a trace. However, this has nothing to do with me. But I appreciate your discretion, Toni. Um, just out of curiosity do you remember the name of the private eye who contacted you?"

"Vito. I believe his last name is Loggia," Moretti answered curtly.

Brandon wasn't surprised that the mysterious man turned out to be Vito, but he didn't feel comfortable saying anything more over the phone. Brandon needed to speak to Moretti privately and in person to make sure she wouldn't change her mind and tell Vito the truth: that Nicole had been his tenant at the time of her disappearance. So what better way to lure a real estate agent to his home than the promise of future business?

"Toni, why don't you come over tonight for dinner? I think I just might be ready to rent out the cottage again after all. Have to get on with life," Brandon said duplicitously.

"Sure, that sounds like a great idea. What time were you thinking?" Moretti asked.

"Make it 7:00 p.m. sharp," Brandon answered. "You still like steak, right?"

"You have a good memory, Brandon. See you then," Moretti answered and hung up the phone.

* * *

Hank volunteered to take the first watch, so she filled a thermos with her favorite cappuccino and made a couple of avocado and cheese sandwiches, the kind that Cary had been so fond of, to take with her. It would be a long night. Hank didn't know for sure where Brandon was at the moment. The time was coming up on six o'clock, so she figured odds were, he was home, probably having dinner. But even if

Hank had guessed wrong, it still made sense for her to head over to Brandon's and begin her surveillance there. After all, he would have to return home sooner or later.

Hank drove to Brandon's estate and parked her car on the side of the road and as far off the pavement as possible. It was already dark, so she didn't think she would be spotted in the brush. Hank unscrewed the top of the thermos and savored the aroma of the coffee. She drank half of the contents and then replaced the lid. Hank was already starving, so she took out one of the sandwiches and devoured it. Hank washed the food down with a bottle of water she kept in the cupholder of her car and tilted her seat back slightly. She took a pair of binoculars out of the glove compartment and stared straight ahead, ever vigilant.

At exactly 6:20 p.m., Hank noticed the headlights of a car exiting the main entrance of Brandon's property. Looking through the lens, she saw that it was Brandon driving the vehicle. Hank put her seat back in its upright position, waited thirty seconds, and then started her car. She managed to keep her distance while never losing sight of him. In ten minutes, Hank found herself in front of a liquor store. Brandon went into the building. He appeared to be in a hurry. A few minutes later, Brandon left the shop carrying a large brown bag. He drove off, with, unbeknownst to him, Hank following closely behind.

They arrived back at Brandon's residence around 6:45 p.m. Hank slowed down as they turned onto Brandon's street and waited for him to pull into the driveway. Then she parked her car where it had been before. Hank thought nothing of the errand Brandon had just run. *If anyone needed a good stiff drink these days, it was Brandon,* she told herself. Hank surveyed the house, as Brandon turned on the kitchen lights. She saw smoke coming out of the chimney. It was a chilly night, so it didn't surprise Hank that her brother would opt for alcohol and a lit fireplace.

The time was now 7:00 p.m., and Hank was already getting restless. Vito was supposed to relieve her at midnight, but that was still five hours away. *Spying was tedious work,* Hank reflected. *Stalkers must have the patience of a saint,* she joked to herself. Just as boredom was setting in, Hank spotted a car heading to the gate of Brandon's home. The doors opened, and the car drove up the driveway and parked near the front entryway. A woman got out of the white BMW and walked up the stairs to the front door. Hank looked through the binoculars to get a better view of the face.

Hank didn't recognize the woman, but as she looked through the lens, she had a thought. She picked up her phone and typed in the name Toni Moretti and the words real estate. Moretti's picture popped up immediately. Hank looked closely at the image on her cell and then back through the binoculars at the woman waiting at the front door. They were one and the same. "Holy shit," Hank uttered. She continued to hold her phone in one hand and the binoculars in the other. As she did so, Brandon answered the door and invited Moretti inside. Then they went out of view.

Hank called Vito immediately.

"Hank? What's up? How's it going? Where the hell are you?" Vito asked.

"I'm right outside Brandon's house. You'll never guess who just showed up. Toni Moretti," Hank declared, waiting for Vito's reaction.

"Okay, that's good. Stay on them. Don't let those two go anywhere. I'm on my way," Vito announced.

"Vito, I don't think we need an entourage out here," Hank said in a worried tone.

"Just wait for me. I'll park my car a block or so away and meet you. Stay put. We'll keep an eye on them together. Shoulda just gone with you, but I'll be there as soon as I can," Vito said in an urgent voice.

"Got it. I'm by the side of the road," Hank instructed him.

"Don't you worry. I'll find you," Vito answered and hung up the phone.

* * *

As Brandon was preparing dinner, he realized he had forgotten to pick up wine of all things for his prey. While he had plenty of expensive bottles in the cellar, he saw no reason to waste them on a real estate agent. So after checking on the roasted potatoes and breaded cauliflower in the oven, he made a mad dash to the liquor store. Boxed wine would have sufficed for an evening such as this, but Brandon decided that would be a low blow. So he purchased a screw-top variety instead.

When Brandon returned home, he took the steaks out of the fridge and threw them in a frying pan. He had decided to try a new recipe tonight. Brandon had to keep close tabs on Moretti now that she had been dragged into the Nicole Schmidt mess courtesy of Vito. He didn't think the woman was the least bit suspicious of him, but better to be safe than sorry. Brandon had to gain her trust and have a handle on whether or not she would change her mind, tell Vito the truth, and betray him.

The buzzer rang at precisely 7:01 p.m. Brandon wiped his hands on his apron and pressed the button on the intercom. After hearing Toni's voice on the other end, he opened the gate and instructed her to park at the top of the driveway. When Brandon got to the front door, he greeted Moretti with a smile and a warm hello. Then he brought her inside. It had been a while since the real estate agent had set foot in Brandon's house. Cary was the last tenant she had procured for him, and it had already been several years since she had moved in. Consequently, Brandon had had no contact with Moretti during that time.

"Here, let me take your coat," Brandon offered. "Let's go to the den. Dinner will be ready in a bit."

Moretti took off her jacket and handed it to Brandon. As they entered the den, she looked around the room and decided nothing had changed. Everything was as she remembered it. Brandon, as she had expected, had lit a fire in the fireplace. The setting was inviting.

"I always loved this room," Moretti commented.

"Why, thank you. It's my sanctuary from the world, as you already know," Brandon responded.

"Are you sure you're ready to rent out the cottage again?" Moretti asked, getting down to business.

Brandon was a bit taken aback by her bluntness, but he had to play along, give her a carrot.

"Well, Toni," he began. "I honestly don't see a reason to put it off any longer. The police have done their job, and Cary's family and friends already cleared the place out. I think it's time."

"Okay, great. Anyone in particular you're looking for? I mean, what type of person do you think I should try to find this time around?" Moretti asked deferentially.

"You know what, hold that thought. Better check on the steaks. Back in a few," Brandon said and left the room.

As Moretti glanced around the den, she noticed a bottle of wine and two glasses on a table in the corner. Brandon must have forgotten to offer her a drink. She assumed his mind was on more important things. The next thing that caught Moretti's eye was the bookcase. It was filled with hundreds of hardcover works, just as she recollected. Moretti walked to the first shelf and browsed through the publications. She noticed a thick book in the middle of the ledge. The title displayed on the spine read *The History of Serial Killers in America.* Biographies on several notorious murderers, including John Wayne Gacy, Dennis Rader, and Danny Rolling, sat on the same shelf. An uneasy feeling settled over her. Moretti realized that despite all the years she had worked for Brandon, she actually knew very little about him.

"Dinner is served," Brandon announced as he entered the room.

Moretti straightened the books and turned around. *Well, aren't we a little snoop?* Brandon contemplated.

"Just need to use the restroom," Moretti said. "If I remember correctly, it's just down the hall."

"You are right," Brandon answered, staring intently at the woman.

"Great, I'll just be a minute," Moretti declared.

"I'll be waiting in the dining room," Brandon said flatly, "if you can find your way there."

Truth be told, Moretti didn't really need to freshen up. What she needed was to get away from Brandon, if only for a moment. Moretti checked herself in the mirror and took the opportunity to wash her hands and flush the toilet in case Brandon was listening. She had never been this ill at ease with him before. Something wasn't right. She could feel it. Moretti had left her purse in the den, and therefore, she didn't have a comb on her. So she opened the vanity mirror on top of the sink and perused the shelves, but there was nothing she could use to fix her hair. The next thing Moretti did was open the top drawer underneath the basin and rifle through it. There was no comb, but something more mysterious glimmered in the light: Nicole Schmidt's gold "N" necklace. Moretti had never seen the young woman without it dangling from her neck.

"My God," Moretti muttered out loud.

She put the jewelry back in the drawer where she had found it and exited the bathroom. When the agent got to the dining room, Brandon was nowhere to be found. As Moretti listened closely, she could hear the sound of dishes clattering in the kitchen. The night couldn't end soon enough.

"Steak medium-rare coming up," Brandon said as he entered the dining room. "Hope you're hungry."

Moretti had to keep her cool, not give off any weird vibes. So she offered to help get the rest of the food from the other room. But Brandon wasn't having it.

"Now, Toni, you're my guest. You have one job: to relax," Brandon said cunningly.

Relaxation didn't appear to be an option at the moment, but Moretti simply smiled and sat down at the opposite end of the table from where she assumed Brandon would sit. He came back with the rest of the food and a large pitcher of water.

"Oh my God, I forgot the wine. It's in the den. Would you mind getting the bottle, Toni?" Brandon asked.

"Certainly," Moretti answered and left the room.

Moretti had forgotten to collect her purse before she went to the dining room, so the first thing she did when she got to the den was look for it. But she was unable to locate the bag. So Moretti grabbed the wine and went back to the dining room where Brandon was waiting.

"Here it is. I couldn't find my purse, though," Moretti said, trying not to sound worried. "Could have sworn I left it there."

Brandon got up abruptly and returned, holding a brown leather pocketbook.

"You mean this?" Brandon asked. "I took it for safekeeping. But if you need it now..." he added.

"No, that's all right. Thanks for keeping an eye on it," Moretti said suspiciously.

Brandon couldn't help but pick up on how uncomfortable she was. He hadn't had time to go through Moretti's purse. But when Brandon went back to the den for a minute while Moretti was still in the bathroom, he noticed the bag on the couch where she had left it. Brandon picked up the purse impulsively and took it back with him to the kitchen. He wasn't even sure why he had taken it; he was just curious to see how the woman would react. The prank revealed her true feelings. Brandon detected a definite lack of trust.

Brandon motioned to the chair across the table from his regular seat, and Moretti sat down obediently. There were three platters on the surface containing the expertly prepared steak, cauliflower, and potatoes. Brandon unscrewed the bottle of wine Moretti had fetched from the den and poured two glasses. He would reward himself with the expensive stuff later. Brandon prepared a plate for Moretti and placed it in front of her.

"Everything looks wonderful," she said self-consciously.

"Why, thank you. Cooking is an expression of love, caring.... More people should try it," Brandon said hypocritically.

"When did you want to begin renting out the cottage?" Moretti asked, suddenly changing the subject.

Brandon knew the only thing keeping the real estate agent there was the promise of more business. But Moretti's unwillingness to simply unwind and enjoy the evening irked him.

"Haven't made up my mind yet. Guess it depends on who the prospects are," he answered slowly.

"I can put out some feelers in the morning, if that's okay with you," Moretti replied.

"That would be wonderful," Brandon answered disingenuously.

Brandon cleared the table and brought out a small apple crumb pie he kept in the freezer for special occasions. Moretti didn't deserve to be rewarded for her behavior tonight, but Brandon thought if he didn't defrost it soon, the pastry would need to be tossed. He warmed two slices and topped each with a scoop of vanilla gelato. Moretti finished her portion first and checked her watch.

"Oh, my, look at the hour. Didn't realize how late it was. I have to be up early. Thanks for a lovely evening," she said.

Brandon walked Moretti to her car, and they said their goodbyes. He went back inside the house convinced that there was something off. Moretti's demeanor had taken a turn for the worse right before dinner. *What am I missing?* Brandon asked himself. And then he remembered that she had excused herself to use the restroom while he waited for her in the dining room.

Brandon put down his glass, which was filled with his most extravagant wine, and headed for the bathroom. He opened the vanity, but nothing seemed out of place. Next, Brandon glanced down at the drawers. He noticed immediately that one of them was slightly open. *Sometimes it pays to be OCD,* he contemplated. Brandon grabbed the handle and pulled.

He looked down and saw something glistening: Nicole's gold necklace. *Fuck no,* Brandon muttered to himself. *Goddamn it.*

Nicole's necklace was the one keepsake Brandon had saved from the night he killed her. But he had gotten trashed after he buried her body and consequently had misplaced the pendant. Brandon had no idea how it ended up in the guest bathroom he rarely, if ever, used. But there it was in plain sight. Brandon could only come to the following conclusion: either Moretti had been snooping around or looking for something potentially innocent like a comb or brush and had come across the jewelry. After all, she had forgotten to take her bag with her when she went to the bathroom.

Losing track of Nicole's necklace was the most careless thing Brandon had ever done. And now Moretti had discovered it in his home. God knows what she would make of the missing woman's chain being in Brandon's possession. Moretti was armed with information that could destroy his life. What worried Brandon the most, however, was how rattled she seemed during dinner. If Moretti didn't suspect him of having anything to do with Nicole's disappearance, surely she would have mentioned finding the piece. The steadfast, reliable real estate agent had outworn her welcome. She was now official loose-end material.

If Brandon put himself in Moretti's place, he knew what he would have done: take the goddamn necklace with him. But he understood why Moretti left the jewelry where she had found it: she was going on the assumption that Brandon knew it was in the drawer. That supposition would turn out to be her fatal mistake. How could he trust that Moretti wouldn't tell Vito the truth? For all he knew she could be on the phone with him right now.

Brandon weighed the pros and cons of killing Moretti. The discovery of the necklace clearly went into the pro column. But he had taken every precaution, eliminating any evidence that could tie him to Nicole's disappearance and probable murder. Her remains were now ashes. People are killed all the time, and their landlords aren't all sitting in jail cells. *Everyone has to live somewhere,* Brandon contemplated. He simply wouldn't allow a tacky gold-plated necklace to be his undoing. Nicole Schmidt's chain with her initial dangling from it wasn't going to send him to prison for life. No fucking way.

* * *

Toni Moretti got into her BMW and sped away from Brandon's estate. What an awkward evening it had turned into. Moretti couldn't get the sight of the necklace out of her head. *Brandon had to have been involved,* she concluded. *How else in God's name would Nicole Schmidt's jewelry be in his powder room?* she asked herself. Moretti's conscience was getting the better of her. But if she was right and Brandon had actually killed Nicole, Moretti thought he would stop at nothing to silence her. She was conflicted, weighing her personal safety against what she knew was the right thing to do: tell Vito the truth.

As Moretti struggled with the decision, she had a thought. Brandon didn't strike her as the type that would take any chances when it came to getting caught. Therefore, whether she stayed quiet or not, he would likely come after her. Maybe telling Vito she had lied to him would actually be the smarter and safer move.

Moretti pulled into her driveway and opened the garage door. She had made up her mind. As she sat in her car, the real estate agent reached into her purse and searched for Vito's card. Moretti picked up her phone and placed the call. Vito answered after two rings. She just didn't know that he was parked outside Brandon's estate, strategizing about his next moves with Hank.

"Toni, I didn't think I'd hear from you again," Vito said, as he put his phone on speaker so Hank could listen. "What can I do you for?"

"We need to talk, in person. I can't say anything more over the phone," Moretti said urgently.

Vito looked at his watch. It was nearly eleven o'clock, but Moretti wouldn't have called him, no less at this hour, unless she had something important to say. Maybe she was the big break they'd been looking for.

"The diner's open all hours of the night. Wanna meet me there?" Vito suggested.

"Perfect. I'll see you soon," Moretti answered. "And, Vito, thanks."

Vito put his phone back in his pocket and turned toward Hank.

"Mind if I give Anna a quick call?" he asked.

"Course not. Go ahead," Hank answered.

The call went straight to voicemail, so Vito figured Anna must've fallen asleep. He left the following message: *Hey babe, there's something I've gotta take care of. Don't wait up for me, but I guess you already haven't*, he added jovially.

"Look, Hank, I know what you're thinking. But it's better if I go in alone. We don't wanna throw her off. Whatever it is that's on her mind it's gotta be really important, we can't risk..." he continued.

"You're right, you're right," Hank repeated. "I'll drop you off at your car, and maybe I can at least follow you there...stay put in the parking lot. Then when it's over, you can tell me what the hell is going on. Sound good?"

Vito knew there was no reasoning with Hank when she got like this, so he agreed to her terms.

"Just don't come inside. Stay in your car, well hidden. After she leaves, I'll find you," Vito told her adamantly. "And cross your fingers cause with any luck, this could blow things up."

* * *

As Vito drove to meet Moretti, he looked in his rearview mirror. Hank was on his tail. *No concept of personal space*, he joked to himself. When he arrived at the diner, Vito pulled into the closest space to the entrance and turned off his car. He checked his watch: it was now nearing 11:45 p.m. As he got out of his vehicle, Vito spotted Hank in the rear of the parking lot. He nodded to her and looked around, hoping to locate Moretti's car. But there was no sign of the white BMW. Vito hoped she hadn't changed her mind.

Xanthe didn't normally work the night shift. It was usually manned with alternating wait staffers. A new girl Vito had never seen before greeted him by the cash register in the front.

"Table for one?" she asked.

"No, sweetheart, waiting on someone. We'll grab a booth in the back when she gets here if that's all right with you," Vito answered cordially.

"Of course. Take your pick. It's pretty empty at this hour," the girl replied, handing Vito two menus.

"Thanks, honey. What's your name?" Vito asked warmly.

"Bree. They just haven't gotten around to giving me a name tag yet," she explained.

"You'll do just fine here, Bree" Vito said encouragingly.

He took the menus and checked his watch: it was five minutes before midnight. *Moretti should have been here by now,* Vito concluded. If she didn't arrive in the next five minutes, he would text her. Vito turned around and perused the bulletin board that hung in the entrance of the restaurant. Just the usual flyers asking for work, offering tutoring classes to college-bound teens, and available dog walkers caught his eye. And then he felt a tap on his shoulder. Vito turned around to find Toni Moretti right in front of him.

"So sorry I'm late," she began. "I...uh..." she continued, but Vito interrupted her.

"No worries. Let's go over there, in the back," Vito suggested, pointing with the menus.

Vito found the furthest booth in the rear of the diner where they would have the most privacy. Not that there were many people around at this hour to bother them, but after midnight, it was not uncommon for a group of drunk adolescents to frequent the place. They took their seats opposite each other, and Vito waited for Moretti to begin the conversation, but she just stared down at the menu in silence. Vito couldn't help noticing that Moretti looked worried and drained. He would have to make the first move.

"So what's so important that it can't wait until the morning?" Vito asked curiously.

"I just had dinner with Brandon...at his house," she began, unaware that Vito already knew as he and Hank had been watching Brandon's every move.

"Go on," Vito nudged her.

"I'm afraid...what I'm trying to say is I wasn't totally honest with you this afternoon when you asked me about Nicole," she said, starting to explain.

"And?" Vito said, prodding.

"I know who Nicole Schmidt is. I rented Brandon's cottage to her. That's where she was living at the time she disappeared," Moretti blurted out.

"Why did you lie to me?" Vito asked, furious.

"I don't know, I really don't, just got a bad feeling. But, Vito, there's something else you need to know. I'm afraid I, um, told Brandon," she continued.

"Told Brandon what exactly?" Vito demanded to know.

"That you showed me Nicole's picture and that I wasn't honest with you, didn't tell you I recognized her," Moretti said contritely.

Vito shook his head and banged his hand on the table.

"I'm sorry, Toni, but what the hell? What changed your mind?" Vito asked.

"That's what I was getting at," Moretti answered. "Something happened at the house...before dinner."

"Am I gonna like this?" Vito asked, exasperated.

"Maybe so...I found something in the bathroom...something incriminating, in my opinion...that, well, that points to Brandon.... Can't really be explained," Moretti continued, a bit disjointedly.

"What did you find?" Vito asked point-blank.

"Nicole Schmidt's necklace in a drawer," Moretti said, as Vito stared back at her stunned.

"Who else have you told? Does Brandon know you found it... found the necklace?" Vito asked, his mind racing in all directions.

"No, God no, I came straight to you, haven't uttered a word to anyone," Moretti reassured him.

"Good...that's good. Where is it? Where's the necklace now?" Vito asked, interrogating her.

"I left it where I found it...in the drawer in the powder room. But Brandon doesn't know anything...he couldn't..." Moretti rambled on.

"Okay, look, go home and try to get some rest. I'll walk you to your car. Just be careful," he emphasized, not wanting to alarm the woman. "We're dealing with a psychopath here."

Vito escorted Moretti to her car as promised. When she reached for the handle of the door, Vito made a suggestion.

"Hang on," he began. "There's someone I'd like you to meet."

Vito spotted Hank's car and motioned to her to join them. Unsure of his intentions, Hank picked up her phone and texted him: *Do you want me to come over?* Vito texted back: *Yes, pronto.* Hank got out of her car and walked straight toward them.

"Toni, this is Detective Hank Nowak. She's been working the case. I'll fill her in on what happened tonight. Just thought that, under the circumstances, it might not be a bad idea for you guys to get to know each other," Vito declared.

"Nice to meet you," Hank said, trying to gain Moretti's trust.

"Yes," Moretti responded uneasily.

"Go home, Toni. I'll be in touch in the morning. And thanks," Vito said sincerely. "You did the right thing."

Vito waited for Moretti to drive away and grabbed Hank by the arm.

"You're not gonna believe this," he began. "I was right. She lied. Moretti knows Nicole Schmidt. She rented Brandon's cottage to her. That's where Nicole was living when she vanished."

"What made her change her mind...tell you the truth?" Hank asked curiously.

"She found Nicole Schmidt's necklace in his house," Vito answered directly.

"Fuck yeah," Hank exclaimed. "Vito, you know what this means, don't you?"

"That we finally have something to tie Brandon to Nicole's disappearance," Vito replied.

"It means that I'd bet my bottom dollar Brandon murdered Nicole Schmidt and hid the body," Hank declared.

"Could just be," Vito agreed.

"I'll update O'Malley tomorrow first thing. Think we can get a search warrant by the morning?" Hank asked urgently.

"You mean to dig up his property? Don't see why not. Depends on the judge, I guess, but..." Vito continued.

"I mean, before it's too late," Hank elaborated.

Vito and Hank knew Brandon was always one step ahead. He must have sensed the noose was tightening after the recent altercations with his sister. Brandon couldn't afford to leave any loose ends, and they knew it.

"We're running out of time, Vito. I can feel it," Hank said anxiously.

"Don't you worry. I told you they always mess up," Vito said with satisfaction in his voice. "Always," he repeated. "You can count on it."

TWENTY-ONE

It had been a long evening for Hank, Vito, Toni Moretti, and Brandon, of course. None of them would be sleeping well tonight. It was a little past one o'clock in the morning, and throughout Fairview County the lights were still on. Moretti lay in bed, wondering what she had gotten herself into. Brandon could be hard to read, but she had gotten a very bad vibe from him as the evening progressed. Therefore, Moretti made sure to set her burglar alarm. Then she took some Ambien and tried to get some rest. God only knew what tomorrow would bring.

Meanwhile, Vito got into bed next to Anna, careful not to disturb her. He wanted to be there when Hank brought O'Malley up to speed. So Vito decided he'd text Hank first thing in the morning and, if she agreed, meet her in Stamford. They needed a warrant to search Brandon's house and property before he destroyed what little, if any, evidence remained. Vito contemplated that Nicole Schmidt's gold necklace was Brandon's fatal mistake, that it could just be the X factor that breaks the case wide open. If they could pin Nicole's disappearance and potential murder on him, Brandon just might confess to everything else and try to make a deal.

Hank got home, exhausted but hopeful that they might finally be getting somewhere. She passed on brushing her teeth and washing her face and climbed into bed with Barry beside her. While her loyal canine slept like a baby, Hank tossed and turned throughout the night. She would meet with O'Malley in the morning and tell him everything. Then they would get a warrant and tear her brother's place apart.

And then there was Brandon, a drink in one hand and Nicole's necklace in the other, staring intently at the fireplace. He wasn't sure if the flames would be hot enough to melt the jewelry. So, ever cautious, and determined to fix his only mistake, Brandon reluctantly got up off the couch and made his way to the incinerator. He threw the gold-plated necklace into the fire and watched as the flames consumed it. Then he made his way back to the house and curled up on the sofa in the den. Brandon had two things to worry about regarding Moretti. One, that she might cave and tell Vito that she knew Nicole and had rented Brandon's cottage to her, and two, that she found Nicole's necklace at his house. He had taken care of the second issue. The necklace was history. But Brandon didn't trust Moretti as far as he could throw her, so he came to one conclusion: he better shut her up before she ruined everything.

* * *

Hank's alarm went off at 6:00 a.m. and startled her, as she had only just managed to nod off a few hours earlier. After going through her normal morning routine, she heard her phone's ringtone emanating from the bedroom. Hank found her cell where she had left it on the nightstand and saw a missed call from Vito. Without bothering to play the message, she called him right back.

"Hey, Vito. I was just about to head out to meet with O'Malley," Hank said.

"That's what I was calling about. Mind if I join you guys there?" Vito asked expectantly.

"Sure, don't have a problem with that. I can pick you up on the way if it's easier. It would give us some time to talk," Hank replied.

"Perfect, I'll be outside," Vito said and got off the phone.

Hank pulled up to Gayle's guesthouse, but Vito was nowhere in sight. As she was debating whether or not to honk the horn, he appeared in the doorway. Vito made his way to the car and got inside.

"Sorry, forgot my wallet. I'm good now. Let's go," Vito said with urgency.

"It's still early, Vito. How 'bout we swing by the coffee shop and grab breakfast to go," Hank suggested. "I'm starving."

"You read my mind," Vito said warmly.

When they got to Coffee 'An, Hank stayed in the car while Vito ran inside, returning with two cups of coffee and a bag of donuts. Hank took one of the coconut twists and washed it down with the caffeinated drink. She headed for I-95 and police headquarters in Stamford.

"We'll explain everything to Joe, and then, we need him to expedite a search warrant," Hank noted.

"Yup, like yesterday," Vito remarked. "Brandon's been covering his ass. I'd bet my life on it. Just hope we're not too late is all. We don't even know for sure if he killed Nicole, much less buried her body on his property. Suspicions aside, we need evidence. Hardcore fucking evidence."

"Don't you think I know that, Vito? There are ways...cutting-edge technology...if he did it, we'll find something. I know it," Hank said, trying to be optimistic. "Nicole's been missing for four years...no word from her...no sign.... She's got to be dead. He had her necklace. She was living in his guesthouse. It all adds up."

"Not saying you're wrong. Just wanna lower your expectations. Cold cases are hard enough even when there is a body, and we have no reason to think we'll find one here. After all this time, God only knows where Nicole's remains could be."

"But circumstantial cases are won all the time even without a body. He killed her. You know he did, Vito, and we'll prove it one way or another," Hank declared.

"There's that Nowak determination," Vito said and rubbed Hank's shoulder lovingly.

They arrived at their destination, and Hank parked in her assigned spot. Then she and Vito made their way to O'Malley's office. It was imperative that they got him on board. The sergeant had to be under a lot of pressure to solve the "Deer Killer" case. Ironically, a prior killing just might end up being Brandon's downfall and O'Malley's saving grace.

O'Malley was on the phone when Vito and Hank entered his office, so he motioned for them to sit down and whispered that he'd be with them in a minute. Hank got the feeling that it was a personal call, but she didn't care one way or the other. She just wanted his attention and a search warrant.

"Sorry, didn't mean to keep you. So what have we got?" O'Malley asked.

"A lot's been going on," Hank began to explain. "Bottom line is I think we may be able to tie Brandon to a cold case: the disappearance of a woman who was living on his estate at the time she went missing, about four years ago. Vito found the real estate agent who rented Brandon's cottage to her, and she identified Nicole Schmidt's photo. She's scared, Joe. Thinks Brandon may be on to her, that he's afraid she'll talk. Anyway, we need a warrant right away so we can look around, dig up his property before he destroys what little evidence may be left. He knows we're on to him..." Hank continued, rambling.

"Slow down. What are you hoping to find?" O'Malley asked, anticipating Hank's answer.

"Nicole Schmidt's remains," Hank responded bluntly.

"That's a stretch, don't you think?" O'Malley asked skeptically. "I mean, after all these years..." he added.

Hank had one last argument to make: an old unsolved murder that could bolster her theory.

"Joe, you remember the Kristin Smart case? It took the police twenty-five years to arrest and charge the guys responsible...allegedly...and they never even found her body. They used ground-penetrating radar, took soil samples, investigated the father's backyard, found human blood in the dirt.... They were able to tell that an area had been dug up and refilled, identified a 'bathtub ring' that indicated a body had been there, in the hole.... We can do this, Joe," Hank said confidently.

O'Malley was impressed with Hank's knowledge of the Smart case and her resolve to bring Brandon to justice. He understood why it meant so much to her to catch him. He had taken away the one thing that really mattered to Hank: Cary.

"You'll have your warrant in a couple of hours and a forensic team to tear Brandon's estate apart, inside and out. No one wants this guy caught more than I do. The higher-ups expected this case to be put to rest like yesterday," O'Malley added, frustrated.

"Thanks, Joe. Vito and I will meet you at Brandon's place around noon then," Hank concluded.

"Yes, I'll bring the search warrant with me. And Hank, Vito, don't tell anyone about this. We can't tip our hand. If Brandon even so much as suspects that we're about to pounce..." O'Malley warned.

"Got it," Vito and Hank said in unison.

And that concluded the meeting.

* * *

The one person Vito felt obligated to give a heads-up regarding the search was Toni Moretti. After all, she had stuck her neck out for them, and if it hadn't been for her, they would never have come this far. So as Vito and Hank sat across from each other, killing the next two hours at the diner, Vito made the suggestion.

"Not sure you're gonna agree with me, but what about bringing Moretti into the loop about this?" Vito asked sheepishly.

"You mean about the search?" Hank responded.

"Yeah, I mean, she's in danger. I know it, and..." Vito began.

"But can we trust her...I mean, to keep her mouth shut, not tell anyone, especially Brandon. If O'Malley..." Hank continued.

"I just think she needs to know. Feels like the right thing to do is all," Vito proclaimed.

"Do it. Call her. But Joe can never know we broke his confidence," Hank declared.

"He won't hear it from me," Vito said and grabbed his phone.

* * *

Hank and Vito got into her car and headed to Brandon's home, his refuge from the world. But his peaceful domain was about to be turned upside down. This was the moment they'd been waiting for. Hank prayed the search would turn up something concrete that would lead to Brandon's arrest. When they pulled up in front of the estate, there were no other vehicles around. It was only 11:46 a.m., Hank and Vito had arrived early.

"Why don't you eat the other half of your sandwich while we wait?" Vito suggested.

"Not hungry," Hank answered, clearly on edge.

"Well, let's get this over with then. O'Malley and the team should be here any minute. Let's just hope Brandon is inside and not doing God knows what God knows where. Can't serve a house with a warrant," Vito said, concerned.

"We had to act. If he's out, we'll just wait until he shows up. We don't know how he's gonna react, but I'll bet anything he'll lose it at some point, the way he did that day with me," Hank concluded.

As Hank and Vito continued their conversation, several vehicles approached. They spotted O'Malley's car, followed by two white police vans.

"Let's just pray Brandon's not looking out the window," Hank whispered to Vito.

O'Malley left his car on the street and walked over to Hank's automobile. When he got to the driver's side door, he motioned to her to put down the window.

"Okay, so this is how it's gonna go. I'll drive up to the gate and press the buzzer. When he answers, assuming he's home, I'll announce myself, and he'll have no choice but to let me in. Then you guys and the vans will follow. Got it?" the sergeant asked.

"Roger that," Vito chimed in.

"Joe," Hank began. "He's really crazy.... He could do anything.... I'm..." Hank continued.

"Right now, your brother thinks he has one up on us, that he still has a lot to lose. Brandon won't do anything to jeopardize that. We have a van full of armed unis, and I can take care of myself," O'Malley added, pulling back his jacket to expose the Glock 19 pistol he kept tucked in his belt.

"Let's go then," Hank said intently.

O'Malley drove his vehicle up to the gate and pressed the button. Hank and Vito were right behind him, followed by the two vans. Brandon answered the beep and waited to see who was interrupting his lunch. As O'Malley identified himself, Brandon peeked out the window and spotted the four vehicles lined up outside the gate.

"Well, well, what a ballsy move," Brandon muttered to himself, as he pressed the buzzer to open the doors. "We'll see who wins this round."

The vehicles drove through the entrance and parked one behind the other at the top of the driveway. O'Malley, Hank, and Vito got out of their cars and headed for the door. The unis and forensic techs stayed in their respective vans, waiting for further instructions. O'Malley rang the doorbell, and they waited for Brandon to appear. As he opened the door, Brandon stood before them, staring coldly at the threesome.

"What brings you fine people here on this beautiful day?" Brandon inquired.

O'Malley reached into his inside jacket pocket and took out the warrant. He handed it to Brandon and waited for his reaction.

"Look anywhere you like, but you won't find anything because I haven't done anything wrong," Brandon said abrasively. "Just wasting your time while you should be looking for the real killer," he added sarcastically.

"Might be better if you stayed put...in one room...while we search the house," O'Malley suggested.

"I believe I know my rights, and I'd prefer to participate," Brandon told the sergeant pointedly.

"Fine, forensics will be looking around inside while some experts search the property," O'Malley explained. "Hopefully we won't be here too long."

"Take all the time you need," Brandon told him. "I'm not going anywhere."

As the technicians entered Brandon's home, he began to process the potential ramifications of the search. The only thing in the house they could find that might pose a problem were the documents he had put back in the bookcase. But Brandon's house was large, and cops were notoriously inept, he told himself, so he wasn't worried. Even if they came across the yellow envelope, all it really proved was that he had traced his DNA like half of America. Brandon had been wise to be proactive and get rid of everything else, from Nicole's remains to the necklace, before any cops showed up banging on his door.

Brandon kept his distance as the team of forensic experts combed through his house. But he was paying attention. *Toni Moretti must have changed her mind after all,* he contemplated. Brandon suspected that she told Vito the truth, identified Nicole Schmidt's picture, and admitted she had rented Brandon's cottage to the missing woman. Otherwise, Brandon saw no reason his estate would be swarming with overzealous cops and canines. He decided his best option was to eliminate the real estate agent from the equation. But this time, Brandon would be driven by revenge, not damage control. She had fucked him over, and he would make her pay later tonight.

* * *

While Brandon's house was being searched, O'Malley, Hank, and Vito accompanied the forensic serologist, archaeologist, and other specialists who were prowling around the property, determining which areas to examine. There was a lot of ground to cover, so they would need to spread out and be strategic. Hank thought it made sense to start with the rear of the estate, as far away from the main house as possible. O'Malley read her mind.

"Listen up, everyone. Let's head toward the property line as far back as we can go," he directed the team.

"That's just what I was thinking, Joe," Hank stated, sensing they were on the right track.

The experts, accompanied by several German shepherds, headed toward the rear of the estate, noting the cabin and small structure that held the incinerator Brandon had put to good use over the past several days. They were looking for any anomalies in the soil that might indicate that a hole had been dug and filled in. As the techs got to the large tree Brandon favored, the dogs began to sniff the ground. The team, led by the canines' reliable noses, continued to walk about another twenty to thirty feet, until the animals' reactions intensified. They put down stakes there.

Using the ground-penetrating radar Hank had mentioned to O'Malley, the technicians began to look for disturbances in the soil and any hint of human remains. It didn't take long for them to conclude that a hole had indeed been dug and then refilled with dirt. The archaeologist began digging until an opening appeared. They spotted the "bathtub ring" that indicated a body may have been buried there and subsequently moved. The serologist and a tech took soil samples for testing, hoping to find fibers or traces of blood.

"I think we're good for now," O'Malley announced to the team. "Let's get this back to the lab, and we'll reassess."

The group collected their equipment and headed back to the front of the estate and their vehicles. Only O'Malley, Hank, and Vito stayed behind to have a word with Brandon. The front door was open, so they went inside. A couple of cops greeted them in the foyer and pointed toward the den to indicate they would find Brandon there.

"Well, did you get what you came for?" Brandon asked sardonically.

"We're gonna run some tests. Be in touch. I wouldn't go anywhere if I were you," O'Malley warned him.

"Wouldn't think of it," Brandon replied. "Now why don't you all get the fuck out of my house?"

* * *

Brandon looked around his home in disgust. *Fucking pigs, literally,* he muttered to himself. Every room was in total disarray. *There oughta be a law,* Brandon reflected. How was it legal for the police to turn someone's house upside down and just leave when it suited them? They needed to clean up their own mess. Brandon had fired his maid a few months after he killed Nicole out of an abundance of caution and never replaced the woman. He had begun to feel self-conscious in front of Lucia and suspected she thought he was somehow involved in Nicole's disappearance. Brandon needed privacy; he couldn't risk having someone underfoot, lurking around, waiting for him to mess up. He would have to straighten up the house himself.

Brandon started with the den. His precious books were completely out of order. He found the section on serial killers and reached behind his favorite book. The envelope was still there, undisturbed. *Cops never disappoint,* he joked to himself. While the thinner books had been shuffled around and left on their sides, the police hadn't bothered to move the coffee-table-sized one on American serial killers; the documents were safe, one less thing to worry about.

After fixing the bookcase, Brandon checked the time. It was already six o'clock, and he had more important matters to attend to. So Brandon decided the rest of the house could wait. The unexpected events of the afternoon had proved exhausting, so Brandon decided to lie down on the couch and take a much-needed nap. The first thing he did when he woke up was to check the time; it was now nearly midnight. But before heading over to Moretti's place to teach her a lesson, Brandon weighed his options. He sat down at his computer and Googled *countries with no extradition to the United*

States. The first nation that came up was China. *Good to know,* he contemplated. As Brandon scanned a number of articles, confusion set in. The answer wasn't as straightforward as he had expected. Brandon would have to figure it out later. But the way things were going, the sooner he left the country, the better, even if he ended up in a somewhat tenuous situation.

* * *

Meanwhile down in Stamford, tests were being run on the soil samples that had been taken from Brandon's property. O'Malley, Hank, and Vito sat in his office, eating takeout Chinese. It was already late and entirely possible that they would be there all night. Max Craven had headed up the search of the interior of Brandon's home. Thanks to a tip from his boss, the evidence tech knew to look in the drawer in the powder room to see what, if any, evidence he could find. Craven was able to extract a single hair from the vanity. DNA tests were being conducted. The hope was the results would be a match to Nicole.

"Who would have thought," Vito began, "that an old toothbrush might just crack this thing."

Toni Moretti was smarter than she looked. After finding the necklace and telling Vito the truth, she remembered that Nicole Schmidt, whose parents were family friends, had spent a couple of nights at her house while she was looking for a place to live. Moretti still had Nicole's toothbrush in her medicine cabinet. Although neither Vito nor Hank had mentioned anything about DNA to the real estate agent, her instincts told her the item could be of help. And so, she turned it over to Vito, who subsequently gave it to forensics, with O'Malley and Hank's approval.

It was getting late, and there was no word yet from the lab. So O'Malley made a suggestion.

"Why don't you guys go lie down in the break room? It should be empty this time of night. I'll wake you when we get the results," the sergeant said.

"Sounds good to me. Wanna come, Hank?" Vito asked.

Hank was exhausted and anxious to boot. She didn't think sleep was in her immediate future.

"You go ahead, Vito. I'll hang out here for a while with Joe. Don't think I could fall asleep if I wanted to," Hank answered.

"Okay then. I'll just be down the hall. Get me as soon as there's any news," Vito declared.

Vito stood up and left O'Malley's office, phone in hand. He curled up on the couch next to the mini-fridge and microwave and dozed off. Hopefully this wouldn't take all night.

"How 'bout I get us a couple of cups of coffee?" O'Malley proposed.

"That'd be nice, Joe. Thanks," Hank responded.

O'Malley crept into the break room quietly as not to disturb Vito and poured two cups of coffee, black. He opened the fridge and grabbed a couple of yogurts and returned to his office.

"Here you go. This should help," the sergeant said, as he handed a cup of each to Hank.

"Joe, do you think they're going to be able to find anything definitive enough to make an arrest from the search today?" Hank asked uncertainly.

"We'll see. We have the best people on it...the most advanced technology.... It's worked before. We just need one lucky break to get an arrest warrant," he stated hopefully.

"Just feels like we've been spinning our wheels. Brandon's losing it, I can feel it. Look how he acted when we left. I'm sure he has someone in his line of fire.... I'm afraid he's going to hurt somebody else while we're pinning all our hopes on a cold case everyone's forgotten about," Hank explained.

"Nicole Schmidt's our best hope at the moment," O'Malley concluded. "Her revenge just might be stopping Brandon in his tracks. Wouldn't that be karma? And what do we all know about karma?"

"It's a bitch," Hank responded, and they locked eyes.

* * *

Brandon knew they were watching him. He could see the uni sitting in a police cruiser parked on the street right outside his gate. *Do they really think they're going to make me a prisoner in my own home?* Brandon contemplated. He would use the rear gate for his departure. Brandon had been keeping his smart car in the woods for a moment such as this. It was time to head over to Toni Moretti's and surprise her. Brandon had prepared the cabin for her arrival. The length of Moretti's stay, however, was yet to be determined.

Brandon pulled up in front of the real estate agent's house and turned off his car. He looked in the visor mirror and fixed his hair. Brandon opened the glove compartment and took out his gun. He opened the cylinder to count the bullets and double-checked that the safety was on. Brandon couldn't afford to have an accident tonight. Everything had to go according to plan.

It was late, but knowing Moretti, Brandon was certain she would answer the door. Curiosity always got the better of people like her. He rang the bell and waited. There was no response, so Brandon hesitated before pressing the button again. Within seconds, he heard Moretti's voice over the intercom.

"Who is it?" Moretti asked, sounding like she had been awakened from an Ambien-induced coma.

"It's me, Brandon," he proclaimed. "I was worried about you and thought I'd come by to check."

"Do you know what time it is?" Moretti asked, unsure of how to handle the situation.

"Yes, so sorry if I disturbed you. But think I could come in for a minute? There's something I need to tell you, and it can't wait," Brandon added, trying to pique her interest.

"Be down in a minute," Moretti replied, unsure if she was doing the right thing.

No one can read people like I can, Brandon decided, congratulating himself. *Dumb fuck. What woman in her right mind would let someone like me into her home in the middle of the night?* he noted.

Moretti's instincts told her she was making a mistake—exactly how big a mistake would become abundantly clear within seconds. She unlocked the front door, opened it, and let Brandon inside. As Moretti closed the door after him and turned around, she saw a shiny silver gun pointed right at her.

"What do you want?" Moretti asked frantically, her body shaking with fear.

"Why don't we go sit down?" Brandon suggested. "I think we need to talk."

As they walked toward the kitchen, Brandon spotted two suitcases leaning against the wall in the front hall.

"Going somewhere, are we?" he asked the terrified woman.

"I was just..." Moretti began to answer.

"No worries. Mind getting me a glass of water? I'm parched," Brandon declared as they entered the room. "Slowly," he cautioned.

Moretti handed Brandon a glass and stood in front of him, pale as a ghost.

"This won't take long," he told her. "Sit down."

"I don't know what you think..." Moretti interrupted.

"I think you told that private eye that you lied, that you know... knew Nicole Schmidt, and that you rented my cottage to her. How am I doing so far, Toni?" he asked derisively.

He doesn't know about the toothbrush...yet, Moretti contemplated. But she didn't know what to say to calm Brandon down, so she stood there in silence.

"No words? Get your things. We're going on a trip after all," Brandon ordered her.

"Where are you taking me?" Moretti asked pleadingly.

"You let me worry about that," Brandon answered sternly. "Here, let me help you with those suitcases."

Brandon didn't see any way he could have been followed to Moretti's. But just to be on the safe side, he thought it would be best if he pulled his car into her garage. No reason to tempt fate. He was coming to the end of the road. So Brandon drove his smart car into the middle stall and opened the trunk. At gunpoint, Moretti crawled into the compartment. Then Brandon put her bags in the back seat of the car. *That dumb bitch thought I was going to put her suitcases in the trunk, and she'd get to sit up front with me,* Brandon reflected. The spontaneous decision amused him. He was good at thinking on his feet.

When they got to Brandon's estate, he drove his car through the rear entrance and popped the trunk. Moretti was a disheveled mess. Still clad in her pajamas and slippers, she looked absolutely deranged.

"Now, now, Toni, it wasn't that bad. Walk. We'll get your things later," Brandon told her.

It took them a couple of minutes to get to the cabin. Brandon dislodged the padlock and opened the door. He used his phone as a flashlight and shoved Moretti inside.

"Have a seat," Brandon said harshly, pointing his gun at the frantic woman.

He tied her arms to the chair and bound her feet together tightly. She wasn't going anywhere. Then Brandon took out a small piece of cardboard: an "Odd Jobs" card. Moretti could see there was something written on the back but wasn't able to make out the words.

"You can't just leave me here," Moretti shrieked in fear.

Her voice echoed in the small space, so Brandon had no choice but to get out the duct tape. He held up his gun and brought it down on top of Moretti's head with a thud.

"Looks like I'll be traveling solo," Brandon mused.

He took the card and stuck it between the duct tape and Moretti's mouth.

"Don't worry, you'll have company shortly," Brandon promised the unfortunate woman. "And I'll make sure to tell them not to shoot the messenger."

TWENTY-TWO

O'Malley had all but nodded off when his phone rang. It was Max Craven on the other end.

"We've got the results. Is now a good time?" the evidence tech asked his boss.

"Get your ass in here now," O'Malley shouted through the phone.

Hank was asleep, sitting upright with her head against the wall. O'Malley touched her shoulder gently.

"What's happening?" Hank asked, disoriented.

"That was Max. He's coming up now with the findings. I'll go get Vito. You stay here," the sergeant instructed her.

Hank took the opportunity to use the restroom and splash water on her face. She wanted to be as alert as possible when Craven announced the results. Their entire investigation, everything they had worked so hard for over the past several months, hinged on this meeting. It had to go right. Hank returned to O'Malley's office and took her seat. The sergeant and Vito arrived a few minutes later. Hank suspected that they had chatted about the case while she was in the bathroom. But she knew they weren't hiding anything from her; they were just worried.

"Max should be here any minute," O'Malley said impatiently. "Then we'll see where we are."

Max Craven entered O'Malley's office holding a folder filled with official papers. He stood behind where Vito and Hank were sitting and cleared his throat.

"Pull up a chair Max and relax," O'Malley said gently. "We're all in this together."

"Thanks, sergeant. Should I begin?" Craven asked.

"Take it from the top," O'Malley instructed his subordinate.

"Well, let's go step by step. First off, the archaeologist, geologist, whatever you wanna call them, found anomalies of interest. The soil showed disturbances beneath the surface...and a 'bathtub ring'...the soil samples had blood...the serologist determined there was human blood...and then there are the fibers..." Craven rambled on.

"Let's cut to the chase, Max. What's the bottom line here?" O'Malley asked intently.

"The geologist concluded there was an area in the rear that had more than likely been dug up and then refilled with dirt. The 'bathtub ring' I mentioned is an indicator that a body had been buried in the hole and then moved. Human blood was found in the soil but no DNA. But the toothbrush Ms. Moretti provided us with, we did get DNA off that," Craven continued.

"And?" O'Malley prodded him.

"And it matched the hair we found in the drawer in the suspect's bathroom," Craven said decidedly.

"Do we have enough to arrest him?" Hank asked prudently.

"And then some," the sergeant answered her. "I'm gonna make a call, and you'll have your warrant in an hour."

Hank turned to Vito, her eyes filled with tears. He took her hand and squeezed it. This was the moment they'd been waiting for. Hank and Vito would stay in O'Malley's office until the warrant arrived. Then the three of them, accompanied by several unis, would head over to Brandon's and give him the surprise of his life.

* * *

It was 4:00 a.m., and Brandon was already on his way to the airport to catch the first morning flight out while the arrest warrant was being processed. He only wished he could have been there when the police found Moretti—or what was left of her—and his cryptic note. But he had no trouble visualizing what their reaction would be. Brandon would wait until he was at the gate to text Hank. He would give himself a head start.

Under normal circumstances, Brandon would have shot the disloyal woman in the head. But he was on the run and didn't really give a shit one way or the other if she lived or died. Brandon had made his point; he would leave it up to fate. But Brandon left the duct tape on Moretti's mouth as a precaution and to keep the "Odd Jobs" card in place.

* * *

A messenger arrived with Brandon's arrest warrant within the hour. But as the sergeant, detective, and private eye were about to leave, a text came in on Hank's phone. *You might want to drop by my place. I left a little something for you. B.*

"What the hell do you make of this?" Hank asked, as she held up the screen for Vito and O'Malley to see.

"That there's no time to lose. Let's go," O'Malley said hastily.

The three of them drove to Brandon's in O'Malley's car, a police cruiser with two uniformed officers trailing behind them. Normally a siren and flashing lights would have been employed, but they didn't want to do anything to put Brandon off in case he was watching them. When the two vehicles pulled up to the estate, Hank and company were surprised to find the front gate wide open. She suspected that her brother had set a trap for them.

"Something's not right," Hank began.

"Tell me about it," O'Malley replied. "Let's poke around and see what we can find."

O'Malley, Hank, and Vito reached for their guns and headed inside the main house. The unis stood guard outside. The trio checked the house, but no one was home.

"What the hell?" the sergeant exclaimed.

Then Hank had a thought.

"We don't know what he left for us to find, but I don't think it's here," Hank started. "What about the other buildings on the property? What do you say?"

"I say, let's do it," Vito responded.

So the three of them headed for the cabin, hoping their instincts would serve them well.

When they got to the small structure, a heavy padlock lay on the ground, and the front door was ajar. Hank had a feeling there was something terribly wrong. O'Malley pointed his weapon and nodded to his colleagues. He stepped inside, followed by Hank, then Vito. O'Malley turned on his flashlight, and Toni Moretti's body came into view, slumped in a chair.

"Oh my God," Hank shrieked.

Vito flipped on the light switch and bent down to untie the rope around Moretti's ankles. Then he gently pulled her head back. As he did so, they noticed the "Odd Jobs" card Brandon had left for them. Hank carefully pried the duct tape from Moretti's mouth and removed the card.

"Where the hell is he?" Hank asked.

She looked down at the card and read Brandon's note on the back. *Race you to JFK? Oh, and don't shoot the messenger. I promised Toni. LOL. B.* Hank handed the card to Vito, and he repeated Brandon's words out loud.

"What about Toni here?" Vito asked.

"We need to get an ambulance right away," Hank interjected.

O'Malley glanced at the poor woman and grabbed his phone to alert the unis out front.

"Call an ambulance. There's a woman back here in the cabin that needs medical attention. Hell, we don't even know if she'll make it. Hurry," O'Malley said urgently.

"Joe, what are you thinking?" Vito asked

"Brandon's planning to leave...flee the country," O'Malley concluded. "But if he's pointing us in the direction of Kennedy, I'd bet my life that's not where he's flying out of."

"Joe, there are three major international airports in the tristate area, and that doesn't include Bradley in Hartford. How can we cover all that ground before his flight takes off?" Hank asked incredulously. "We don't even know where he's going."

"I agree with what you said, Joe, but I think it would be a mistake to chalk off JFK just in case he's using reverse psychology," Vito interjected. "Manipulative son of a bitch."

"We need to make a plan. Time isn't working in our favor. Brandon's given himself a head start. For all we know, he's already on a plane heading God knows where," O'Malley concluded, distressed.

"What about countries with no extradition to the US? Might narrow down the destination," Hank said in desperation.

"There's no time. Too many places...countries with no treaty but who don't return criminals anyway.... We're fucked," O'Malley replied.

"Then there's only one option because we can't give up, let him get away...win," Vito interrupted. "We're gonna have to spread out...hit JFK, LaGuardia, and Newark; see if we can catch him. Check international terminals because this guy ain't stickin' around."

O'Malley glanced at his watch. They had to act quickly.

"Vito, why don't you and Hank head over to Kennedy? I'll hit Newark. And the unis can go to LaGuardia. Sound good?" O'Malley proposed.

"Joe, we only have two cars here. We drove together, remember?" Hank said.

"Damn it, that's right. Okay, listen, you guys take my car. The unis can ride in the ambulance. I'll drive their vehicle and call headquarters and have them send another cruiser to LaGuardia. Let's go," O'Malley declared.

"We're not gonna get him, are we?" Hank asked despondently. "He royally fucked us, didn't he?"

"Don't think like that. I'll make some calls on the way. Maybe we'll get a break...pin down the airline...country...it ain't that easy to disappear," Vito concluded. *Tell that to Nicole Schmidt,* Hank reflected. She thought Vito was grasping at straws. People vanish all the time. *Brandon had gotten the best of them,* Hank contemplated. *Fuck.*

* * *

Brandon purchased his ticket in cash and only brought one carry-on bag with him; the envelope containing the potentially damning DNA documents was inside it. He could buy more clothes and toiletries along the way. Brandon sipped his coffee as he waited at the gate to board the flight to Miami. While the three stooges were scrambling around making a futile attempt to catch him, Brandon was relaxing. In a few hours, he would be at a bar in South Beach killing time before his next flight. Miami was like New York City: open day and night.

The JFK challenge was a nice touch. Brandon was certain the brain trust would fan out to the three major New York area airports searching for international flights. They would never have thought to check out a domestic airfield such as Westchester. *There's more than one way to leave the country, dumb fucks,* Brandon contemplated. As there weren't any direct flights from the Westchester airport to Los Angeles, a layover in Miami was the perfect bridge to his final destination: Tasmania. *Guess I got the brains in the family,* Brandon joked.

"Now calling flight #529 to Miami, expected to arrive on time," the announcer proclaimed. "Anyone traveling with children, a disability, and all first-class passengers, please come to the gate. You may board at this time."

Brandon stood up, fixed his baseball cap so it covered most of his forehead, and made his way to the ticket agent. He handed the young man his boarding pass and walked down the galley and onto the plane. As they taxied down the runway and achieved lift off, Brandon noticed a stunning young woman across the aisle. He couldn't help thinking, that while his sister, the sergeant, and a private detective were stuck in the past, he had a whole new world ahead of him to explore. Checkmate.

EPILOGUE

Hank sat in O'Malley's car, Vito in the front passenger seat beside her, pounding her fist on the steering wheel.

"How is it even possible that Brandon's not on any manifest for departing international flights?" Hank asked, distraught.

"Maybe we got it wrong," Vito began. "His note about JFK...it could have been a trick. He might not be flying anywhere. How the hell are we supposed to know what his plans are...what he's thinking. Brandon's been messing with us from day one."

"He's gonna get away...get away with all of it," Hank concluded. "Evil always finds a way to win."

"It's not over yet, Hank, not by a long shot. Gonna call O'Malley again...see if they're setting up roadblocks. Brandon's probably behind the wheel of a car right now driving God knows where," Vito surmised.

Hank leaned back on the head rest and tried to think. But nothing useful came to mind. She couldn't help but remember the line in *Monster* after Charlize Theron unknowingly shot and killed a cop, thinking he was just another "John." *You can't get away with your shit forever. Sooner or later, it's gonna catch up with you. When in God's name will Brandon get his?* Hank asked herself. Unless a miracle happened, *the fucking tenth of never* was her answer.

* * *

Brandon made his connecting flight from Miami to Los Angeles and then boarded the plane to Sydney. The two-hour layover at LAX had given him a little time to grab a decent cup of coffee and reflect on recent events. The fourteen-hour journey from California to Australia was just what Brandon needed. *Travel is one of the only pleasures left in this world,* he pondered. Brandon couldn't help wondering if Hank and Vito had stuck their heads in an oven yet. The thought amused him. *Their professional egos must be crushed,* he contemplated. But it wasn't over, not quite yet.

While Brandon had disposed of the remaining items that could have incriminated him, he intentionally left something behind: the GoPro camera and recording. Before he left, Brandon moved the device from the cabinet in his study to underneath the floorboards in the cabin. On the off chance the police would get that far, there would be one more surprise waiting for them: Nicole Schmidt's right index finger bone. The experts would, of course, assume the fragment belonged to Caity—*mix and match,* Brandon joked to himself.

Your average shrink would likely opine that the decision on Brandon's part indicated that subconsciously he wanted to get caught—*simpletons.* There was simply no point in being a fugitive from justice if you didn't have a little fun with it. *Let's see if they can find me, no less extradite my sorry ass back to the States,* Brandon speculated.

* * *

As Brandon settled into his pod, a child in the row behind him started banging his foot against Brandon's seat. The little tyke's parents buried their heads in books, trying to ignore the situation. *First-class isn't what it used to be,* Brandon reflected. He assumed the family of three was returning from a trip to Disneyland. *These people belong in a bus station.* Brandon wasn't sure he could take fourteen hours of their bullshit. But if an annoying child and his obnoxious guardians was the price Brandon had to pay for all his evil, he could live with that. However, if the boy's *mum* failed to get him under control soon,

Brandon contemplated that she just might be his first victim down under. *Good day, mate,* Brandon whispered to himself and nodded off to sleep.

ACKNOWLEDGMENTS

First, I would like to thank Anthony Ziccardi, Kelsey Merritt, Ashlyn Inman, Maddie Sturgeon, Sara Stickney, and everyone at Post Hill Press for their dedication and professionalism in bringing *Retribution* to life. As always, they were a total delight to work with.

Next, I have to recognize Lenore Riegel and Jerome Charyn, my mentors at large, who generously gave their time and advice no matter the question or hour.

To Nancy Grace, my forever guardian angel, whose continuous support of the book and my writing journey means the world to me.

To my friends and colleagues Rita Cosby, Jack Ford, Rikki Klieman, Ashleigh Banfield, Gregg Jarrett, Kimberly Guilfoyle, Robi Ludwig, Diane Dimond, and Jerry Boyle, I am eternally grateful for your encouragement and for believing in me.

To fellow thriller authors Tessa Wegert, Wendy Walker, Lynne Constantine, Brian Cuban, Deborah Goodrich Royce, Lisa Gardner, Deborah Levison, and Jon Land I so appreciate your advice and willingness to help bring *Retribution* to the attention of crime enthusiasts everywhere.

To Ana Crespo who started it all and Vincenza Carovillano for her unending support and loyalty.

I want to thank Dennis Baker for his assistance in promoting *Retribution* and help in all aspects of marketing a book.

To all of my Court TV and *Nancy Grace* friends and colleagues, I appreciate your enthusiastic support of both novels.

A note about the Dedication: Although I chose Tracy Paules and Channon Christian to dedicate the book to, unfortunately I could have filled endless pages with the names of so many others. But the heartbreaking murders of Tracy and Channon have haunted me for years and I therefore used them to represent the rest. May their families find some kind of peace knowing they will never be forgotten; not by me.

And finally, to Norton, our precious boy, your struggle is over; now ours begins.

ABOUT THE AUTHOR

Wendy Whitman has a unique background through her decades-long work as an executive and producer for Court TV and HLN, covering almost every major high-profile murder case in America. Through her knowledge of the most detailed aspects of the crimes, Ms. Whitman has become an expert on the subject of murder in America. Before attending Boston University School of Law, Whitman worked for comedians Lily Tomlin and George Carlin. After graduating from law school, the author embarked on what turned out to be a twenty-year career in television covering crime. She spent fifteen years at Court TV and another several at HLN for the *Nancy Grace* show, where she appeared on air as a producer/reporter covering high-profile cases. Whitman received three Telly Awards and two GLAAD nominations during her tenure at Court TV.

Wendy Whitman attended Tufts University, graduating with a degree in English and Photography. Her first book, *Premonition*, was published in 2021.